MARIE NDIAYE was born in France in 1967. She published her first novel at seventeen, and has won the Prix Femina (*Rosie Carpe* in 2001) and the Prix Goncourt (*Three Strong Women*, 2009). Her play *Papa doit manger* has been taken into the repertoire of the Comédie Française. In 2013 she became the youngest writer to be selected as a finalist for the Man Booker International Prize.

JOHN FLETCHER is Research Fellow in French at the University of Kent. Their translation of *The Georgics* by Claude Simon won him and his then co-translator Beryl Fletcher the Scott-Moncrieff Prize.

"A writer of the highest calibre . . . NDiaye is a hypnotic storyteller with an unflinching understanding of the rock-bottom reality of most people's lives. This clearsightedness – combined with her subtle narrative sleights of hand and her willingness to broach essential subjects like the fate of would-be migrants to the rich North – gives her fiction a rare integrity that shines through the sinuous prose"

FERNANDA EBERSTADT, *New York Times*

"A novel that is more than the sum of its parts is a hard act to pull off. Marie NDiaye, one of France's most exciting prose stylists and playwrights, succeeds with elegance, grit and some painful comedy . . . The prose compels with its astonishing range and precision"

MAYA JAGGI, *Guardian*

"A great read . . . NDiaye soon establishes herself as a writer who dissects her characters with impressive forensic detail . . . The novel has a passion, daring and individuality th~~. . .~~

Marie NDiaye

THREE STRONG WOMEN

Translated from the French by
John Fletcher

MACLEHOSE PRESS
QUERCUS · LONDON

First published in the French language as *Trois femmes puissantes*
by Éditions Gallimard, Paris, 2009
First published in Great Britain in 2012 by MacLehose Press
This paperback edition published in 2013 by

MacLehose Press
an imprint of Quercus
55 Baker Street
7th Floor, South Block
London W1U 8EW

This book is supported by the French Ministry of
Foreign Affairs as part of the Burgess Programme run by the
Cultural Department of the French Embassy in London.

Liberté • Égalité • Fraternité
RÉPUBLIQUE FRANÇAISE

www.frenchbooknews.com

A CIP catalogue record for this book is available
from the British Library.

ISBN (PB) 978 0 85705 107 3
ISBN (Ebook) 978 1 78087 360 2

2 4 6 8 10 9 7 5 3 1

Typeset in Roos by Patty Rennie
Printed and bound in Great Britain by Clays Ltd, St Ives plc

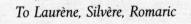

To Laurène, Silvère, Romaric

ONE

AND THE MAN WHO WAS WAITING FOR HER AT THE ENTRANCE TO his big concrete house – or who happened by chance to be standing in the doorway – was bathed in a light so suddenly intense that his whole body and pale clothing seemed to produce and project it: this short, thick-set man standing there, glowing as brightly as a neon tube, this man who had just emerged from his enormous house displayed no longer, Norah straight away realised, any of the stature, arrogance and youth that was once so mysteriously characteristic of him as to seem everlasting.

He held his hands crossed over his belly and his head tilted sideways; his hair was grey, and under his white shirt his belly sagged limply over the waistband of his cream trousers.

There he was, bathed in cold light, looking as if he had dropped onto the threshold of his pretentious house from the branch of one of the flame trees the garden was filled with, because – Norah said to herself – she had approached the house staring through the railings at the front door, but had not seen it open to let her father out: and yet there he stood in the sunset, this glowing, shrunken man who had apparently been dealt an enormous blow on the head that had reduced the harmonious proportions of Norah's recollection to those of a fat man with no neck and short, thick legs.

He stood there watching her as she approached; nothing in his rather lost, rather hesitant look showed that he was expecting her or that he had asked, even begged her to come and see him (in so far as a man like that, she thought, was capable of requesting help of any kind).

There – quite simply – he was; he had perhaps flitted down from the thick branch of the flame tree in the yellow shade of which the house stood, and had landed heavily on the cracked concrete of the doorstep: it was as if Norah had approached the railings at that instant by pure chance.

And this man who could transform every entreaty on his part into an appeal made to him by others watched her opening the gate and entering the garden. He had the look of a host who was rather put out but was trying to hide the fact; he was shading his eyes even though the fading light had plunged into shadow the doorway that was however lit up by his strange, shining, electric person.

"Well, well," he said, "it's you." His speech was muffled and weak; despite his mastery of the language he was hesitant in French, as if a touchy sensitivity he had always felt over certain mistakes that were difficult to avoid caused his very voice to tremble.

Norah said nothing.

She gave him a quick hug but did not hold him tight: from the almost imperceptible way the flabby skin on her father's arms shrank under her grasp she remembered how much he detested physical contact.

She thought she noticed a musty smell.

A smell emanating from the lush, wilting vegetation of the flame tree which thrust its branches over the flat roof of the house and perhaps hid amongst its leaves this withdrawn and self-assured man, who was on the alert – Norah thought in her embarrassment – for the slightest sound of footsteps approaching the gate and ready to take flight and land clumsily on the doorstep of his vast house with its rough concrete walls; or emanating – this smell –

from her father's body or his clothes or his old, wrinkled, ashen skin: she could not say what it was, she had no idea where it might be coming from.

The most she could say was that he was wearing that day – and probably, she thought, wore all the time now – a crumpled, sweat-stained shirt and trousers that were pale, shiny and hideously baggy at the knees, either because he was too heavy a bird and fell over each time he landed, or – Norah reflected with rather weary compassion – because he had after all become a slovenly old man, indifferent or blind to personal hygiene while still clinging to habits of conventional elegance, dressing as he had always done in white and cream and never appearing on the threshold of his unfinished house without tightening the knot on his tie, whatever dusty room he had emerged from or whatever flame tree, exhausted by flowering, he had flown down from.

On landing at the airport Norah had taken a taxi, then walked in the heat for a long while because she had forgotten her father's exact address and only found her way after she had recognised the house. She felt sticky, dirty and exhausted.

She wore a sleeveless lime-green dress covered with little yellow flowers rather like those strewn over the doorstep under the flame tree, and flat sandals in the same soft green.

And she noticed with a start that her father wore plastic flip-flops, he who had always made a point, it seemed to her, of never appearing in anything other than off-white or beige polished shoes.

Was it because this untidy man had lost all right to cast a stern, critical or disapproving eye over her, or because, as a confident thirty-eight-year-old, she no longer cared above all else what people thought of her appearance? Whatever the case, fifteen years earlier – she said to herself – she would have felt embarrassed and mortified to have appeared tired and sweating in front of her father whose appearance and bearing was never affected in those days by the slightest sign of weakness or sensibility during a heatwave, whereas now she could not care less about that and even, without looking away, showed him a bare, shiny face that she had not bothered to powder in the taxi, saying to herself with some surprise "How could I attach any importance to all that?"; telling herself, too, with a rather sour, rancorous cheerfulness, "He can think what he likes of me", as she remembered the cruel, insulting, offhand remarks made by this superior male when, as teenagers, she and her sister came to see him: remarks that always turned on their lack of elegance or absence of lipstick.

She would have liked to say to him now: "You realise, don't you, that you spoke to us as if we were women whose job it was to make themselves attractive, whereas we were just kids, and your own daughters into the bargain."

She would have liked to say this to him in a flippant, mildly scolding tone of voice, as if all that had been just a rather crude form of humour on his part, and she would have liked them to see the funny side of it together, and for her father to show a little contrition.

But seeing him standing there in his plastic flip-flops on the concrete doorstep strewn with rotting flowers which he perhaps had knocked off as he flew down from the flame tree on his tired, heavy wings, she realised that he no more cared to scrutinise her appearance and formulate a judgment about it than he would have understood or grasped the most insistent allusion to the unkind comments he once used to make.

He had a rather fixed, vacant, distant look.

She wondered then if he actually remembered writing to ask her to come.

"Shall we go in?" she said, slipping her bag from one shoulder to the other.

"Masseck!" he shouted, clapping his hands.

The icy, bluish light seemed to shine more intensely from his misshapen body.

A barefoot old man in bermudas and torn polo shirt hurried forward.

"Take the bag," Norah's father said.

Then, turning to her, he said "It's Masseck, d'you recognise him?"

"I can carry my bag," she said, immediately regretting her words which could only offend the servant who, despite his age, was used to lifting and carrying the most awkward burdens, then passing it to him so impetuously that, taken unawares, he tottered, before recovering his balance and tossing the bag onto his back, and then going back into the house, stooping as he did so.

"When I last came," she said, "it was Mansour. I don't know Masseck."

"What Mansour?" her father said with a suddenly wild, almost dismayed look that she had never seen before.

"I don't know his surname, but that Mansour, he lived here for years and years," said Norah, who felt herself being slowly gripped with a nauseating, stifling feeling of discomfort.

"It was perhaps Masseck's father, then."

"Oh no," she said, "Masseck is far too old to be Mansour's son."

And since her father seemed increasingly bewildered and even close to wondering if she was not deliberately trying to confuse him, she quickly added:

"Oh, it really doesn't matter."

"You're mistaken, I've never employed anyone called Mansour," he said with a subtle, arrogant, condescending smile that was the first manifestation of his former personality. However irritating that tiny, scornful smile had always been, it warmed Norah's heart; it was as if, to this conceited man, it mattered less to be right than to persist stubbornly to have the last word.

For she was certain that a diligent, patient, efficient Mansour had been present at her father's side for years on end, and that even if she and her sister had come to this house scarcely more than three or four times, all in all, since they were children, it was Mansour whom they had seen here and not this Masseck, whose face she did not recognise.

Once inside, Norah noticed how empty the house was.

Outside, it was now quite dark.

The big living room was dark too, and silent.

Her father switched on a lamp, the kind that uses forty-watt bulbs and gives a poor light. Nevertheless it revealed the middle of the room and its long, glass-topped table.

On the roughly plastered walls Norah recognised the framed photographs of the holiday village which her father had owned and run and which had made him rich.

He took much pride in his success, and a large number of people had always lived in his house. Norah had always thought that this was not so much because he was a generous man as because he was keen to show that he could provide his brothers, sisters, nephews, nieces and sundry other relatives with free board and lodging. As a result, at whatever time of day she happened to be there, Norah had never seen the living room empty.

There were always children on the sofas, sprawling belly-up like well-fed cats, men drinking tea and watching television, and women moving to and fro between the kitchen and the bed-rooms.

That evening the room was empty, crudely exposing the harsh

materials used in its construction, the shiny floor-tiles, the cement rendering on the walls, the narrow window-frames.

"Isn't your wife here?" asked Norah.

He picked up two chairs from the big table, moved them closer to each other, then changed his mind and put them back again.

He switched on the television, and then turned it off before it had time to light up.

He moved about the room without lifting his feet, so that his flip-flops scraped on the tiles.

His lips trembled slightly.

"She's away travelling at the moment," he said finally.

"Oh," Norah said anxiously to herself, "he daren't admit that she's probably left him."

"And Sony? Where's Sony?"

"Likewise," he said.

"Sony's off travelling too?"

The thought that her father who had had so many wives and children, that this not particularly handsome but brilliant, clever, quick-witted and ruthless man who had been born into poverty but who, once he had made his fortune, had always lived surrounded by a crowd of grateful and submissive associates, that this spoilt individual now found himself alone and perhaps abandoned, pandered to an old hazy grudge that Norah harboured in spite of herself.

It seemed to her that her father was at last being taught the lesson he should have learned much earlier.

But what sort of lesson?

It made her feel petty and cheap, to think that.

For even if her father had always kept open house to spongers, even if he had never had any true friends, honest wives (with the exception, Norah thought, of her own mother) or loving children, and if now, old, ravaged and probably much weakened, he wandered alone around his gloomy house – in what way did that reinforce a solid moral absolute, in what way could that be a matter of satisfaction for Norah, just on the strength of her being a jealous daughter avenged at last for never having belonged to the charmed circle surrounding her father?

And feeling petty and cheap she was now ashamed of her hot, damp skin and her crumpled dress.

As if to make up for her spiteful thoughts, as if to make sure he would not be left alone for too long, she asked, "Will Sony get back soon?"

"He'll tell you himself," her father said.

"How come, if he's away?"

Her father clapped his hands and shouted "Masseck!"

Small yellow flame tree flowers fluttered down from his neck and shoulders on to the tiled floor, and with a swift movement he crushed them under the toe of one of his flip-flops.

It gave Norah the impression that he was crushing her dress, covered in similar flowers.

Masseck came in pushing a trolley laden with food, plates and cutlery, and proceeded to lay the table.

"Sit down," her father said, "and let's eat."

"I'm going to wash my hands first."

She found herself adopting the tone of peremptory volubility which she never used with anyone other than her father and which served to forestall any attempt on his part to get Masseck or, before Masseck, Mansour, to do what she proposed doing; she knew that he so hated seeing his guests carrying out the slightest tasks in his house and appearing thereby to cast doubt on his servants' competence that he was quite capable of saying to her "Masseck will wash your hands for you" and not for a moment imagining that she would not obey him as those around him, young and old, had always obeyed him.

But her father had hardly heard her.

He had taken a seat and was staring vacantly at what Masseck was doing.

She found that his skin was blackish, less dark than before, and dull-looking.

He yawned, his mouth wide open, not making a sound, just like a dog.

She felt certain that the sweet fetid smell which she had noticed at the threshold came both from the flame tree and from her father's body, because his whole person was steeped in the slow putrefaction of the yellowy-orange flowers – and this was the man, she said to herself, who had taken such care over his appearance, who had worn none but the most chic of perfumes, this haughty and insecure man who had never dreamt of giving off his own odour!

Poor soul, who would have thought he would turn into a plump old bird that moved clumsily and gave off a strong smell?

She walked towards the kitchen along a concrete corridor lit imperfectly by a bulb covered in fly-specks.

The kitchen was the smallest and least user-friendly room in this badly proportioned house, and that too Norah remembered, having added it to the inexhaustible list of her grievances against her father, knowing full well that she would not mention any of them, neither the serious ones nor the less serious, and that she could never, face to face with this unfathomable man, summon up the courage – which she possessed in abundance when far away from him – to express her disapproval, and as a result she was not at all pleased with herself but, rather, very disappointed, and all the angrier for bending the knee and not daring to say anything to him.

Her father could not have cared less about making his servants work in a tiring, uncomfortable place, since neither he nor his visitors ever set foot in it.

Any such consideration would have been incomprehensible to him. Indeed – she said to herself with resentful fury – he would put it down to the sentimentality that characterised her sex, the world she inhabited and a culture he did not share.

"We don't live in the same country, societies are very different," he would say more or less, in a pedantic, condescending manner, and perhaps summon Masseck to ask him in front of her whether the kitchen suited him – to which Masseck would say yes – and her father, not even looking at her triumphantly since that would give the subject an importance it did not merit, would simply consider the matter closed.

"There's no point, there's no sense in having a father you literally can't communicate with, whose feelings for you have always been open to question," she said to herself yet again, but this time calmly, not shaking with rage, impotence and despondency as so often in the past when, through force of circumstance, she came up against the fundamental differences of perception, outlook and education that came between herself, a vulnerable person with strong feelings, and this cold, passionless man who had spent only a few years in France, whereas she had lived there all her life.

And yet here she was, in her father's house. When he had called her, she had come.

If she had possessed to a lesser degree this capacity for emotion which he so heartily despised (lumping together, with his own daughter, the entire limp-wristed, feminised western world), she would have found any excuse to avoid having to make such a journey (". . . *and you would do me a great honour and give me signal pleasure if you were able – if you felt strong enough – to leave your family for a time, even for quite a while, and come here, to your father, because I've important things to say to you . . .").*

Oh, how she regretted already having weakened, how she longed to return home now and get on with her life.

At the tiny sink in the kitchen a slim young girl in a T-shirt and threadbare skirt was washing some cooking-pots.

The table was covered with dishes about to be served, Norah realised, to her father and herself.

Stunned, she noticed roast chicken, couscous, saffron rice, a dark meat in a peanut sauce, and other dishes she could just make out under their steamy glass covers. The profusion was staggering. It was beginning to make her feel queasy.

She slipped between the table and the sink and waited until the girl, who was laboriously rinsing out a large stew-pot, had finished.

The sink was so narrow that the pot kept hitting the edges or the tap and, since there was no draining-board, the girl had to crouch to put the vessel down to dry on a tea towel spread out on the floor.

Once again, it exasperated Norah to see how little her father cared about his servant's wellbeing.

She quickly washed her hands, all the while smiling and nodding to the girl.

And when she had asked her name and the girl – after a brief silence as if, Norah thought, to embed her answer in a setting worthy of it – had replied "Khady Demba", her calm assurance, firm voice and limpid gaze both surprised and soothed Norah, calming her jumpy weariness and feelings of irritation and resentment.

At the end of the corridor her father's voice rang out.

He was calling her impatiently.

She made haste to rejoin him and found him in a state of some annoyance, anxious to tuck into the prawn and fruit *tabbouleh*

Masseck had served in the two plates placed opposite each other.

She had hardly sat down when he started eating greedily, with his face almost in his plate, and this voraciousness, entirely devoid of pretence and small talk, was in such sharp contrast to the old-fashioned manners of this rather affected man that Norah nearly asked him if he had been depriving himself of food, thinking that he was quite capable – if his financial difficulties were such as she supposed them to be – of trying to impress her by concentrating on this dinner all the provisions of the three preceding days.

Masseck brought one dish after another, at such a pace that she could not keep up.

She was relieved to see that her father was paying no attention to what she ate.

He only raised his head to scrutinise greedily and suspiciously what Masseck had just put on the table, and when at one point he looked furtively at Norah's plate, it was with such an air of child-like apprehension that she realized he was simply making sure that Masseck had not served her more generously than himself.

That really upset her.

Her father – normally so loquacious, so full of fine words – remained silent. The only sounds to be heard in the desolate house were the clatter of plates, the slip-slap of Masseck's feet on the tiles, and perhaps too the rustle of the top branches of the flame tree brushing against the tin roof. She wondered vaguely whether the lone tree was calling out in the night for her father to come.

He went on eating, moving from the grilled lamb to the chicken in sauce, hardly pausing for breath between mouthfuls, joylessly stuffing himself.

For dessert, Masseck put a mango cut in pieces before him.

He pushed one piece into his mouth, then another. Norah saw him chewing with difficulty, and trying to swallow. In vain.

He spat out the mango pulp onto his plate.

Tears were pouring down his cheeks.

Norah felt her own cheeks burning.

She got up, heard herself mumbling something, she could not tell what, went over and stood behind him, and then did not know what to do with her hands, never before having found herself in a position either to comfort her father or show him anything other than a stiff, forced respect tinged with resentment.

She turned round, looking for Masseck, but after clearing the table he had left the room.

Her father, his face expressionless, was still weeping silently.

She sat down next to him and leaned forward to bring her head as close as possible to his wet, tear-streaked face.

She could smell, beyond the odour of the food and the spicy sauces, the sickly-sweet scent of the rotting flowers of the big tree, and since her father kept his head lowered, she could see the grubby shirt-collar round his neck.

She remembered a piece of news which, two or three years earlier, her brother Sony had passed on, but which her father had not seen fit to divulge to her sister or to herself. She had resented this, but before long she had forgotten both the news and the bitterness she had felt at not having been told. The two things now went through her mind simultaneously and as a result her tone was rather acerbic even though she had tried to make her voice sound comforting.

"Tell me, where are your children?" she asked.

She remembered that he had fathered twins, but could not recall what gender they were.

He looked at her, distraught.

"My children?"

"The last ones you had. Or so I believe. Has your wife taken them with her?"

"The little girls? Oh, they're here, yes," he murmured, and turned his head. It was as if he were disappointed, as if he had hoped that she would talk about something he did not know and had not grasped all the implications of, something which, in a strange, magical way, would save him.

She could not contain a slight shiver of vengeful spite.

So Sony was the only son of this man who did not care much for girls, or have much time for them.

"Overwhelmed, weighed down by useless, mortifying females who weren't even pretty," thought Norah calmly, thinking of herself and her sister; for their father, they had always had the irremediable defect of being too like him, that is, quite unlike their mother, testifying to the pointlessness of his marriage to a Frenchwoman, because what good had it done him? No almost-white children, no well-built sons . . .

And it had been a failure.

Upset, overwhelmed by a feeling of ironic compassion, she laid her hand lightly on his shoulder.

"I'd like to meet them," she said, adding at once so as not to give him time to ask her what she meant, "your two daughters, the little girls."

Her father shook her hand off his fat shoulder in an involuntary gesture which signified that nothing could justify such familiarity on her part.

He rose heavily and wiped his face on his shirt sleeve.

He pushed open an ugly glazed door at the other end of the room, switched on the solitary bulb that lit another long, grey concrete corridor off which, she recalled, doors opened on to small square rooms like monastic cells that once were inhabited by her father's numerous kindred.

From the way their feet echoed in the silence, and from the

sound made by her father's noisy, irregular breathing, she was sure that the rooms were now empty.

They seemed to have been walking already for several long minutes when the corridor swung first to the left, then to the right, getting darker all the while, and so stuffy that Norah nearly turned back.

Her father stopped in front of a closed door.

He grasped the handle and stood still for a moment with his ear against the panel. Norah could not tell if he was trying to listen to something inside or was summoning up the will to open the door. But the attitude of this man, at once scarcely recognisable and inherently implausible – oh, what incorrigible naivety to think, even though she had not seen him for years, that time would have altered him and brought them closer together – worried and annoyed her now more than it ever had in the past when she could never be sure whether, in his brazen recklessness and arrogant flippancy, and quite without humour, he was not going to throw some unforgettably cruel remark at her.

With a quick movement, as if to catch someone *in flagrante*, he opened the door.

With an air of fear and repugnance, he stood aside and let Norah in.

The tiny room was lit by a lamp with a pink shade. It stood on a small table placed between two beds, on the narrower of which sat the girl whom Norah had seen in the kitchen and who had told her she was called Khady Demba. The lobe of her right ear, Norah noticed, was slit in two.

Sitting cross-legged on the mattress, she was sewing a small green dress.

Looking up briefly, she smiled at Norah.

Two little girls were asleep on the other bed, lying face-to-face under a white sheet.

With a tightening in her chest, Norah thought that the faces of the two children were the most beautiful she had ever seen.

Awakened perhaps by the stuffy heat from the corridor flooding into the air-conditioned room, or by an imperceptible change in the quiet atmosphere surrounding them, the two little girls opened their eyes at the same time.

They looked at their father gravely and without warmth or feeling. They showed no fear at seeing him, but no pleasure either. As for him, Norah noted with surprise, he seemed to melt under their gaze. His shaven head, his face, his neck in its shirt-collar, all were suddenly dripping with sweat and giving off the strong, acrid odour of flowers crushed underfoot.

This man, who had managed to surround himself with a climate of dull fear and who had never let anyone intimidate him, now seemed terrified.

"What could such small girls be making him afraid of?" Norah wondered. They – the miraculous offspring of his old age – were so marvellously pretty that they must have made him overlook the fact that they belonged to the weaker sex, and caused him to forget the plainness of his first two daughters, Norah and her sister. How could he possibly be scared of such enviable children?

She went towards the bed and knelt down. Looking into the two small identical faces, round, dark and delicate like the heads of seals resting on the sand, she smiled.

At that moment the first bars of "And here's to you, Mrs Robinson . . ." rang out in the room.

Everyone jumped, even Norah who was familiar with the ringtone of her mobile. She reached for it in the pocket of her dress. She was about to turn it off when she noticed that the call was coming from her own house. Embarrassed, she put the phone to her ear. The silence of the room seemed to have changed in nature.

Instead of being calm, ponderous and lethargic, it had suddenly become attentive and vaguely hostile, as if in the hope of hearing clear, definitive words that would enable them to choose between keeping her at arm's length or welcoming her into their midst.

"It's me, Mummy!" Lucie's voice rang out.

"Hello, darling! You don't have to shout, I can hear you quite clearly," Norah said, red in the face. "Is everything O.K.?"

"Yes! At the moment we're making pancakes with Grete. Then we're off to the cinema. We're having a lovely time."

"Splendid," said Norah softly. "Lots of love! Speak to you soon."

She snapped the phone shut and slipped it into her pocket.

The two little girls pretended to be asleep. Their eyelids flickered and their lips were pressed together.

Disappointed, Norah stroked their cheeks, then got up, nodded to Khady and left the room with her father, who closed the door carefully behind him.

She thought bad-temperedly that, once again, he seemed to have failed to establish a straightforward loving relationship with his children. She felt that a man who was greeted with such a pitiless look did not deserve the beautiful little girls born when he was old, and that nothing, no-one, could change a man like that unless they tore his heart out first.

But as she followed him back down the gloomy corridor she could feel the mobile knocking gently now against her thigh, and she admitted with grim annoyance that the irritation she felt against her father was increased by the exaggerated excitement she had sensed in Lucie's voice; that the bitter things she could not or would not dare to say to Jakob, the man she had been living with for a year, were going to be planted there, in her father's back, as he walked innocently before her, bowed and overweight, along the gloomy corridor.

For in her mind's eye she could see her beloved Paris flat, the intimate, modest symbol of her perseverance, of her discreet success, into which, having lived for a few years alone with Lucie, she had introduced Jakob and his daughter Grete, and at a stroke had let in aberration and disorder, whereas the idea behind the purchase of the three-room apartment in Montmartre (financed by a thirty-year loan) had precisely been her spiritual longing to put an end to the lifelong confusion agonisingly incarnated in her now elderly, threadbare father, his wings folded under his shirt, cutting a huge and incongruous figure in the gloomy corridor.

Oh, she had been quick to sense in Lucie's tone – panting, urgent and shrill – that the flat was at that very moment the scene of those demonstrations of fatherly enthusiasm which she detested and which were characterised by Jakob's ostentatious refusal to lay down any limits or exercise the slightest authority over the two seven-year-old girls, and by his habit of undertaking with extravagant commentary, great energy and much enthusiasm culinary preparations which he usually lacked the ability, will or patience to see through; the pancake-batter or cake-mix was never set to cook, because in the meantime he would suddenly suggest going out or doing something else, in a similar panting, urgent, shrill tone which the girls copied, and which got them so overexcited that they often ended up exhausted, fretful and in tears, a situation made worse, Norah thought, by a vague feeling that, despite all the screaming and the laughter, the day had been pointless, awkward and weird.

Yes, she had been quick to sense all that in Lucie's voice. She was already worried about not being back there. Or rather, the disquiet which she had started to feel as the day of her departure approached and which she had firmly suppressed, she now gave free rein to. Not that there was anything that could objectively be considered dangerous in leaving the girls in Jakob's care, but she was concerned that the values of discipline, frugality and lofty morality which, it seemed to her, she had established in her little flat and which were meant to represent and adorn her own life and form the basis of Lucie's upbringing, were being demolished in her absence with cold, methodical jubilation by a man. As for bringing the man into her home, nothing had obliged her to do that: only love, and hope.

Now she was unable to recognise that love any longer; it lay smothered by disappointment. She had lost all hope of an ordered, sober, harmonious family life.

She had opened her door and evil – smiling, gentle and stubborn – had entered in.

After years of mistrust, having left Lucie's father and bought the flat, after years spent austerely constructing an honourable existence, she had opened her door to the destruction of that existence.

Shame on her! She could not tell anyone about it. Nothing seemed explainable or understandable in the mistake she had made: a mistake, a crime against her own efforts.

Neither her mother nor her sister, none of her few friends could conceive how Jakob and his daughter Grete – both of them gentle and considerate, well-brought-up and likeable – were working subtly to undermine the delicate balance that had finally been achieved in the lives of Norah and Lucie, before Norah – as if blinded in the end by an excess of mistrust – had obligingly opened her door to the charming incarnation of evil.

How lonely she felt!

How trapped, how stupid she felt!

Shame on her!

But what words could she find that were sufficiently precise to enable them to comprehend the anger and disquiet that she had felt two or three days previously, during one of those family rows which epitomised for her Jakob's malevolent underhandedness and her own feebleness of mind – she who had so aspired to simplicity and straightforwardness, she who had been so afraid of warped thinking while she and Lucie lived alone together that she would run a mile at the slightest hint of it, determined never to expose her child to eccentric or perverse behaviour?

But she had been ignorant of the fact that evil could have a kindly face, that it could be accompanied by a delightful little girl and that it could be prodigal in love. The fact was, though, that Jakob's vague, impersonal and inexhaustible love cost him nothing; she knew that now.

As on every other morning, Norah had got up first, made Grete's and Lucie's breakfast and got them ready for school. It was then that Jakob, who normally only woke up when the three of them had left the house, emerged from the bedroom just as Norah was finishing off her hair in the bathroom.

The girls were putting on their shoes, and what should he do but start teasing them, undoing one girl's laces and pinching the other's shoe, running and hiding it under the sofa with howls of laughter like a mocking child, oblivious of the time and of the distress of the children who, amused at first, ran around the flat in pursuit, begging him to stop his tricks, on the brink of tears but trying to smile because the situation was supposed to be funny and light-hearted. Norah had to intervene and order him, like a dog, in that falsely gentle tone, throbbing with suppressed anger, which she used only with Jakob, to bring the shoe back at once, which he did with such good grace that Norah, and the girls too, suddenly looked like petty, sad women whom an impish teaser had tried to cheer up.

Norah knew that she had to hurry now if she were not to be late for the first appointment of the day, so she refused tartly when

Jakob suddenly offered to go with them. But the girls had encouraged him and backed him up, so Norah, weary and demoralised all of a sudden, gave in. Standing silently in the passageway with their coats, shoes and scarves on, they had to wait for him to get dressed and join them. He was gay and light-hearted, but in a way that seemed to Norah forced, almost threatening. Their eyes had met as she glanced anxiously at her watch. All she saw in Jakob's look was cruel spite, bordering on hardness, under his stubbornly effervescent manner.

Feeling giddy, she wondered what kind of man she had allowed into her home.

At that time he had taken her in his arms and embraced her more tenderly than anyone had ever done. Feeling miserable, she had once more said to herself: "Who, having once known tenderness, can willingly give it up?"

They then squelched through the muddy slush on the pavement and clambered into Norah's little car. It was cold and uncomfortable.

Jakob had got into the back with the girls (as was his annoying habit, Norah thought: as an adult, wasn't his place in the front, next to her?), and, while she let the engine warm up, she had heard him whisper to the girls that they need not fasten their seat belts.

"Oh, why needn't we?" Lucie, stopped in her tracks, had asked in astonishment.

"Because we're not going far," he had said in his silly, excited voice.

Norah had gripped the steering-wheel, and her hands had begun to tremble.

She had ordered the girls to fasten their seat belts at once, and the fury she felt against Jakob had hardened her tone. Her anger had seemed aimed at them, which Grete and Lucie had felt to be unfair, because they had looked at Jakob with a pained expression.

"We're really not going far," he had said. "In any case, I'm not going to fasten my seat belt."

Norah had moved off.

She, who made a point of never being late, was certainly late now.

She was on the brink of tears.

She was a lost, pathetic creature.

After some hesitation, Grete and Lucie had given up fastening their seat belts and Norah had said nothing, furious with Jakob for seeking always to cast her in the role of a tiresome or unpleasant person, but also disgusted with herself for being, she felt, cowardly, unworthy.

She had felt like driving the car into a bus, just to show him that fastening seat belts was not pointless, but he knew that perfectly well.

That was not the issue. What was *she* up to? What did she want from this man who was hanging on her back with his adorable child in tow? What did she want from this man with the soft, pale eyes, who planted in her flank his tiny painless barbs which, however much she tried to duck and weave, she could no longer shake off?

That was what she could not, dare not, explain to her mother or her sister or her few remaining friends: the sheer ordinariness of such incidents, the narrowness of her thinking, the nullity of such a life beneath the appearance of normality which – such was the terrible power of enchantment wielded by Jakob and his daughter – so easily took in mother, sister and friends.

Norah's father stopped in front of one of the cells that lined the corridor.

He opened the door carefully and immediately stood back.

"You'll be sleeping here," he said.

Gesturing towards the far end of the corridor, he added, as if Norah had shown a slight hesitation where this particular room was concerned, "There are no longer any beds in the other rooms".

Norah switched on the ceiling light.

The walls were covered with posters of basketball players.

"Sony's room," she said.

Her father nodded.

He was breathing more loudly, with his mouth wide open, his back against the wall.

"What are the girls called?" asked Norah.

He shrugged, pretending to think.

She laughed, slightly shocked.

"Don't you remember?" she asked.

"Their mother chose their names, rather strange names, I can never remember them," he said, laughing too, but mirthlessly.

To her great surprise she sensed in him an air of desperation.

"What do they do during the day, when their mother isn't there?"

'They stay in their room," he said abruptly.

"All day?"

"They've all they need. They don't lack for anything. That girl takes good care of them."

Norah then wanted to ask why he had summoned her.

But though she knew her father well enough to be aware that it could not have been for the simple pleasure of seeing her after so long and that he must be wanting something special from her, he seemed at that moment so old and vulnerable that she refrained from asking the question. "When he's ready, he'll let me know," she said to herself, but she could not help telling him: "I can only stay a few days."

She thought of Jakob and the two overexcited girls, and her stomach tightened.

"No, no," he said, agitated all of a sudden, "you must stay a lot longer, it's absolutely essential! Well, see you tomorrow."

Slipping into the corridor, he trotted away, his flip-flops clacking on the concrete, his fat hips wiggling under the thin fabric of his trousers.

With him went the bitter-sweet smell of rotting flowers, of flowers in full bloom crushed under an indifferent foot or bitterly trampled upon, and when she took her dress off to go to sleep she took particular care to spread it out on Sony's bed so that the yellow flowers embroidered on the green cotton cloth remained fresh and intact to the eye and bore no resemblance to the flame tree's wilting flowers and their guilty, sad smell left in her father's wake.

She found her backpack at the foot of the bed.

She sat in her nightdress on her brother's bed. It was covered with a sheet bearing the emblems of American basketball clubs. She cast a pained look at the small chest of drawers covered with dusty knick-knacks, the child's desk with its low top, the basketballs piled up in a corner, most of them burst or deflated.

She recognised every object, every poster, every piece of furniture.

Her brother Sony was thirty-five and Norah had not seen him for many years, but they had always been close.

His room had not changed at all since his adolescence.

How was it possible to live like that?

She shivered in spite of the heat.

Outside the small square window everything was pitch black and totally silent.

No sound came from within the house nor from outside it,

except perhaps – she could not be sure – from time to time that of the flame tree's branches rubbing against the corrugated-iron roof.

She picked up her mobile and phoned the flat.

No reply.

Then she remembered that Lucie had mentioned going to the cinema, which annoyed her because it was Monday and the girls had to be up early the next day for school, and she had to struggle against a sense of impending catastrophe, of terrifying disorder, that swept over her every time she was not there to see, simply see, what was going on, even if she could not always do much about it.

She considered such worries as failings on her part, not as weaknesses.

Because it would be too arrogant to think that she alone knew how to organise Lucie's and Grete's life properly, that she alone, through the power of her reasoning, of her anxious concern, could prevent disaster from crossing the threshold and entering her life.

Had she not already opened her door to evil in a kindly, smiling form?

The only way to mitigate the effects of this major blunder was to be constantly, anxiously, on the alert.

But in response to her father's call she had gone and left.

Sitting on Sony's bed, she now regretted it.

What was her father – this selfish old man – to her, compared with her daughter?

What did her father's existence matter now, when her own hung in the balance?

Although she knew that, if Jakob was sitting in a cinema at that moment, it was pointless, she still dialled his mobile.

She left an exaggeratedly cheery message.

She could see his affable face, the calm, clear, sensible look in his eyes, the slight droop of his lips and the general pleasantness of his finely wrought features. She was still able to acknowledge that such amiability had inspired her with confidence, to the extent that she had not dwelt on the puzzling aspects of the life of this man who had come from Hamburg with his daughter, or on the slightly differing versions he had given of his reasons for coming to France, or the vagueness of his explanations for the lack of assiduity he displayed in his attendance at law school, or the fact that Grete never saw and never spoke about her mother who, he claimed, had stayed in Germany.

She knew now that Jakob would never become a lawyer or anything else for that matter, that he would never contribute meaningfully to the expenses of the household even if he did receive from time to time – from his parents, he said – a few hundred euros which he spent immediately and ostentatiously on meals that cost a lot and on clothes the children did not need, and she knew too – finally admitting it to herself – that she had quite simply established in her home a man and a little girl whom she had to feed and care for, whom she could not throw out, and who had got her boxed in.

That was the way it was.

She dreamt sometimes that she would return home one evening to find Lucie all by herself, relaxed and happy as she used to be in the past, not given to the hollow excitement Jakob gave rise to, and that Lucie would tell her calmly that the others had left for good.

That was the way it was. Norah knew that she would never have the strength to throw them out.

Where would they go, how would they manage?

You could not do such a thing.

Only a miracle, she sometimes thought, could rid her of them, could free Lucie and herself from having to live with this amiable but subtly evil couple.

Yes, that was the way it was, she was trapped.

She got up, took a toilet bag out of her backpack, and went into the corridor.

So deep was the silence that she seemed to hear it quivering.

She opened a door which she remembered as being likely to be that of the bathroom.

But it was her father's room. It was empty and the double bed had not been slept in. Something about the stillness of the air and of everything else made her think that the room was no longer used.

She followed the corridor to the living room and felt her way through it.

The front door was not locked.

Hugging her toilet bag to her chest and feeling her nightdress brushing against the back of her knees, she went outside. With her bare feet on the warm cement she felt herself trampling on the invisible flowers that had fallen from the flame tree. She dared at last to look up at the tree, in the vain hope of seeing nothing there, of not discerning in the crisscross of branches the pale shape, the cold luminescence of her father's hunched body. She thought she could hear, coming from the shadows, loud, painful breathing, desolate panting and even stifled sobs and little groans of distress.

Overcome with emotion, she wanted to call out to him.

But what word could she use to address him by?

She had never been comfortable saying "Daddy", and could not imagine using his first name, which she barely knew.

Her urge to call out to him remained stuck in her throat.

For a long while she watched him rocking very slightly above her head. She could not see his face, but she recognised, gripping the biggest branch, his old plastic flip-flops.

The body of her father, this broken man, shone palely.

What a bad omen!

She wanted to run away from this funereal house as quickly as possible, but she felt that having agreed to return to it and having managed to locate the tree her father was perching in, she was now too deeply committed to be able to abandon him and go back home.

She returned to Sony's room, having given up on the idea of trying to find the bathroom, so fearful was she now of opening a door on a scene or situation which would make her feel guilty.

Sitting on Sony's bed again, she toyed with her mobile, deep in thought.

Should she try again to call home, at the risk of waking the children if they had got back from the cinema?

Or go to sleep with the guilty feeling of having done nothing to avert a potential catastrophe?

She would have liked to hear Lucie's voice again.

A hideous thought went through her mind, so fleetingly that she forgot the exact form it took, but long enough to feel the full horror of it: would she ever hear her daughter's voice again?

And what if, in hastening to her father's side, she had unwittingly chosen between two camps, two possible ways of life, the one inevitably excluding the other, and between two forms of commitment that were fiercely jealous of each other?

Without further ado she dialled the number of the flat, and then, since no one picked up, the number of Jakob's mobile, also in vain.

Having slept little and badly, she got up at dawn, slipped on her green dress and sandals and went in search of the bathroom which was, in fact, next door to Sony's room.

She went back to the little girls' room.

She gently opened the door.

The young woman was still asleep. The two little girls were awake and sitting up in bed. Their perfectly identical eyes were wide open, gazing sternly at Norah.

She smiled at them, murmuring from a distance the tender things she habitually said to Lucie.

The little girls frowned.

One of them spat at her. The thin spittle dribbled on to the sheet.

The other began to imitate her, puffing out her cheeks.

Norah shut the door, not offended, but ill at ease.

She wondered: should she be doing something for these little waifs, and in what capacity, that of a half-sister, a kind of mother, an adult morally responsible for every child one came across?

She once again felt her heart bursting with impotent rage against her father, that thoughtless man who after so many failures could not wait to marry again and produce children who meant nothing to him; a man whose capacity for love and for showing consideration to others was limited, having seemingly in his youth used it all up in his relationship with his old mother, long dead, whom Norah had never known.

It was true he had shown some affection towards Sony, his only son.

But what need had he for a new family, this man without feeling, incomplete, detached?

He was already eating when she re-entered the living room. He was sitting at the table as on the previous evening, dressed in the same pale shabby clothes, his face bent over his plate, stuffing himself with porridge, so that she had to wait until he had finished and had hurled himself backwards as if after enormous physical exertion, panting and sighing. Only then could she ask, looking him straight in the eye, "Now, what's it all about?"

That morning her father had a look that was even more evasive than usual.

Was it because he knew that she had seen him in the flame tree?

But how could that embarrass him, this cynical man who had never batted an eyelid over much more degrading situations?

"Masseck!" he shouted hoarsely.

He said to Norah, "What'll you have? Tea? Coffee?"

She tapped on the table lightly with her fingers, thinking, with a vacant, worried air, that it was time for Lucie and Grete to get up and go to school, and that Jakob would perhaps have forgotten to set his alarm-clock, which would mean that the whole day would bear the mark of failure and neglect. But she herself, was she not excessively virtuous, punctual and scrupulous? Was she not in reality the tiresome woman who she reproached Jakob with trying to turn her into?

"Coffee?" asked Masseck, offering her a full cup.

"Will you please tell me why I came?" she said calmly, looking her father in the eye.

Masseck scurried away.

Her father then started breathing so violently and with such difficulty that Norah leapt from her chair and went up to him.

She stood there, awkwardly, and would have put her question to him again if she had been able.

"You must go and see Sony," he said painfully.

"Where's Sony?"

"In Reubeuss."

"What on earth's Reubeuss?"

No answer.

He breathed less painfully, slumped in his chair, his stomach sticking out, surrounded by the syrupy odour of flame tree flowers in full bloom.

Then, deeply moved, she saw tears running down his grey cheeks.

"It's the prison," he said.

She jumped, almost leapt, backwards.

"What have you done to Sony?" she said. "You were supposed to be looking after him!"

"He was the one who committed the offence, not me," he said, almost inaudibly.

"What offence? What's he done? Oh God, you were supposed to be taking care of him and bringing him up properly!"

She stepped back and sank on to her chair.

She gulped down the coffee, which was acrid, lukewarm and tasteless.

Her hands trembled so much that she dropped the cup on to the glass-topped table.

"That's another broken cup!" her father said. "I spend all my time buying crockery in this house."

"What did Sony do?"

He got up, shaking his head, his old wizened face ravaged by the impossibility of talking.

"Masseck will drive you to Reubeuss," he said.

He walked backwards towards the door to the corridor, slowly, as if he were trying to escape without her noticing.

His toenails were long and yellow.

"So," she said calmly, "is that why there's no one here any more? Is that why everyone has left?"

Her father's back met the door, he groped behind him, opened it and scuttled away down the corridor.

Once, in a meadow in Normandy, she had seen an old abandoned donkey whose hooves had grown so much that he could hardly walk.

Her father was quite capable of trotting along when it suited him!

Her immense feeling of resentment lit up her mind and sharpened her thoughts.

No-one, nothing, could ever excuse their father for his failure to keep Sony on the straight and narrow.

Because, when, thirty years earlier, wishing to abandon their mother and leave France where he was stuck in a mediocre office job, he had suddenly left, taking with him Sony, then aged five (abducting Sony, in truth, because he knew that he would never get their mother's agreement to take the little boy), when he had thereby plunged into despair Norah, her sister and their mother who had never really got over it, when he had promised in a letter left on the kitchen table to take greater care of the child than of his own life, his business affairs and his personal ambitions, their mother, overcome with grief, had clung to that promise, had convinced herself that Sony would have a brilliant career and great opportunities which she, a simple hairdresser, would perhaps not have been able to give him.

Norah could not recall, without gasping for breath, the day she came home from school and found her father's letter.

She was eight, her sister nine, and in the bedroom the three children shared Sony's things had gone: his clothes in the chest of drawers, his bag of Lego, his teddy-bear.

Her first thought was to hide the letter and, by some miracle, the reality of Sony's and their father's departure, so that her mother would not notice.

Then, grasping how powerless she was, she had wandered round the small dark flat, dizzy with worry and pain, staggered by the realisation of what had happened, of the huge suffering already inflicted and certain to go on being inflicted, and of the fact that nothing could undo the terrible event which had occurred.

She had then taken the *métro* to the *salon* where her mother worked.

Even now, thirty years later, she could not summon the strength to recall precisely the moment when she told her mother what had happened and what suffering still lay in wait.

All she could do was bring back to mind, little by little, her mother's wild, staring eyes as she sat on Sony's bed, frantically smoothing the pale blue chenille bed-cover and repeating shrilly, monotonously, "He's too young to live without me. Five years old, that's much too small!"

Their father had phoned the day after his arrival. He was triumphant, full of gusto, and their mother had made an effort to be conciliatory, to sound almost calm, fearing above all that this man who hated open conflict would break off all relations if he thought she was making a big fuss.

He had let Sony talk on the phone but had grabbed the handset back when the child, hearing his mother's voice, had started to cry.

Time had passed and the bitter, heartrending, unacceptable situation had become diluted in the routine of everyday life, had melted in the normality of an existence only disrupted at regular intervals by the arrival of a clumsy, stilted letter from Sony which Norah and her sister had to answer in a similarly formal way so that – their mother calculated – it would appear to their father that he would not run any risk if he allowed greater contact.

How accommodating and sadly devious this gentle, benumbed woman had shown herself to be in her distress! She had gone on buying clothes for Sony, folding them carefully and putting them away in the little boy's chest of drawers.

"For when he gets back," she would say.

But from the outset Norah and her sister had been fully aware that Sony would never come back, knowing as they did their father's lack of empathy, his indifference to the feelings of others, and his penchant for imposing his iron will on his entourage.

If he had decided that Sony was his by right, he would ignore everything that could set limits to his ability to have his only son at his side.

He considered the unhappiness that Sony felt about his exile of little importance, just as he viewed the suffering of his wife as un-avoidable but purely temporary. For he was like that: implacable and terrifying.

Throughout the time when their mother still expected Sony to return, Norah and her sister knew that she had not got the full measure of her husband's intransigence. He would stubbornly re-fuse, for instance, to send the boy back to France for the holidays.

For he was like that: implacable and terrifying.

The years passed and the painful subservience of their mother was rewarded only by an invitation to Norah and her sister to visit their brother.

"Why won't you let Sony come and see us?" their mother shouted down the phone, her face contorted in grief.

"Because I know that you wouldn't let him go again," their father probably answered, calm and self-assured, slightly annoyed per-haps because he loathed weeping and shouting.

"Of course I would, I swear to you!"

But he knew she was lying, and she knew it too. Choking and gasping for breath, she could not go on.

That their father would never want to be burdened with his two daughters, that he would do nothing to keep them by his side, was so blindingly obvious that their mother let them go and see him, sending Norah and her sister as emissaries bearing witness to her immense affliction, to her somewhat disembodied love for a boy whose photograph his father from time to time sent to her, a badly taken picture, always blurred, which invariably showed Sony smiling broadly, in excellent health, amazingly handsome, and expensively dressed.

Their father had acquired a holiday village while it was still under construction. He had given it a complete, luxurious make-over, and it was now making him a wealthy man.

Meanwhile, in Paris, in a symmetrical but contrary manner as if she felt she had to atone for her misfortune by letting things slide, their mother was experiencing money troubles. She kept getting into debt and having to negotiate endlessly with credit-card companies.

Their father sent a little money at irregular intervals, different amounts each time, doubtless because he wished to convey the impression that he was doing all he could.

He was like that, implacable and terrifying.

He was incapable of compassion and remorse and, because as a child he had been tormented by hunger on a daily basis, he was determined now to gorge himself and put his quick intelligence to work with the sole aim of ensuring his comfort and establishing his power. He had no need to say to himself "I've deserved all this," because never did he question for a second the assumption that his privileges and rapidly amassed wealth were his by right.

On the other hand their conscientious, desperate, insecure mother was getting into a mess with her accounts. She tried to keep her books in order but, given her modest income, she could never get them to balance.

That meant she had to move. In the rue des Pyrénées they took a two-bedroom flat that looked on to an inner courtyard. Sony's drawer was stocked with fewer and fewer new clothes.

So when the two girls, aged twelve and thirteen, arrived for the first time in their father's enormous house, paralysed by emotion and exhausted by the heat, they brought with them the seemly, austere, repressed sadness in which they lived and which was betrayed by their short, simply coiffed hair, their denim dresses bought too big so as to last longer and their graceless missionaries' sandals. It aroused overwhelming feelings of disgust in their father, made worse by the fact that they were neither of them very pretty, that they suffered from acne and were overweight. As they grew older they shed the surplus pounds, but they would always, in a way, look fat in the eyes of their father, because he was like that: a man deeply shocked and repelled by ugliness.

That's why, Norah thought, he had loved Sony with as much love as he was capable of.

Their younger brother had appeared on the threshold of the house. He had not dropped from the flame tree, which was still a small and delicate shrub, but had just dismounted from a pony on which he had been slowly trotting round the garden.

Dressed in a cream-coloured riding outfit and wearing real riding boots, he stood with one foot forward, his riding hat tucked under his arm.

No smell of rotting flowers clung to his lithe, elegant frame. The nine-year-old boy's narrow chest was not lit from within by any unusual glow.

He was simply there, smiling, happy, and magnificent, stretching his arms out to his sisters, as dazzling and carefree as they were dull and serious.

And Sony treated them with extreme simplicity and kindness

throughout their stay, during which, scared and reproachful, they tasted a life of luxury beyond their wildest imaginings.

He greeted every remark they made, every question they asked, with a gentle smile and a few non-committal words, making a joke of it, so that they failed to notice that they never got a straight response to anything.

He remained silent whenever they mentioned their mother.

He gazed into space and his lower lip quivered slightly.

But it did not last, he quickly became once again the happy, calm, unpretentious, smooth-skinned, almost-too-gentle boy whom their father would gaze at proudly, obviously comparing him favourably with his two lumpish daughters with that anxious look in their eyes, saying to himself – Norah supposed – that he had done the right thing in not leaving Sony behind, in removing him from his mother's baleful influence which had transformed two amiable little girls into a pair of tubby nuns, particularly because the beautiful woman with the scornful expression and slightly bulging eyes whom he had married two or three years earlier and who wandered silently around the property with a weary, irritated, melancholy and intimidating air, had not yet given him a child and never would.

When at the end of three weeks Norah and her sister returned home they were very upset at leaving Sony behind but relieved to escape a way of life which their loyalty to their mother made them feel duty-bound to condemn ("Mummy has money troubles," they had found the courage to tell their father, on learning that Sony was being sent to a celebrated private school, to which he had responded with a sigh, "My poor dear girls, who doesn't have money troubles!").

Standing on the threshold with one foot in front of the other, dressed this time in full basketball gear, his ball under his arm, and making every effort to smile, Sony had said goodbye, his lower lip trembling slightly, with the same smooth, kind, inscrutable and submissive air he always had.

Their father was there too, standing up straight beneath the scanty foliage of the young flame tree, looking elegant, his narrow hips slightly turned away.

He had laid his hand on Sony's shoulder and the boy had seemed then to cringe, to be trying to huddle up and, greatly surprised, Norah had thought, "He's afraid of our father," before getting into the car driven by Mansour and rejecting the idea, since it bore no relation to anything she had seen during their stay.

Because their father, that terrifying, unbending man, had always treated Sony with great kindness.

He had even shown him some tenderness.

But Norah had tried to imagine how distraught her five-year-old brother must have been when he had found himself in this unknown country, alone in a hotel with his father, then in this hastily rented house invaded soon by numerous relatives; when it had slowly dawned on him that he was embarking on a new existence and that there was no longer any question that he could once again live with his mother and sisters in the little flat in the twelfth *arrondissement* that until then had constituted his whole universe.

She had felt very sorry for Sony and no longer envied him his father's love or the pony in the garden.

And the life of the three of them, grim, sombre, thrifty and meritorious, suddenly appeared free and desirable to her compared with that of Sony, the pampered little prisoner.

Their mother, hungry for news, listened dejectedly and in silence to the cautious account given by the two sisters of what they had seen and heard.

Then she burst into tears and kept repeating "So he's lost to me, lost!" as if the education and affluence Sony enjoyed were erecting an impenetrable barrier between herself and the boy, even if she could see him again.

It was at this time that their mother's behaviour changed.

She left the hairdresser's where she had been slaving away for twenty years or more and began going out in the evening. Although Norah and her sister never suspected it at the time, they gathered years later that their mother must have worked as a prostitute and that this activity, despite her outward cheerfulness, was the particular form her grief took.

Norah and her sister went back to their father's on holiday once or twice.

No longer, now, did their mother ever want to be told anything about what they had seen there.

She had adopted a hard, determined look; her face was smooth under her makeup; and at the drop of a hat, with a sarcastic curl of the lip and an angry sweep of the hand, she was given to saying, "Oh, what do I care?"

This new demeanour and this gritty bitterness enabled her to meet exactly the kind of man she was looking for. She married a bank manager who like her was divorced. Still her husband today, he was an uncomplicated, likeable and well-paid man and showed Norah and her sister much kindness, even – at their father's invitation – taking the three of them to see Sony all together for the first time.

Their mother had not seen the boy since he had left.

Sony was now sixteen.

On learning that their mother had remarried, their father had at once sent her and her new husband an invitation and had reserved several nights' accommodation for them in the town's best hotel. It was as if – Norah thought – he had been waiting for their mother to make a new life for herself to cease worrying that that she would try to abduct Sony.

And that was how they had all found themselves, like a big happy reconstituted family, Norah and her sister, their mother and her husband, Sony and their father, seated in the hotel dining-room eating local delicacies, their father and the husband discussing calmly, with a touch of embarrassment, the international situation, whilst the boy and his mother, sitting close together, shot furtive, awkward glances at each other.

Sony was as usual superbly dressed; he wore a dark linen suit; his skin was soft and smooth, and he had a short afro haircut.

Their mother's face wore its new fixed expression. Her mouth was slightly twisted, her heavily lacquered hair was dyed pale blonde, and Norah noticed that in asking Sony about his school and favourite subjects she took care not to make mistakes of grammar and syntax because she thought Sony was much better educated and more refined than herself, and that made her feel miserable and uncomfortable.

Their father looked at them with an air of happy relief, as if at long last he had managed to reconcile a pair of old enemies.

"Is that what he really thinks now?" Norah had wondered crossly, with astonishment. "Has he managed to convince himself that it was Sony and our mother who, throughout all those years, were the ones who refused to meet each other?"

Long before, their father had said to their mother, when, wild with grief, she had told him on the telephone that, since he refused to send Sony to spend the holidays with her, she was going to borrow the air fare to visit her son in his house, "If I see you getting off that plane, I'll slit his throat and mine under your very eyes!"

But was he really man enough to cut his own throat?

There he was now, seated at the head of the table, handsome, charming, exquisitely polite, his cold dark eyes shining with love and pride whenever he gazed at Sony's adorable face.

Norah noticed that her brother never looked anyone straight in the eye. His affable, impersonal gaze flitted from one person to another without dwelling on any particular face and, when spoken to, he stared fixedly at an invisible point in the distance without ceasing to smile or to adopt an expression of formal interest in whatever was being said to him.

He was particularly careful, Norah thought, not to be caught unawares by their father's gaze. Even then, even when their father looked at him and Sony glanced elsewhere, he seemed to withdraw, to curl up in the depths of his being where he was safe from every judgement, every feeling that involved him.

He exchanged a few words with his mother's husband, and then with her, haltingly, because she had reached the limit of what she dared ask him.

After the meal they went their separate ways, and although a few days were left before their departure, Sony and their mother never saw each other again and their mother never mentioned him again.

Their father had organised a lavish tourism programme, had hired a guide and a chauffeur for their mother and her husband and even paid for a few supplementary nights in one of the chalets in his holiday village at Dara Salam.

All that, however, their mother turned down, dismissing the guide and the chauffeur, and she brought forward their departure date.

She no longer left the hotel. She just went back and forth between her room and the pool, smiling in the same mechanical, distant, very calm way that Sony did, and Norah and her sister took on the task of entertaining the husband who took pleasure in everything and found nothing to complain about, and on the last evening, at a loss to think where to go, they took him to dinner at their father's, where the two men chatted until two in the morning, parting with reluctance and promising to see each other again.

That had really annoyed Norah. "He was making fun of you the whole time," she said to the husband, with a knowing snigger, as they went back to the hotel.

"What? Not at all. He's a very nice chap, your dad!"

And Norah immediately felt guilty for her spiteful remark, telling herself that it was indeed perfectly possible that their father had genuinely enjoyed the husband's company and that she was simply feeling angry with the two of them for appearing to trivialise her mother's immense unhappiness, telling herself too that her mother had conceived the unseemly idea of bringing her husband to their father's house in the obscure hope no doubt of provoking an almighty row, at the end of which she and Sony would be avenged and their father confounded, his cruelty having been exposed and owned up to; but ought she not to have understood that this ideal husband was not the sort of person to make a scene?

Their mother never saw Sony again, never once wrote to him or telephoned him, never even mentioned his name.

She and her husband had moved to a house in the outer suburbs. From time to time Norah brought Lucie to see her. She had the impression that her mother had never stopped smiling since their return, with a faint smirk that seemed disconnected from her face and to float lightly in front of her, as if she had snatched it from Sony to mask her pain.

Norah continued passing on to her the odd bits of news she got from Sony or their father – about Sony's studies in London, or his return to their father a few years later – but she often felt that their mother, who smiled and nodded, was trying not to listen.

Norah spoke about Sony to her less and less, then stopped doing so altogether on learning that, after getting a very good degree, he had ended up in his father's house, where he led a strangely passive, idle, lonely existence.

Her heart of course often missed a beat when she thought of him.

Ought she not to have gone to see him more often, or made him come and see her?

Was he not, despite his money and opportunities, deprived?

As for Norah, she had managed, all alone, to train to become a lawyer. She had not found life easy, but she had kept her nose to the grindstone.

No-one had helped her, and neither her mother nor her father had ever told her that they were proud of her.

And yet she did not bear a grudge and even felt guilty about not going to help Sony in some way.

But what could she have done?

A devil had possessed the five-year-old boy and had never let go of him.

What could she have done?

That was what she kept asking herself as she sat on the back seat of the black Mercedes driven by Masseck. As the car moved slowly down the deserted street she gazed in the rear-view mirror at her father standing motionless by the gate, waiting perhaps to be on his own to flit heavily up again into the deep shade of the flame tree and sit on the branch stripped and polished by his flip-flops. That was what she kept wondering as she fiddled with the extensively rubber-stamped official documents which her father had given her: had she not, out of carelessness, let Sony down badly?

The Mercedes was dirty and dusty, and the seats were covered in crumbs.

In the past her father would never have put up with such slovenliness.

She leaned towards Masseck and asked him why Sony was in prison.

He clicked his tongue and sniggered. Norah realised that he had been badly put out by her question and would not answer it.

Deeply embarrassed, she forced herself to laugh too.

How could she have done that?

Obviously it was not his place to tell her.

She was confused. She felt ashamed.

Just before getting into the car she had tried to contact Jakob. In vain: the phone rang in the flat but no one answered.

It seemed to her unlikely that the children had already left for school, and equally unlikely that all three were sleeping so soundly that they had not been aroused by the phone's insistent ringing.

So what was going on?

Her legs were shaking nervously.

She would have been grateful, at that moment, to take refuge in the fragrant golden semi-darkness of the big tree!

She smoothed her hair back, retied her bun and, as she stretched forward to see her reflection in the rear-view mirror, thought that Sony would perhaps have difficulty recognising her because, when they had last met eight or nine years earlier, she had not had those two lines on either side of her mouth or the rather thick, podgy chin against which she remembered having struggled ferociously when younger, guiltily aware that her father found rolls of fat disgusting; later, without remorse, and even with a feeling of satisfied provocation, she had allowed it to develop in full know-ledge of the fact that such a chin would offend that slim man with a preference for thin women, and from that moment she had resolved to be free, to cast aside all concerns about pleasing a father who did not love her.

As for him, well, he had gone completely to fat.

She shook her head, afraid and lost in thought.

The car was crossing the town centre and Masseck was driving slowly in front of the big hotels, calling out their names in rather a grand tone of voice.

Norah recognised the one where their mother and her husband had briefly stayed, back in the days when Sony, a first-rate student at high school, seemed destined for great things.

She had never tried to go into the reasons why Sony had returned to live with his father after studying political science in London, and above all why he seemed to have made nothing of his life or his gifts.

That was because she considered him at the time to be much luckier than she was. She had had to work her way through college waiting at tables in a fast-food restaurant, so she did not think she was under any obligation to worry about her spoilt younger brother's mental state.

He had fallen into a devil's clutches and had never been able to break loose.

Sony must in truth have suffered greatly from clinical depression. "Poor, poor boy," she thought.

It was at that moment that she saw Jakob, Grete and Lucie sitting at the hotel terrace where they had all had lunch before.

Her blood ran cold. She closed her eyes.

When she opened them again, Masseck had turned into another street.

They were running along the coast road and the car was filled with the smell of the sea.

Masseck had fallen silent and his face, which Norah could see in profile, had taken on a sullen, stubborn, hurt look as if, in being made to drive to Reubeuss, he was being personally slighted.

He parked opposite the high grey walls of the prison.

Standing in the hot, dry wind, she queued behind a large number of women. Noticing that they had all put down on the pavement the baskets and parcels they had brought with them, she did the same with the plastic bag Masseck had handed to her, telling her grudgingly, with an air of outraged scorn, that it contained coffee and food for Sony.

Then, having to wait for her, he settled down in his seat with his door wide open so that it did not get too hot in the car, and turned his face away from her.

"There's nothing to be ashamed of," she nearly told him.

But she stopped herself from doing so, wondering whether it was in fact true.

Her stomach was churning. Who, in reality, were the three people she had seen on the hotel terrace? Herself and her sister, when they were small, accompanied by some stranger?

Oh no, she was sure it was her daughter and Grete with Jakob. The children were wearing little striped dresses with matching sunhats which she recognised from having bought them the previous summer. She had had a spasm of guilt as she left the shop, she remembered, because the outfits were perhaps too elegant for little girls, not at all the sort she and her sister had ever worn.

What devil had got her sister into his clutches?

After a long wait outside the prison she was called into an office where she handed over her passport together with the documents her father had given her which certified that she had the right to visit her brother.

She also handed over the bag of food.

"Are you the lawyer?" said a warder. He wore a tattered uniform. He had reddened, shining eyes, and his eyelids twitched nervously.

"No, no," she said, "I'm his sister."

"It says here you're the lawyer."

Circumspectly she said, "I am a lawyer, but today I'm just here to see my brother."

He hesitated and gazed fixedly at the little yellow flowers on Norah's green dress.

Then she was shown into a big room with pale blue walls, divided down the middle by metal grating. The women who, like her, had waited on the pavement outside were already there.

She went up to the grating and then saw her brother Sony entering at the other end of the room.

The men who came in with him rushed towards the grating, making such a din that she could not hear Sony's greeting.

"Sony, Sony!" she said.

She felt giddy and clung to the grating.

She got as close as she could to the dirty, dusty metal grating in order to be able to see clearly this thirty-year-old man who was her younger brother. Under the blemished skin, behind the eczema scars, she recognised his long handsome face and gentle, rather vague expression. When he smiled, it was with the same distant, radiant smile she had always associated him with and which – as in the past – tugged at her heart-strings, because she had sensed then, and now knew, that this smile served merely to keep secret, untouched, an unhappiness which he could never express.

His unshaven cheeks were covered in stubble and his hair, some strands of which were long and some short, stood up on his head – where, that is, it was not flattened, on the side he slept on, no doubt.

He was talking to her, smiling – smiling all the time – but she could not hear a word because of the din.

"Sony!" she said, "What was that you said? Speak up!"

He was scratching his forehead savagely. It was pale with eczema.

"You need a cream for that?" she said. "Is that what you're saying?"

He seemed to hesitate for a moment, then nodded, as if it did not matter much if she had misunderstood, as if "cream" was as good a reply as any.

He shouted something, a single word.

This time Norah clearly heard the name of their sister.

A fleeting sensation of panic drove every thought out of her mind.

For a devil had grabbed hold of her too.

Now it seemed impossible to explain to Sony, to shriek at him that their sister had become an alcoholic and was so heavily addicted – as she herself acknowledged – that the only way out for her was to seek refuge in a mystical sect from which she occasionally wrote Norah wild, fanatical, sloppy letters enclosing the odd photo that showed her with long grey hair, as thin as a rail, meditating on a dirty rubber mat and sucking on her lower lip.

Norah could not bellow at Sony: "And all that because our father took you from us when you were five!"

She could not, no, she could not say anything to this haggard face, those hollow, dead eyes and those dry lips which seemed detached from the smile that played on them.

The visit was over.

The warders were leading the prisoners out.

Norah glanced at her watch. Only a few minutes had elapsed since she had entered the room.

She waved to Sony and said "I'll be back again!" as he moved away, dragging his feet, tall and gaunt, dressed in a grubby T-shirt and an old pair of trousers cut off at the knee.

He turned and made the gesture of putting a spoon to his lips.

"Yes, yes," she said, "there's coffee there, and something for you to eat!"

The room was stiflingly hot.

Norah clung to the grating afraid, if she let go, of fainting.

She was then dismayed to find that, without realizing it, she had lost control of her bladder, suddenly conscious that she felt a warm liquid running down her thighs and calves and into her sandals. But she could do nothing about it and even the awareness of micturition seemed to elude her.

She stepped away from the puddle in horror.

But in the rush for the exit no-one appeared to have noticed.

She was shaking so violently with fury against her father that her teeth were chattering.

What had he done to Sony?

What had he done to them all?

He was present everywhere, he was installed with impunity in each one of them, and even when dead he would go on hurting and tormenting them.

She asked Masseck to drop her at the hotel.

"You can go home," she said, "I'll manage, I'll take a taxi."

To her intense embarrassment the smell of urine soon filled the Mercedes.

Without saying a word Masseck lowered the windows in front.

She was relieved to find the hotel terrace empty.

But the vision of Jakob and the girls continued to haunt her. The subtle but clearly perceptible shadow of their cheerful, conspiratorial presence hung over her, so that when she felt a puff of wind she looked up. But all she could see above her head was a large bird with pale feathers outlined against the sky. It flapped its wings heavily and clumsily, casting over the terrace a huge, cold, unnatural shadow.

Once again she felt a spasm of anger, but it passed as soon as the bird did.

She went into the hotel and looked for the bar.

"I'm due to meet M. Jakob Ganzer," she said to the man on the reception desk.

He nodded and Norah made her way to the bar in her wet sandals. The green carpet with its golden leafy pattern was the same as it had been twenty years earlier.

She ordered tea and went to the toilet to wash her legs and feet.

She took her pants off, rinsed them in the basin, squeezed the water out of them and held them for a long while under the hand dryer.

She was afraid of what awaited her in the bar, where she had noticed that there was a computer connected to the internet for customers' use.

Sipping her tea slowly, so as to postpone as long as possible the moment when she would have to start her internet search, she eyed the barman as he watched a football match on the big screen above the bar, and she kept thinking that there was no worse fate for the children of a dangerous man like her father than to be loved by him.

Because Sony was certainly the one who had paid most dearly for being the child of such a man.

As for herself, well, it was true that nothing irreparable had happened yet, just as it was possible she had not yet understood what was in store for her and Lucie, possible, too, that she had not yet realised that the devil had gripped her too, that he was crouching, biding his time.

She paid for thirty minutes' connection and soon found, in the archives of the paper *Le Soleil*, a long article about Sony.

She read and reread it with increasing horror as she went over the same words again and again.

Holding her head in her hands she stammered, "Oh my God, Sony, oh my God, Sony", unable at first to make any connection between her brother and such an appalling crime, then, almost despite herself, lingering on precise details, such as his date of birth and physical description, which banished all hope that it could have been a case of mistaken identity.

And who else could have been the son of the father mentioned in the article? Who else could have shown, in the midst of such horror, the immense kindness which the writer of the article singled out as being a particularly despicable trait?

She started to moan "My poor, dear Sony", but immediately swallowed the words as if they were a mouthful of saliva, because a woman was dead and Norah normally stood up for women who had died in such circumstances and felt no pity for their tormenters even if they were gentle, smiling, unhappy men caught in the grip of a devil since the age of five.

She carefully logged off from the newspaper's website and walked away from the computer, eager now to get back as soon as possible to her father's house to ply him with questions, almost afraid, if she lingered, that he would have flown off for good.

She was crossing the terrace when she saw them – Jakob, Grete and Lucie – sitting where they had been before. They were being served bissap juice.

They had not seen her yet.

The two little girls, wearing sunhats that matched the red-and-white striped dresses with short puff sleeves and smocked tops that she had later regretted buying (had she thought her father would have approved of the choice, of the vague longing to transform the girls into expensive dolls?), were chatting gaily, addressing the occasional remark to Jakob which he answered in the same cheerful, level tone.

And that was what Norah noticed straight away: their calm, ready banter. She was filled with a strange melancholy.

Could it be that the unhealthy excitement which she suspected Jakob of provoking and sustaining was triggered by her presence, and that in the end everything went well when she was not there?

It seemed to her that she had never been able to envelop the children in the serene atmosphere which she now observed bathing the little group.

The pink shade of the parasol cast a fresh, innocent blush on their skin.

Oh, she thought, that unhealthy feverishness, was she perhaps the source of it?

She went up to their table, pulled up a chair and sat down between Grete and Lucie.

"Hello, Mum," Lucie said, getting up to kiss her on the cheek. And Grete said, "Hello, Norah."

They went on with their conversation, about a character in a cartoon they had been watching that morning in their room.

"Have a taste of this, it's delicious," said Jakob, pushing his bissap juice towards her.

She found that he had already got a tan, and as for the long fair hair that hung over his forehead and down the back of his neck, it seemed as if the sun had bleached it even more.

"Go up and get your things," he told the girls.

They left the table and went into the hotel with their arms around each other. One girl was fair and the other dark. Their closeness had never seemed entirely credible to Norah because, while they got on very well together, they were always silently jockeying for the first place in Norah's and Jakob's affections.

"You know my brother Sony," Norah said quickly.

"Yes?"

She took a deep breath but could not help bursting into tears, into floods of tears which her hands were powerless to wipe away.

Jakob picked up a tissue, dried her cheeks, took her in his arms, and patted her back.

She suddenly wondered why she had always had the vague feeling, whenever they made love, that he was making an effort, that he was paying for his and Grete's keep because, at that moment, she felt great tenderness in him. She held him tight.

"Sony's in prison," she said quickly, her voice breaking.

Glancing around to make sure the children were not back in earshot, she told Jakob that four months earlier Sony had strangled his stepmother, the woman whom his father had married a few years before but whom Norah had never met.

She remembered that Sony had informed her at the time that their father had remarried and that his new wife had given birth to twin girls, something the old man had not seen fit to tell her himself.

But Sony had not revealed that he had embarked on a relationship with his stepmother, nor that, as the article in *Le Soleil* put it, they had planned to run away together. He had never told her that he had fallen head over heels in love with the woman who was about his own age, nor did he mention that she changed her mind, broke off the affair and asked him to move out of the house.

He had lain in wait for her in her bedroom, where she slept alone.

"I know why my father wasn't there," Norah said. "I know where he goes at night."

Standing by the door Sony had waited in the shadows while she put her children to bed in another room.

When she entered he grabbed her from behind and strangled her with a length of plastic-coated clothes-line.

He had then carefully lowered the woman's body on to the bed and gone back to his own room, where he had slept until morning.

All that he had himself described, without prompting and with dazzling affability, as the newspaper article very disapprovingly stressed.

Jakob listened closely, gently shaking the ice cubes at the bottom of his glass.

He was wearing jeans and a newly laundered blue shirt that smelt nice and fresh.

Norah said nothing, afraid she might be about to urinate again without realising it.

It came back to her, the burning, suffocating, scandalised feeling of incomprehension she had experienced on reading the article, but her indignation refused stubbornly to focus on Sony. Their father alone was to blame. He had got into the habit of replacing one wife with another, of making too young a woman, a woman he had bought in one way or another, live with his ageing body and damaged spirit.

He who had been perching for so long on the big branch of the flame tree that his flip-flops had made it shine, by what right had he snatched from thirty-year-old men the love that was their due, by what right had he helped himself so freely to that store of burning passion?

Grete and Lucie came out of the hotel with their backpacks on and stood beside the table, ready to leave.

Norah gazed intently, sorrowfully, at Lucie's face. It suddenly seemed to her that this beloved face meant nothing to her any more.

It was the same face, with its delicate features, smooth skin, tiny nose and curls on the forehead, but she did not recognize it.

She felt at once vibrant and, as a mother, distant, distracted.

She had always loved her daughter passionately, so what was happening?

Was it simply that she was humiliated to feel that, behind her back, Jakob and the children had taken advantage of her absence to establish a close understanding?

"Right," said Jakob, "let's go, I've already paid the bill."

"Go where?" asked Norah.

"We can't stay in the hotel, it's too expensive."

"True."

"We can go to your father's, can't we?"

"Yes," said Norah airily.

He asked the girls if they had separated their things carefully into their two backpacks and left nothing behind. Norah could not fail to notice that he was now able to talk to them with the gentle firmness she had always wanted so much to see in him.

"And school?" she asked casually.

"The Easter holidays have begun," Jakob said, somewhat surprised.

"I'd forgotten that."

She was upset and started trembling.

Things like that had always been her responsibility.

Was Jakob lying to her?

"My father never liked girls much. Now there are suddenly going to be two more!"

Faced with their serious expression, she giggled nervously,

feeling sheepish at having such a father and for making fun of him.

Because all that ever emerged from that house was heartbreak and dishonour.

In the taxi she had some difficulty indicating precisely where her father lived.

She had only a rough idea of the address, just the name of the district, "Point E", and so many homes had been built in the last twenty years that she was soon quite lost. She once again misdirected the driver and for a moment thought that Jakob and the children were going to think that she had made it all up, the existence of the house and of its owner.

She had taken Lucie's hand in hers and was alternately squeezing it and stroking it.

In her distress she thought that genuine motherly love was slipping through her fingers: she no longer felt it, she was cold, jittery, dysfunctional.

When they stopped at last in front of the house she jumped out and ran to the door where her father appeared, still wearing the same rumpled clothes, his long yellow toenails sticking out from the same brown flip-flops.

He gazed suspiciously past Norah at Jakob and the girls taking their bags out of the boot.

She asked him nervously if they could stay in the house.

"The brunette is my daughter," she said.

"So you have a daughter?"

"Yes, I wrote to you when she was born."

"And him, he's your husband?"

"Yes."

"You're really married?"

"Yes."

She lied, knowing how much the proprieties mattered to her father, but it none the less made her cross.

He smiled with relief and shook hands affably with Jakob and then with Grete and Lucie, complimenting them on their nice dresses, speaking with the same urbane, winning drawl that he had used when showing V.I.P.s round his holiday village.

After lunch – during which he once again tortured himself with gluttony, leaning back heavily in his chair to get his breath back every so often, his mouth wide open and his eyes closed – Norah led him off to Sony's room.

He showed great reluctance to go in but, bloated with food, he could do nothing but flop down on the bed.

He was gasping like a dying animal.

Norah stood leaning against the door.

He pointed towards a drawer and she opened it. She found on Sony's T-shirts the framed photo of a very young woman with round cheeks and laughing eyes who was making her thin white dress swirl around her slender, beautiful legs.

Norah felt bitter, full of pity for this woman, and said to her father, "Why did you marry again? What more did you want?"

He made a limp, slow gesture with his hand and muttered that he was not interested in being lectured at.

Then, slowly getting his breath back, he said: "I asked you to come because I want you to take on Sony's defence. He hasn't got a lawyer. I can't afford a lawyer."

"He hasn't got a lawyer yet?"

"No, I tell you. I can't afford a good lawyer."

"Can't afford it? What about Dara Salam?"

She did not like the sound of her voice, nor its spiteful, nagging tone. She did not like being aware that she was having a row with this baneful man, her father, when she had tried so hard to keep their relationship bland and innocuous.

"I know where you spend your nights," she said, more calmly.

He glanced at her askance. There was hostility and menace in his hard round eyes.

"Dara Salam went bankrupt," he said. "So there's nothing doing there. You'll have to take on Sony's case."

"But that's not possible, I'm his sister. What makes you think I can be his defence lawyer?"

"It's not forbidden, is it?"

"No, but it's not done."

"So what? Sony needs a lawyer, that's all that matters."

"You still love Sony?" she said, trying to understand.

He turned over on the bed and put his head in his hands.

"That boy is all I have to live for," he said.

He lay there, curled up in a foetal position, old and enormously fat, and Norah suddenly realised that one day he would be dead. Until then she had always thought, with some annoyance, that nothing human could ever happen to him.

He stirred, and sat on the edge of the bed. He then had difficulty getting up.

He turned his eyes from the pile of balls in a corner of the room to the photo Norah still held in her hand.

"She was evil, that woman, it was she who ensnared him. He would never have dared look at his father's wife."

"That may be so," Norah said, "but she's the one who's dead."

"How much will Sony get? What do you think?" he said in a tone of utter helplessness. "He won't surely spend the next ten years in jail. Or will he?"

"She's dead, he strangled her, she must have suffered a great deal," Norah said. "The little girls, the twins, what did you tell them?"

"I didn't tell them anything, I never speak to them. They're no longer here."

He looked stubborn and annoyed.

"What do you mean, no longer here?"

"I sent them north this morning, to her family," he said, jutting his chin at the photo of his wife.

Suddenly Norah could not bear to look at him any longer. She felt trapped. He had got her in his grip. In truth he had them all in his grip, ever since he first abducted Sony, thereby putting the stamp of his ferocity on their very existence.

By sheer strength of will she had got herself an education that had led to her securing a partnership in a law firm. She had given birth to Lucie and bought a flat. But she would willingly have given up all that in return for being able to turn the clock back and prevent Sony being snatched from them.

"You said once, if I remember rightly, that you would never fail Sony," her father said.

A few yellow flowers had stained the sheet. They had fallen from his shoulders and been crushed beneath his bulk.

How heavy the devil must now be who held Sony in his grasp, Norah thought.

It was at dinner that night, when Jakob and her father were chatting amiably, that Norah heard him say: "When my daughter Norah lived here . . ."

"What are you talking about? I've never lived in this house!" she said.

He was holding a leg of roast chicken. He bit off a chunk, took his time chewing it, then said calmly, "No, I know. I meant when you were living in this town, at Grand-Yoff."

He then looked as if a wad of cotton wool had got stuck in his throat. His ears started throbbing gently.

The voices of Jakob and her father, and of the girls who were conversing in an exaggeratedly level-headed way, seemed to be fading away, becoming muffled and almost inaudible.

"Listen," she said angrily, "I've never lived at Grand-Yoff, nor anywhere else in this country."

But she was not sure of having spoken or, if she had, of being listened to.

She cleared her throat and repeated more loudly: "I've never lived at Grand-Yoff."

Her father raised his eyebrows in amused astonishment.

Jakob looked hesitantly first at Norah, then at her father, and the girls had stopped eating, so that Norah, dismayed at appearing to beg to be believed, felt obliged to say, yet again: 'I've never lived anywhere but France, you ought to know that."

"Masseck!" her father shouted. He said a few words to Masseck, who went to fetch a shoe-box which he put on the table. Norah's father started rummaging in it impatiently.

He pulled out a small square photograph which he held out to Norah.

As with all the photographs her father took, the picture was, deliberately or otherwise, somewhat blurred. "He manages to make them fuzzy so as to be able to say what he likes about them," Norah thought.

The young, plump woman was standing in front of a little house with pink walls and a blue corrugated-iron roof. She was wearing a lime-green, yellow-flowered dress.

"That's not me," Norah said with relief. "That's my sister. You've always mixed us up, even though she's older than I am."

Without answering her, he showed the photograph to Jakob,

then to Grete and Lucie. Embarrassed, the girls gave it a cursory glance.

"I'd have thought it was you, too," Jakob said with a nervous laugh. "You're very alike."

"Not really," Norah said. "It's a bad photograph, that's all."

Her father waved the photograph in front of Lucie, who had lowered her eyes and was blushing slightly.

"Come on, Lucie, it's your mother in the photograph, isn't it?"

Lucie nodded vigorously.

"You see," he said, "your own daughter recognises you."

Furtively, but harshly as always, he glanced sideways at her.

"You didn't know your sister once lived at Grand-Yoff?" Jakob said, trying obviously to be helpful. "But," Norah said to herself, "I don't need anyone's help with this."

How absurd it all was!

She suddenly felt very tired. "No, I didn't know. When she's away proselytising with her funny sect, my sister hardly ever tells me what she's up to or where she's going." Without looking him in the eye, Norah said to her father: "What was she doing here?"

"It was you who were here, not your sister. You must know why you came. I do know, after all, how to tell my children apart."

In the night, leaving Jakob asleep, she left the oppressive atmosphere of the house and went outside, knowing full well that she would not find any peace there either, because he was on the alert up in the branches of the flame tree.

And although in the pitch-black darkness she could not see him, she could hear him, hear the noises he made in his throat, and hear the tiny movements of his flip-flops on the branch. All those sounds were amplified in her skull, to the point almost of deafening her.

She stood there, motionless, with her bare feet on the rough warm concrete of the threshold, aware that her arms, legs and face were paler than the night and would probably be shining with an almost milky brightness, and that doubtless he could see her as she could now see him, his face in shadow, crouching in his white clothes.

She was torn between satisfaction at having found him out and horror at sharing a secret with this man.

She now felt that he would always resent the fact that she had a share in this mystery even though she had in no way sought to know anything about it.

Was that the reason why he had tried to muddy the waters with that story about a photo taken at Grand-Yoff?

She could not even remember ever having set foot there.

The only troubling detail – as she freely acknowledged – was that her sister was wearing a frock very similar to hers, because her mother had made the lime-green, yellow-flowered dress thanks to a Bouchara fabric voucher which Norah had found.

It would not have been possible for her mother to make two dresses out of that one piece of cotton cloth.

Norah went back inside and walked along the corridor to the twins' room, where Masseck had put up Grete and Lucie.

She pushed the door open gently and, on sniffing the warm smell of the children's hair, suddenly felt overwhelmed by the love that had deserted her.

Then it faded away, vanished, and she once again felt hard, distracted, remote, as if possessed by something that had calmly and without justification entered her being and now refused to yield to anyone or anything.

"Lucie, my poppet, my little dark-haired darling," she murmured. Her disembodied voice made her think of Sony's smile, or their mother's, because it did not seem to come out of her body but to hover in front of her lips, a pure product of the air. Nothing tangible seemed to inhabit any longer those words which she had so often uttered.

Once more she found herself in front of Sony, separated from him by the grating against which they both had to stick their lips if they were to have any hope of hearing each other.

She told him that she had brought him some ointment for his eczema, and that the medicine would be given to him in the prison sickbay once it had been checked. Sony burst out laughing, saying, in the affable tone he always adopted whatever the subject, that he would never get to see it.

Despite the thinness of his body, the scabs on his skin and his unkempt beard, she could now recognise her brother's kindly, saintly face, and tried to discern upon it signs of distress, suffering or remorse.

There was none of that.

"I can't believe it, Sony," she said.

She thought, with pain and bitterness, of the many occasions when she had heard the same words uttered pitifully, fruitlessly, by a criminal's family.

But Sony had been, really, a sort of ecstatic.

Scratching his face, he shook his head.

"I'm going to defend you. I'm going to be your lawyer. I'll have the right to visit you more frequently."

Still scratching his cheeks and forehead furiously, he kept shaking his head.

"It wasn't me, you know," he said calmly. "I wouldn't have done anything to hurt her."

"What? What's that you're saying?"

"It wasn't me."

"It wasn't you who killed her? Oh my God, Sony!"

Her teeth hit the grating. Her lips tasted of rust.

"So who killed her, Sony?"

He shrugged his painfully thin shoulders.

He had already told her that he was hungry the whole time because, among the hundred or so prisoners with whom he shared his vast cell, there were some who stole part of his rations every day.

All he now ever dreamt about at night, he told her with a smile, was food.

"It was him," Sony said.

"Our father?"

He nodded, moistening his dry lips with his tongue over and over again.

Then, knowing that the visit was nearly over, he started speaking very quickly: "You remember, Norah, when I was little and we were still living together, there was this game we played: you'd pick me up, swing me up and down, and shout 'with a one, with a two,' and on 'with a three!' you'd throw me on to the bed saying it was the ocean, and that I had to swim back to the shore, do you remember?"

Throwing his head back, he chuckled with delight, and Norah recognised at once, with a violent shock, the little boy with the wide-open mouth whom she used to throw on the blue chenille counterpane that covered his bed.

"How are the twins?" he said.

"He's sent them to their mother's family, I believe." She spoke with difficulty. Her teeth were clenched and her tongue was thick.

As he moved away from the grating, following the other prisoners, he turned round and said gravely: "The little girls, the twins, they're my daughters, not his. He knew that, you understand."

For a long while, in the scorching midday sun, she walked up and down the pavement in front of the prison, trying to summon up the strength to rejoin Masseck in the car.

"So everything is falling into place at last," she said to herself, with icy exultation.

She seemed to be staring into the eyes of the devil that held her brother in his clutches, thinking: "I'll make him let go, but what is it all about, and who can ever restore what has been taken away over the years?"

What, indeed, was it all about?

Masseck took a different route back from the usual one, she noticed, but she did not pay it much attention until he stopped in front of a little house with pink walls and a blue corrugated-iron roof, turned the engine off and put his hands on his knees. She was determined not to ask any questions, having decided that she would not take a single step towards a possible trap.

For Sony's sake, and her own, she had to be a strong, skilled tactician. "The unsuspected will never again get the better of me," she said to herself.

"He told me to show you this house," Masseck said, "because that's where you lived."

"He's wrong, my sister did."

Why was she so reluctant to look closely at the house?

Feeling awkward, she cast an eye over the faded pink walls, the narrow balustrade in front and, close by, the humbler houses where children were playing.

Since she had seen the photograph, she thought she could no longer stop herself remembering the place.

But did the memory not come from further back?

Were there not, behind the pink walls, two small rooms with dark blue tiles, and at the back, a tiny kitchen that smelt of curry?

During dinner she noticed that Jakob and her father enjoyed talking to each other and that, if the latter could scarcely pretend to be interested in children, he none the less sometimes made an effort to make faces at Lucie and Grete, accompanied by funny noises which were supposed to make them laugh.

He was relaxed, almost merry, as if – Norah thought – she had lifted the terrible weight of Sony's incarceration off his shoulders, as if all he had to do now was wait until she sorted the matter out, as if she had taken upon herself the moral burden and thus relieved him of it for ever.

In her father's attitude to the girls she sensed an element of flattery towards herself.

"Masseck showed you the house?" he said suddenly.

"Yes, he showed me where my sister must have lived."

He gave a knowing, offhand laugh.

"I know," he said, "why you came to Grand-Yoff, I've given it some thought, and now I remember."

She was dizzy all of a sudden and felt like jumping up from her chair and rushing into the garden, but she thought of Sony and suppressed all her fears, doubts, unease and disillusionment.

It did not matter what he might say to her, because she would get him to disgorge it.

"You came in order to get closer to me, yes. You must have

been, I'm not sure exactly, twenty-eight or twenty-nine."

He spoke in a very neutral tone, as if he wanted to dispel all hint of conflict between them.

Jakob and the children were listening carefully. Norah felt that her father's affable manner, together with the air of authority conferred on him by his years and by the vestiges of his wealth, ensured that the three gave him the benefit of the doubt in a way she no longer could: indeed, they were now inclined to believe him and not her.

Perhaps they were right?

Were not all her educational principles being called into question, their rigour, their fierceness, their lustre?

For if Jakob, Grete and Lucie were to think that she had lied, dissembled or begun to suffer rather oddly from amnesia, she would seem all the more culpable for having, in the life they shared, preached such rectitude and laid so much stress on it.

A warm dampness slid along her thighs and insinuated itself between her buttocks and the chair.

She felt her dress anxiously.

With a feeling of despair she wiped her wet fingers on her napkin.

"You were keen to know what it was like to live near Sony and me," her father said in his kindly voice, "so you rented that house at Grand-Yoff. I suppose you wanted to be independent, because of course I'd never have refused to put you up. You didn't stay long, did you? You'd probably imagined, I don't know, that things would be like the way they are in your country now, where people are always blathering on about 'opening up', 'asking for forgiveness', inventing all sorts of problems and banging on about how much they love each other, but I had work to do at Dara Salam and in any case baring my soul's just not my thing. No, you didn't stay long, you must have been disappointed. I don't know. And Sony wasn't exactly on top form at the time so perhaps he disappointed you too."

Norah did not budge, so concerned was she to let no-one realise just how wretched she felt.

She raised her feet and held them above the little puddle under her chair.

Her face and her neck were burning.

She said nothing, kept her eyes lowered, and remained seated until everyone had left the table. Then she went to the kitchen to fetch a floorcloth.

That evening before dark she went outside and stood in the doorway, knowing she would find her father there, waiting patiently as always for the moment he could make the leap.

In his grubby shirt he shone as never before.

He looked at the beige dress she'd put on, pursed his lips and said, almost kindly: "You peed yourself just now. It doesn't matter, you know."

"Sony told me you strangled your wife," Norah said, ignoring his remark.

He did not jump, nor even shoot a sideways glance at her; he was already somewhat absent, absorbed no doubt by his awareness of the coming night and his eagerness to find again his dusky retreat in the flame tree.

"Sony affirms that he did it," her father said at last, as if dragged back to a tedious present. "He's never said, and never will say, anything different. I know him. I've every confidence in him."

"But why all this?"

"I'm old, my girl. Can you see me in Reubeuss? Come on.

Besides, you weren't there, so far as I'm aware. What do you know about who did what? Nothing. Sony confessed, they've wound up the investigation, so that's that."

His thin, dreamy voice became fainter and fainter.

"My poor dear boy," he said.

In the bedroom turned into a temporary office she read for the umpteenth time the file on Sony's case.

Jakob and the girls had gone back to Paris as she was moving into the little house with pink walls and blue corrugated-iron roof. She had reached an agreement with her colleagues that she could conduct Sony's defence.

She occasionally looked up from the file to gaze with pleasure at the small, white, bare room. She accepted the idea that she had perhaps, ten years earlier, slept in this same room, because it was now much simpler freely to acknowledge that possibility than to reject it fearfully and angrily. As a result she was not afraid any longer of being overwhelmed by a feeling of *déjà-vu* which could just as well have been provoked by a dream she had experienced as by what she was currently living through.

There she was, alone in the intense brightness of a strange house, sitting on a cool, hard, shiny metal chair. Her whole body was at peace and her mind was equally calm.

She understood what had happened in her father's house. She understood all of those involved as if she were the devil gripping each one of them.

For this is what Sony had told the examining magistrate:

"I hid in my step-mother's bedroom. I stood in a corner between the wardrobe and the wall. I had in my pocket a bit of cord I'd taken from the cupboard under the kitchen sink, a piece left over from the clothes-line in the garden. I knew my stepmother would enter the room alone after putting the twins to bed because that was what she did every evening. I knew my father would not be joining her because he'd stopped sleeping in that room, I can't say where he sleeps, I know but I can't tell you. That means I acted with premeditation throughout, because I knew that my step-mother would go towards the wardrobe and that it would be easy to put the cord round her neck. She was on the tall side, but quite slim and not particularly strong. Her slender arms were not very strong, so I knew she wouldn't struggle much. I'd hugged her often enough in that same room, I'd put my arms around her often enough, to know that I was a great deal stronger than she was. She was so delicate that my hands almost touched my shoulders when I hugged her. Then everything went as planned. She came in, closed the door behind her, walked to the wardrobe, I reached out to her and did it. Her throat gurgled, she tried to grip the cord around her neck but she was already too weak. She slumped a little, I lifted her up again and put her on the bed. I left the room and closed the door. Back in my own bedroom I pumped up all my basketballs. I knew that no-one was going to pump them up for quite a while and I feel better if they're correctly inflated. I went to bed and slept soundly. At six I was awoken by the twins scream-ing. They'd gone to see their mother and it was their screams that aroused me. A little later the police arrived and I told them what had happened, just as I'm telling you today. I did it because my stepmother and I were involved in a love affair that had been going on for three years. She was my age and it was the first time I'd ever been in love. I loved her more than anything or anyone in the whole world. When my father married and brought her home, it was love at first sight. It was very hard, I felt guilty, I felt dirty. But she had fallen for me too and we started making love. It was my first time, I'd waited until then, I'd never dared before. I found her gay and beautiful, I was very happy. She got pregnant and I became very fond of the twins: I was sure they were mine. I was happy with the situation because my father didn't suffer at all, I wasn't afraid of him any more and he took no interest in me. But she began to tire of me. She wasn't capable of loving me for the rest of her life as I was capable of loving her for the rest of mine. She was discontented and started hating me. She said I had to leave the house and make my life elsewhere. But where could I go and what could I do and who else could I love? My home was in my father's house and I was irrevocably married to my father's wife and my father's children were my children. As a result my father's secrets were my secrets too, which is why I can't speak about him even though I know everything about him."

And the young Khady Demba, eighteen, had said:

"I was in the kitchen and I heard the two little girls shouting loudly. I left the kitchen and went to the bedroom where the girls were screaming. They were standing close to the bed and their mother was stretched out on it. I saw that her eyes were open and her face wasn't its normal colour."

And the father had said:

"I'm a self-made man and I think I'm entitled to take some pride in that. My parents had nothing, no-one around me had anything, we lived by our wits and survived thanks to various dodges, but each day the benefits were outweighed by the amount of intellectual effort involved. I was a clever lad so I went to study in France. Then I returned with my son Sony, who was aged five at the time, and went into business. I bought a half-built holiday village at Dara Salam and I managed to turn it into a popular resort and make it profitable. But times changed and I had to sell Dara Salam. As you see me today I have to make do with very little, but I don't care, I haven't much pride left. When I entered the house I was greeted by all that screaming. If my son Sony affirms that he did this, I accept that, and I forgive him because I've always loved my son the way he is, even though people sometimes tell me, 'Your son has never made good use of his intelligence,' but he's made what use he could of it, he's done what he wanted, it's not my concern. My wife betrayed me, he didn't. He's my son and I accept and understand what he's done because I see myself in him. My son Sony is better than me, his generosity of spirit is greater than that of anyone else I've ever known, nevertheless I can see myself in him and I forgive him. I accept what he's affirmed, I've nothing to add, nothing else to say, and if he were to withdraw his confession I'd accept that likewise. He's my son and I raised him, that's all. My wife, I didn't raise her. I don't know her and I can't forgive her and my hatred of this woman who cuckolded me in my own house and didn't care a fig for me will never fade."

At the end of the afternoon, when the shade made the heat less oppressive, Norah went to see Sony.

She left each day at the same time, walking slowly so as not to sweat too much.

And she went over in her mind the questions she would put to Sony, well aware that he would only answer with a smile and would never go back on his resolve to protect their father, but she wanted to show him that she was herself determined to save him and was therefore prepared to confront him fair and square.

She walked joyfully along the familiar street. She was at peace with herself and her body was behaving itself.

She said hello to a neighbour who was sitting at her door and thought "What good neighbours I have," and if one or other of them, the Lebanese baker or the old woman who sold fizzy drinks in the street, spontaneously spoke to her about herself, claiming they had known her ten years earlier, she was not upset by that.

She accepted it humbly, unreasonably, as a mystery.

In the same way she had stopped wondering why she no longer doubted that her love for her child would be rekindled once she had done all she could for Sony, once she had delivered them both from the devils that had sunk their claws into them when she was eight and Sony five.

Because that was the way it was.

And she was able to contemplate with calm gratitude the way Jakob was taking care of the children. His way of doing it was perhaps no worse than her way, and so she was able to think of Lucie without feeling any anxiety about her.

She was able to think of her brother Sony's radiant expression when, in the old days, she used to play at throwing him on the bed. She could think of it now without suffering the torments of the damned.

Because that was the way it was.

And she would watch over Sony and bring him back home.

That was the way it was.

COUNTERPOINT

He felt near him a breath other than his own, another presence in the branches. For some weeks now he had been aware that he was not alone in his hideout, and patiently, without irritation, he was waiting for the stranger to reveal herself even though he knew what it was all about since it could not be anyone else. He was not annoyed because in the tranquil darkness of the flame tree his heart was beating languidly and his mind was lethargic. No, he was not cross: his daughter Norah was there, close by, perched among the branches that now were bereft of flowers, surrounded by the bitter smell of the tiny leaves; she was there in the dark, in her lime-green dress, at a safe distance from her father's phosphorescence. Why would she come and alight on the flame tree if it was not to make peace, once and for all? His heart beat languidly, his mind was lethargic. He heard his daughter breathing and it did not make him angry.

TWO

THROUGHOUT THE MORNING, LIKE THE VESTIGES OF A TROUBLING, rather degrading dream, the thought kept coming back to him that he would have done better, in his own interest, not to have spoken to her like that. Going round and round in his unquiet mind the idea soon became a certainty, even though he could no longer remember the precise reason for the quarrel. But the troublesome, degrading dream left a bitter aftertaste.

He ought never, never, to have spoken to her in that way. That was all he could now remember about their argument; and that was what made it impossible for him to concentrate, that was what stopped him deriving any benefit from the row, anything that could prove useful when he returned home and found himself face to face with her again.

Because, he thought confusedly, how was he going to assuage his conscience if his truncated memories of their disputes merely served to highlight his own guilt, over and over again, as in those troubling, degrading dreams in which whatever you say, whatever you decide, you are the one who is always irrevocably to blame?

And, he also wondered, if he could not manage to assuage his own conscience, how was he going to calm down and become a proper father? How could he get people to love him again?

He certainly ought not to speak to her like that; no man had the right to do so.

But the thing which had pushed him into letting slip certain words that ought never to be uttered by a man whose passionate desire was to be loved as he once had been, that was what he could not easily recall, as if the terrible phrases (but what were they exactly?) had exploded in his head, obliterating everything else.

So was it fair that he felt he was so much to blame?

If only, he thought, he could prove before his own inner tribunal that he had had a valid reason to get so terribly angry, he would be better able to feel sorry for his behaviour and his whole character would be softened thereby.

Whereas his present swirling, excited, chaotic shame only served to make him lose his temper.

Oh, how he longed for clarity, for peace and quiet!

Why, with his fine younger days drifting away from him, and why, with the years slipping by, did he feel that it was only the lives of others – the lives of almost all the people around him – that were proceeding naturally, along an increasingly unencumbered path illuminated already by the warm, gentle rays of the light shining at the end? It was something that made it possible for all the men in his circle to lower their guard and adopt a relaxed, subtly caustic attitude towards existence, an attitude inspired by a discreet awareness of having acquired wisdom at the price of perfect health, a supple, flat stomach and hair unflecked by grey.

Being plunged in grief, I find myself mightily dejected.

He, Rudy, could see what this wisdom consisted of, even if he himself seemed to be making painfully slow progress along a path choked with tangled undergrowth which no light could penetrate.

From the depths of his chaotic feebleness he felt he understood the fundamental insignificance of his suffering, and yet he was incapable of deriving any advantage from his awareness of it, lost as he was on the fringes of the true existence which everyone has the power to influence.

So that – he said to himself – he, Rudy Descas, had seemingly not yet, despite his forty-three summers, acquired that chic, relaxed level-headedness, that sardonic tranquillity which he saw informing the simplest actions and the most ordinary utterances of other men, of people who spoke calmly and with unstudied naturalness to their children, who read newspapers and magazines with wry interest, who looked forward to a pleasurable lunch with friends the following Sunday, to ensure the success of which they would cheerfully and generously spare no effort, without ever having to strive to conceal the fact that they had only just emerged from yet another bout of squabbling and from a painful, degrading dream.

I find myself mightily dejected.

He was never, ever, vouchsafed any of that.

But why, he wondered, why?

That he had behaved badly at such-and-such a moment and in such-and-such a situation where it was important to measure up to the joy or to the tragedy involved, *that* he was perfectly happy to acknowledge, but where was the joy, what constituted the tragedy in the diminished life led by himself and his family, and what were the particular circumstances he had been incapable of confronting as a fully rounded person?

Exactly. It seemed to him that his great fatigue – his fury being no less considerable, Fanta would say with a snigger; just like him to claim to be consumed by it when the permanent muted rage he imposed on his nearest and dearest wore them out more than him: true, Rudy? – that his great fatigue arose from the efforts he was making to steer their poor tumbrel, their load of painful, degrading dreams in the right direction.

Had his desire to do the right thing ever been rewarded?

No, not even – no, not even acknowledged, let alone praised and honoured.

In defence of Fanta, who always seemed to be blaming him silently for all their setbacks and misfortunes, he had to acknowledge that he was quick to forestall any judgement of that kind by his feeling that he was himself obscurely accountable for all the bad luck that came their way.

As for the rare strokes of good luck, he had got into the habit of greeting them with considerable scepticism, and his mistrustful face demonstrated so eloquently his having done nothing to bring about the brief moment of happiness in their house that it would not have occurred to anyone to show him any gratitude.

Oh yes, Rudy was well aware of that.

He felt this look of almost nauseous suspicion starting to show on his face the moment he suggested to Fanta, for example, or to Djibril, that they go out for a meal, or go for a spin to the canoe club; and in return (when the child, unable to fathom his father's secret intentions, turned to catch his mother's eye) he saw anxiety or slight distress sweeping across the two beautiful faces, so similar, of his wife and his son; and he could not suppress his resentment and would get very cross, saying to them, "What? Aren't you ever pleased?" while the two beautiful faces of the only creatures he loved on this earth became expressionless, revealing nothing more now than dismal indifference towards himself and towards all his suggestions for doing things that might give them pleasure, pushing silently out of their lives, their thoughts and their feelings this surly and unpredictable man whom a malevolent fate obliged them to put up with for the time being, like the after-effects of a bad, shameful dream. *Everything that was going to happen to me has happened.*

He pulled up sharply on the verge of the little road that every day led him straight to Manille's, once he had passed the big roundabout in the middle of which there now stood a curious white stone statue of a naked man whose bent back, lowered head and outstretched arms seemed to be waiting with terrified resignation for the fountains to drench him with water when summer came round again.

Rudy had followed every stage in the construction of this fountain as he drove slowly past the roundabout every morning in his old Renault Nevada before turning off to the Manille offices, and without his being aware of it his mild curiosity had changed into embarrassment, then into a deeper malaise when he thought he discerned a close resemblance between the statue's face and his own (the same wide, flat, square forehead, straight but rather short nose, prominent jaw, big mouth and angular chin so characteristic of proud men who know precisely where each one of their resolute steps is taking them – something more comic than pathetic when one was happy to flog one's guts out at Manille's, eh, Rudy Descas?) and his distress had increased at the sight of the monstrous genitalia which the artist, a certain R. Gauquelan who lived locally, had carved on his hero's crotch, forcing Rudy to feel himself the subject of a cruel act of mockery, so pitiful was the contrast between the statue's weak, spineless attitude and its enormous scrotum.

He tried now to avoid looking at the statue as he drove past the roundabout in his clapped-out Nevada.

But a malevolent reflex sometimes caused him to glance at the stone face that was his own, at that large, pale figure stooping with fear, and at the testicles out of all proportion to the rest, and he had come to resent and almost hate Gauquelan who had managed, Rudy read in the local paper, to sell his sculpture to the municipality for around a hundred thousand euros.

The news had caused him considerable anguish.

It was, he said to himself, as if in his innocence or during his sleep Gauquelan had taken advantage of him and got him to feature in a ridiculous pornographic photograph that had made Gauquelan richer and Descas poorer and more grotesque – as if Gauquelan had dragged him from a tiresome dream and plunged him into a degrading one.

"A hundred thousand euros, I can't believe it," he had said to Fanta, sniggering to hide his distress. "No, I really can't believe it."

"What's it matter?" Fanta must have replied. "In what way does the fact that others do all right diminish you?" she asked with that irritating habit she had recently adopted of appearing to look at every situation from a lofty, magnanimous, detached viewpoint, abandoning Rudy to his envious, petty thoughts which, like all the rest, she no longer wished to share with him.

But she could not prevent him thinking – nor reminding her, imploringly – of the good years, not so long ago, when, sitting cross-legged side by side like two old chums in their darkened bedroom, puffing on the same cigarette, it had become one of their dearest pleasures to dissect with brutal frankness the habits and personalities of their acquaintances and neighbours. From the harshness the two shared, mingled with a very conscious bad faith, they would derive comic effects which they would never have been able – or dared – to attempt in the company of others, but which were peculiar to the pair of good friends that, in addition to being man and wife, they had once been.

He now wanted her to remember this, she who claimed to believe that she had never enjoyed a moment's fun with him, but (given the grovelling manner he had adopted in spite of himself) it was not, by a long chalk, the best idea he could have come up with: to show himself reduced to begging her to accept and acknowledge that, however it had come about, what had been was no longer the case, that the amusing companion which he might once have been was now probably dead for ever, and that it was all his fault, and his alone.

And he always came back to this intolerable aspect, this tacit accusation which grabbed him by the throat that, for all eternity, it was his fault, and the more he struggled to free himself from what was strangling him, killing him, the more he shook his heavy head and the more angry he got and the worse he made things.

In fact, they had not had any friends for a long while, and the neighbours cold-shouldered him.

Rudy Descas could not care less; he thought he already had enough worries without having to trouble himself with what was displeasing in his attitude, but he could not make fun of anyone with Fanta any more, even if she had been capable of wanting him to.

They lived isolated lives, very isolated, that was what he had to accept.

It seemed that their friends (who were they exactly, what were they called, where had they all gone?) had drifted away as Fanta started to turn her back on him; it was as if the love she had felt for him had, like a dazzling outsider between the two of them, been the only thing they had liked and been interested in, and that once this beautiful witness had vanished into thin air, Fanta and he – but he above all – had finally appeared to those friends in all the starkness of their banality, their poverty.

But Rudy could not care less.

He had need only of his wife and of his son – and, as he had already admitted to himself with some embarrassment, he had a lot less need of his son than of his wife, and less need of his actual son than of his son as a mysterious and seductive extension of his wife, as a fascinating, miraculous development of the personality and beauty of Fanta.

Where the presence of these formless shadows who had acted the part of friends was concerned, all he missed was their warm, kindly looks, assuring him that Rudy Descas was a nice chap, a pleasant man to be with, whose wife (who had come from afar) loved him unreservedly. He was then truly himself, Rudy Descas, just as he saw himself, present in this world, and not the unlikely, discordant figure emerging from some tiresome, shameful dream that no dawn would manage to chase away. *What has become of my friends whom I loved so much and was so close to?*

He looked at his watch.

He had only five minutes before work started at Manille's.

He had stopped in front of the only nearby telephone box, by the side of the little road which, boldly and cheerfully, opened up a route between the expanses of vines.

The sun was already beating down.

Not a breath, not a scrap of shade until you got to the tall evergreen oaks far away that surrounded the wine-producing château, an austere dwelling with closed shutters.

How proud he had been when he introduced Fanta to this region where he was born, where they were going to live and prosper, and particularly to this building the owners of which his mother knew slightly, people who made an excellent Graves that Rudy could no longer afford to drink.

He was obscurely aware, beyond all reasonable hope, that the proud delight he had taken in showing Fanta the small dark château, almost dragging her into the drive and up to the gate, up to the evergreen oaks, approaching it with a confident air on the pretext that his mother knew the owners slightly (she must have replaced their usual cleaner for a few weeks at the outside), he was obscurely aware that his proud delight in doing this came from the fact that he had convinced himself that one day the property would belong to them, to Fanta and to himself, that it would be passed on to them in some way, though he did not yet know how.

This feeling of certainty had not been affected by the fact that three enormous dogs had shot out from the back of the dwelling and rushed towards them, although he had then been seized by a sensation of pure horror.

Oh, Rudy Descas wasn't *that* courageous a man.

Those friends have really failed me.

Had the unleashed Dobermans wanted to punish him for his presumptuous and absurd desires, for the heavy possessive hand he had (in thought) laid on the property?

Their invisible master had whistled to the dogs and stopped them in their tracks. Rudy meanwhile was slowly backing away, holding his arm out in front of Fanta as if he had wanted to dissuade her from leaping at the three monsters' throats.

How useless and futile he had felt on this warm spring day in the bright, tranquil silence that had followed the dogs' retreat and their own return to the car, how pale and trembling he had felt beside Fanta who had hardly batted an eyelid.

She doesn't bear a grudge for my putting her in harm's way, he had thought, not because she is a good person, though she is, but because she had never had an inkling that she might be in danger. Is that, he wondered, what it is to be courageous, whereas all I am is foolhardy?

For, while God was assailing me, I never saw a single one at my side.

Out of the corner of his eye he had glanced at his wife's impassive face and at her big brown irises as she looked down at the gravel path, prodding at it absently with the end of a stick, a hazel twig she had picked up just before the dogs came charging at them.

Something in the naturalness of the placidity shown by a woman who was above all an intellectual, something in the seeming un-awareness of her own composure on the part of a woman who usually got to the bottom of everything, appeared to defy all under-standing, he thought almost admiringly, but also a trifle uneasily.

He gazed at the broad, high plane of her smooth cheek, her thick black eyelashes, her not particularly prominent nose, and the love he felt for this unfathomable woman put the fear of God into him.

Because she was strange, too strange for him, perhaps, and he was wearing himself out trying to prove that he was a lot more than he seemed, that he was not just an ex-schoolteacher who had come back to live in the region of his birth, but a man chosen by fate to bring something truly original to fruition.

For Rudy Descas, to have no other duty than that of loving Fanta would have sufficed, indeed he would have welcomed such an obligation with open arms.

But he had the feeling that it was too little for her even if she was unaware of the fact, and that, having dragged her from her familiar surroundings, he owed her a lot more than a heavily mort-gaged, rather ugly little house in the country and the kind of life that went with it, all the pettiness that drove him mad .

And now here he was, standing on the edge of this same cheer-ful little road, several years after the dogs had nearly torn them both apart (but had not Fanta's coolness stopped them in their tracks, had they not retreated, perhaps with a growl, intimidated by a vague awareness that she was not like other human beings?) on a balmy warm May morning very like this one, except that his discomfiture on that occasion had barely dented his confidence in the future, in their chances of success, in their amazing good fortune, whereas now he knew that nothing would ever turn out right.

They had driven off in the same old Nevada from which he was now extricating himself, because, yes, it was even then a nasty old-fashioned car, painted greyish-blue in accordance with the prudent taste of Rudy's mother from whom he had bought it when she had abandoned it for a Clio, and since he had been sure then of being able very soon to get himself something much better (an Audi or a Toyota). He had led Fanta to view their car as a rather treacherous dirty creature, sad and weary, whose last days they were patiently seeing out, only starting it up to have it serviced.

He had treated the poor Nevada with disdainful offhandedness, but was it not a sort of loathing he felt now for its very sturdiness, its unfailing courage typical of a good old uncomplicated car, its decency almost, its selflessness?

Nothing could be more wretched, he thought, than to hate one's car, how did I come to this and can I sink any lower? Oh yes, I can, he said to himself, since that was a mere trifle compared to what he had said to Fanta that morning before leaving for work at Manille's, to take the very same route that once used to cut a merry path through the vines . . .

What had he said to her exactly?

The wind was blowing in front of my door and it bore them away.

He left the car door open and stood there, his knees knocking, stunned by the extent of the damage he had very probably caused.

"You can go back where you came from."

Was it possible?

He smiled weakly, nervously, unamused – no, Rudy Descas would not speak like that to the woman he so ardently wished to be loved by once again.

He raised his eyes and shielded them with his hand. Sweat was already making his forehead and blond fringe wet.

Blond too was the world around him on this mild, clean morning, blond the walls of the small château over there which some foreign people or other (Americans or Australians, thought his mother, always on the *qui-vive* for news that would feed her *penchant* for voluptuous lamentation) had recently bought and restored, and the blond spots of light under his eyelids danced whenever he blinked – if only they would flow at last, the tears of anger he felt weighing heavily within, pressing against his eye-sockets.

But his cheeks stayed dry and his jaw remained tense.

He heard behind him the roar of a car approaching. He crouched down at once behind the door of his own car, not being keen to wave to the driver, who – given where they happened to be – he would very likely be acquainted with, but he straight away began shaking with a rather doleful fit of the giggles at the thought that he was the only person in these parts who drove a blue-grey Nevada and that the vehicle betrayed the presence of Rudy Descas as surely as the silhouette of Rudy Descas himself would have done, indeed even more so, since at a distance Rudy Descas could well have looked like someone else.

For it seemed that everyone could afford to buy a car that was no more than ten to twelve years old except himself, and he could not understand why.

When he stood up he realised he could not now avoid arriving late for work, so he would have to come up with a fairly unfamiliar excuse as he passed through Manille's office.

That thought satisfied him, in a vague sort of way.

He knew that Manille was tired of him, of the way he was frequently late for work, and of his grumpiness – at least that was what Manille, a naturally affable and commercially astute man, called it whenever Rudy made it clear that keeping his own counsel figured among the basic rights which, as a poorly paid employee, he was prepared to defend fiercely; and although in some ways Rudy thought quite highly of Manille, he was glad that Manille, who was typical of the sort of pragmatic, dodgy, narrow-minded men who, within the extremely narrow limits of their faculties, were astonishingly gifted, almost talented, did not think particularly highly of him.

He knew that Manille would have liked and respected him, and even excused his bloody-mindedness, had Rudy shown some skill at getting customers to purchase new kitchens; he knew that Manille would not have rated the ability to earn money for the firm as highly as good, solid competence in a particular domain, just as he knew that in Manille's eyes he was not skilled nor clever nor committed, nor – to compensate for his utter uselessness – even straightforwardly pleasant.

Manille only kept him on, Rudy thought, out of a peculiar form of indulgence, a complicated sort of pity, because why, really, would Manille feel pity for him?

What did he know about Rudy's precise circumstances?

Oh, very little, since Rudy never confided in anyone, but a wily, amiable rough diamond of a person like Manille must have realised that in his way Rudy was just a square peg in a round hole and that when it came to the crunch it behoved people like himself – people who felt perfectly happy with their place in the world – to protect someone like Rudy.

So Rudy understood Manille's reasoning even if Manille would never have put it quite like that.

Although he was grateful, he felt humiliated by the situation.

Go to hell, I don't need you, you crummy little man, to hell with your rustic-kitchens business.

But what will become of you, Rudy Descas, when Manille kicks you out with a genuinely upset and sincerely apologetic air but is unable to conceal the fact that you brought it all upon yourself?

He was sure it was to his mother that he owed the fact that he had been taken on, even though she would never have admitted that she had gone to talk to Manille (or confessed that she had been obliged to beg him, the corner of her drooping eyelids damp and pink, her long nose red with shame at what she was asking Manille to do), and the reason Rudy had had to seek work in the first place was so painful he could not summon up the courage to raise the issue with her.

I couldn't care less about Manille, no.

How could he waste time thinking about Manille when he could not recall the exact words he had used to Fanta that morning and which he should never have uttered in the first place, because it was clear that, if she decided to take them literally and seized the opportunity to put them into effect, they would rebound on him in the most terrible way imaginable, and that he would achieve the precise opposite of what he had long been striving for.

"You can go back where you came from."

He was going to telephone her and ask her to repeat the exact words he had used during their violent quarrel and to tell him what had given rise to it.

It was not possible that he had said that to her.

He thought he had – so he believed – because of his tendency to feel more guilty than he really was, to accuse himself where she was concerned of the worst, since she was incapable of mean thoughts or ambiguous designs, because she was so helpless and – quite rightly – so disappointed, so disappointed!

The sweat poured down his face and neck at the very thought

that she might indeed carry out what he had so horrendously told her to do.

Then, almost immediately, he began to shiver violently.

With a child-like feeling of despair he sought to extricate himself from that cold, interminable, monotonous dream in which Fanta was about to leave him because he had in a way – even if he could not remember the exact words – ordered her to, and because nothing more horrible could now befall him. He knew that, didn't he, because she had already done so, already tried to do so: isn't that true, Rudy Descas?

He hastily banished the thought, the intolerable memory of Fanta's flight (as he called it, to lessen the impact of what had been nothing less than an act of betrayal), in favour of the monotonous coldness of the interminable bad dream which, to his great surprise, his life had become – his life, his poor life.

He opened the door of the telephone box and slipped in between the walls covered in scribbles and graffiti.

In much the same way as he was reduced to driving around in a clapped-out Nevada, he had recently had to cancel his mobile-phone contract, and this decision which – given the tightness of his monthly budget – he ought to have been prepared to look upon as a reasonable one, seemed to him inexplicable, strange and unjust, a form of self-inflicted cruelty, because apart from himself he knew of no-one, and had never heard of anyone, who had had to give up their mobile.

Even the gypsies who lived in a permanent encampment they had set up below the little road, just beyond the vines planted along the slope, the green mossy roofs of whose caravans must be visible, Rudy mused, from the small château with its new inhabitants (American or Australian), even the gypsies whom Rudy often saw hanging about in front of Manille's shop-window, gazing intently and scornfully at the kitchens on display, did not have to do without a mobile telephone.

So how, he wondered, did all those people manage to have so much better a life than he did?

What stopped him from being as smart as the others, since he was no stupider than they were?

He, Rudy Descas – having long believed that his lack of shrewdness and cunning was amply compensated for by his singular sensibility, the spiritual, idealistic and romantic scale of his ambition, by its very imprecision – was now beginning to wonder if such singularity had any value, if it was not ridiculous, secretly contemptible, like a potent man confessing to a *penchant* for spanking and cross-dressing.

He was trembling so much he had to have three goes at dialling his own number.

He let it ring for a long time.

Through the glazed walls of the telephone box his eyes wandered over the small, blond, tranquil château nestling in the cool shade cast by the dense, well-ordered foliage of its dark oaks. Then his gaze returned to the glass panel in which, as if imprisoned in matter, he contemplated his own transparent, sweaty face and wild stare, the blue of his irises darkened by anguish, and saw clearly in his mind's eye the room in which the telephone was vainly ringing, ringing, the undecorated lounge of their small house frozen in its hopeless, unfinished state, with its unpointed wall-tiles, its ugly brown flooring on which stood their poor furniture: an old suite of varnished wood and flowered upholstery (a hand-me-down from one of his mother's bosses), the garden table covered with a plastic tablecloth, a pine dresser, the small bookcase crammed to overflowing with books, all the sad ugliness of a place that neither an indifference to one's surroundings nor a lively cheerfulness on the part of its inhabitants (feelings here conspicuous by their absence) could hope to illuminate or soften. It all constituted one big eyesore that was never meant to be more than temporary, and Rudy loathed it; he was hurt by it every day, and even now, just imagining it as he stood in the telephone box, he was pained and angered by it, trapped as he was in an interminable nightmare, the unending discomfort of a cold, monotonous dream.

But where could she be at this hour?

She had no doubt walked Djibril to the spot where the school bus drew up, as every morning, but she should have been back long before this, so where was she, why was she not answering the telephone?

He hung up and leant against the wall of the telephone box.

His pale blue short-sleeved shirt was soaked. He could feel it, warm and damp, against the glass.

Ah, how tiresome, unsettling and humiliating it all was, how it made him want to hide away and weep once his anger had cooled.

Could it be, could it be that she had . . . taken literally the words which he was not even certain of having uttered and which in any case he was certain of never having formulated inside his head?

He picked the receiver up again so sharply that it slipped through his fingers, struck the glass and dangled at the end of its cord.

From the pocket of his jeans he pulled out his ancient dog-eared notebook and looked up Madame Pulmaire's number even though he was sure, having telephoned the old trout several times before, that he knew her number by heart.

She was not actually all that decrepit, hardly older than his mother in fact, but she put on a *vieille dame* act and made a show of suppressing her awareness of her own virtue in order to be able to descend to the level of the complicated and slightly disgusting favours which, ever since they had become neighbours, Rudy was wont to request – while she, no doubt, made it a point of honour never to ask them for anything.

As he expected, she answered straight away.

"It's Rudy Descas, Madame Pulmaire."

"Ah."

"I just wanted to know whether . . . whether you could go and have a peep next door and check that all's well."

He felt his heart thumping madly as he tried to sound casual and relaxed. Madame Pulmaire would not for a second be fooled by that, and he was prepared to pray, weeping and moaning, to his mother's god, that nice little god who seemed to have heard her prayers and eventually answered them, instead of which he held his breath, sweating, chilled to the bone despite the stifling atmosphere in the telephone box, feeling suddenly isolated in immobile duration (for everything round about him – the foliage of the holm-oaks, the leaves on the vines and the fluffy clouds in the petrified blue sky – seemed frozen in time and in anguished suspension). The only thing that could propel this state of immobility forward again would be the news that Fanta was at home, was feeling happy, was still in love with him, and had never stopped loving him.

That, though – no, Pulmaire wouldn't tell him that, would she?

"What's the matter, Rudy," she said, in an affectedly gentle tone. "Is anything wrong?"

"No, nothing in particular, I was just wondering . . . seeing as I don't seem to be able to get hold of my wife . . ."

"Where are you phoning from, Rudy?"

He knew that she had no right to ask, knew too that he would not dare tell her to get lost before she had deigned to heave her useless august mountain of flesh as far as the Descas household to look through the bare windows or ring the doorbell so that this peculiar wife he had got, this Fanta, who had run away once before, could prove that she had neither done a runner nor collapsed in a corner somewhere in that sad little half-done-up house – oh, how weary he was of understanding *la Pulmaire* so well, how sullied he felt by acquaintanceships of that sort.

"I'm in a telephone box."

"Aren't you at work, Rudy?"

"No!" he said. "So what, Madame Pulmaire?"

There was a silence; it was protracted, but it betrayed neither shock nor surprise. Old Pulmaire was above such childish reactions, being invested with a weighty dignity which, if Rudy had an ounce of respect, would soon make him contrite.

He could hear her panting into the receiver.

Just as earlier that morning when Fanta had defied him by something she had said (or perhaps by her silence, he could no longer remember which), he could feel welling up inside him again that hot, almost gentle, almost cordial anger which he knew he should resist but which, too, it felt so nice, so good, so comforting, not to impede in any way, that he found himself wondering sometimes whether this familiar anger was not all he had got left, whether he had not lost everything except that. But would he finally tell her just how long a man who fights for the survival of his honour as a man, a father, a husband and a son, who every day strives to prevent the collapse of everything he has built, just how long such a man can put up with being the butt of the same old reproaches, spoken (or unspoken: merely a watchful, pitiless, bitter look), and whether he can put up with it smilingly, not batting an eyelid, as if saintliness too constituted one of his obligations; would he finally tell her that, he who had been abandoned by his friends?

He clamped his lips onto the damp plastic.

"Now get your fat arse into gear and go and do what I ask!" he said.

Madame Pulmaire hung up at once, without a word or a sigh.

He slammed his hand two or three times on the cradle, then once again dialled the telephone number of his home.

He had now learned to call it that – "my home" – even if that annoyed and hurt him as much as it ever had, but the expression matched what Fanta clearly felt, what her whole attitude betrayed, that she no longer considered the poor shaky house their home but solely his home, and not because of its ricketiness, he knew, not because of the irremediable ugliness of the place which at bottom he knew she could not care less about, but because he had chosen the house, given it its name and, in a sense, had invented it.

This building, he had decided, would be a temple for their happiness to dwell in.

Fanta was now withdrawing from the house, taking along with her the child, little seven-year-old Djibril, with whom Rudy had never felt much at ease (because he realised, without being able to do anything about it, that he frightened the little boy).

Fanta was there, she had no choice but to be there, but – Rudy said to himself – she gave the house the cold shoulder, she refused to lavish care and affection on her husband's home, to envelop her husband's wretched house with anxious, maternal concern.

Taking his cue from her, it was in a rather uncommitted frame of mind that the child occupied the house, flitting lightly over the floor, sometimes seeming to hover above the ground as if wary of all contact with his father's house, in the same way – Rudy thought – as he kept his father at arm's length.

Oh – he wondered in a dazzlement of pain, all anger spent, with the ringtone vibrating in his ear, and seeing on the other side of the glass the vines and oaks and little baby clouds come back to life again in the minuscule wind – what had happened to the three of them that his wife and son, the only people he loved in the whole world (for he felt only a vague, formal, inconsequential tenderness for *maman*) should look upon him as their enemy?

"Yes?" Fanta said in a tone so flat, so sullen, that at first he almost thought he had phoned Madame Pulmaire again by mistake.

He was so surprised at this that his heart missed a beat.

So that was how Fanta spoke when she was alone at home and did not think he was around (whenever she talked to him her voice took on a tone of hardness and rancour which made her tremble), so that was how Fanta spoke when she was herself and not involved with him: with such sadness, with such glum disappointment, and with such a melancholy re-emergence of her accent.

Because, as far back as he could remember, she had always tried to conceal an accent which he found endearing, and though he never quite approved of her desire to appear to come from nowhere, finding it even a little absurd since her features were obviously foreign, he had always connected it with Fanta's energy, her vitality that was greater than his, and with her courageous struggle since childhood to become an educated and cultured person, to escape the interminable reality – so cold, so monotonous – of poverty.

It was cruelly ironic that it had been he, Rudy, who had pushed her back into what she had managed, courageously, all by herself, to escape from, whereas he should have shielded her more effectively from everything and helped her conquer the misfortune of being born in the Colobane district, whereas he ought not to have buried her alive – still young and beautiful – in the depths of . . .

"It's me, Rudy," he said.

"Hold on a moment, there's someone at the door."

Now she knew whom she was speaking to, her voice became a little less sullen, as if an automatic reflex of guarded wariness had reset her reaction mechanism and prevented her letting slip any word that he could use against her during the next slanging match, although to tell the truth, he thought, Fanta never answered back but simply countered his attacks with a stubborn silence, a distant, rather sulky look, her lips swelling and her chin drooping; he, Rudy, knew only too well that she watched too carefully the little she said for any word of hers to provoke his outburst, and he, Rudy, also knew only too well that what made him angry was the very indifference – so deliberate, so studied – of her expression, and the crosser he became, the more Fanta shut herself off and the more he got bogged down in his fury at her falsely unruffled manner until, as if he were spitting in her face, he spoke the words he later regretted so despairingly even if, as this morning, he was not sure he had really uttered them.

How hopeless it was, he thought, did she not understand that a few innocent, ordinary words from her, spoken with the requisite warmth, would have been enough to make him once more the good, calm, affable Rudy Descas that he had still been, it seemed to him, two or three years earlier, not very practical-minded, perhaps, but curious in outlook and pretty energetic for all that, did she not understand . . . ?

"I love you, Rudy," or "I've never stopped loving you," or even – that would have done just as well – "I'm fond of you, Rudy."

He felt himself blushing, ashamed of these thoughts.

She understood all right.

No entreaty, no fit of anger (but as far as he was concerned were the two not connected?) would ever make her say anything like that.

He was convinced that even if he beat her up and pushed her face down hard on the rough floor she would still have said nothing, and as for telling a white lie just to be let off the hook, she was quite incapable of that.

Through the receiver he could hear Fanta's footsteps sliding, dragging a little as she made towards the door, then Madame Pulmaire's high-pitched, anxious voice followed by Fanta's murmuring. Could he, at that distance, discern a note of immense weariness in his wife's voice, or was it merely the effect of distance and his own shame?

He heard the door slam, then the slow progress of Fanta's bare feet once again, that weary, exhausted gait which she displayed these days from the moment she got up, as if the prospect of another day in a place she refused obstinately to take any interest in ("Why do I have to do everything in this house?" he often shouted in exasperation) hobbled her slim ankles with their dry, shining skin, those same ankles which used to run swiftly, indefatigably in their dusty pumps or trainers through the alleyways of Colobane towards the *lycée* where Rudy had first set eyes on her.

Back then those ankles had seemed winged, because how else could they, those two slender, rigid, valiant straight little sticks covered in gleaming skin transport with such lightness and speed Fanta's youthful, slim, long, compact, muscular body, how could they, he had wondered rapturously, without the assistance of two small invisible wings, very similar to those which made the skin between Fanta's shoulder-blades quiver gently in the neckline of her sky-blue T-shirt as he stood behind her waiting his turn in the teachers' queue at the cafeteria of the Lycée Marmoz, how, he had wondered, as he gazed at the bare nape of her neck, her dark strong shoulders, her delicate quivering skin . . .

"That was the neighbour," she said laconically.

"Ah."

And since she did not add anything, since she did not specify, in that tone of gloomy sarcasm she was apt to use, the reason why Madame Pulmaire had called, he surmised that the old girl had shielded him, after a fashion, by saying nothing about his telephone call, probably inventing some trivial excuse, and he felt relieved, but at the same time embarrassed and annoyed, at becoming complicit with Madame Pulmaire behind Fanta's back.

His reaction was to feel deeply sorry for Fanta, because it was, if not his fault exactly, at least his doing, that the ambitious Fanta of the winged ankles no longer flew over the reddish mud of the streets of Colobane, still hard up, certainly, and held back in her ambitions by many constraints at home but, in spite of all, heading towards the *lycée* where she was a fully fledged French literature teacher; was it not his doing, with his lovesick gaze, tanned features, fair hair (a lock of which always kept falling over his eyes), his fine words and serious manner, his promise of a comfortable, intellectual, altogether elevated and attractive way of life, was it not his doing that she had given up her neighbourhood, her town, her (red, dry, very hot) homeland to end up unemployed (he should have known that she would not be allowed to teach French literature here, he ought to have made enquiries and found out that she could not and then drawn the proper conclusions as to how that would affect her) in the depths of a quiet provincial region, dragging her leaden feet through a house a little better than the one she had left but which she had refused to grace with a single thought, gesture or look of consideration (whereas he had seen her sweep patiently, systematically, the run-down two-room flat with sea-green walls she shared in Colobane with an uncle, aunt, and several cousins, so patiently, so systematically!): if it was not his fault, was it not his doing if she seemed trapped and lost in the icy mists of an eternal, monotonous dream?

He, Rudy Descas, with the terribly persuasive force of his love, with his tanned face, suave manners and the unusual impact over there of his blondness, the particularly striking quality . . .

"Do you want to know why I'm ringing?" he asked at last.

"Not particularly," she said after a moment, her voice no longer tinged with the slack, utter disillusionment that Rudy had been moved by, but with something that was almost its opposite, the controlled, metallic, perfection of her mastery of the French accent.

"I'd like you to tell me why we had an argument this morning. Listen, I don't know what started that off, all that . . ."

He was aware of a particularly striking quality in the ensuing silence, a weakly panting silence which sounded as if he was telephoning a far-off country with rudimentary communications, his words needing all these slow seconds to arrive, though it was only the echo of Fanta's anxious breathing as she pondered the best way of answering his question in order to safeguard he knew not what – he dared not imagine what – future interests she might have (then a bubble of anger suddenly exploded in his head: what possible future could she envisage that did not include him?). Yes, he recalled, as he let his eyes wander over the green vines with their tiny bright-green grapes, over the green oaks beyond them which the new owners of the property, those Americans or Australians (who fascinated and upset his mother because she believed the vineyard should have stayed in French hands) had had pruned so savagely that the trees looked humiliated, punished for having the nerve to let their shiny, fade-resistant foliage grow so dense as to partially conceal the once greyish, now blond and fresh stonework of what was after all only a large house of the kind on which people in these parts bestowed the respectable name "château"; yes, he recalled, the particularly striking quality in Fanta's homeland of his own blondness, his own freshness . . .

"I don't know," Fanta said in a low, cold voice.

But he was convinced that she was only answering in the least compromising manner possible, and that whatever appeared least likely to commit her to anything involving him in any way, be it only a simple exchange of words, had become the sole yardstick of her frankness.

Besides, if he wanted (but did he really?) to be straight with himself, he thought, as he looked up again at the distant sunny outline of the château which he sensed more than actually saw, knowing it so well that he often dreamt about it during those monotonous, cold, grey dreams he regularly had, full of precise details which he could only have heard, though he had no memory of doing so, from *maman* who had perhaps stood in on one of two occasions for the previous owners' cleaning woman (the maid who did everything, preparing and serving the meals, the hoovering, the ironing), but passed on with that tiresome and degrading habit his mother had of pretending to look down on everything she described (the many unused fully furnished rooms, the fine china, the silver) while her drooping little pinkish clear eyes shone with frustrated longing – and his own limpid pale eyes were once again raised towards the outline of the château as if he ought to be receiving some kind of striking, definitive response from that large, drab, cold house (no longer grey, perhaps . . .), but what could the property possibly have to tell him except that it would never be his or Fanta's or Djibril's, so, if he wanted to be straight with himself . . .

"By the way," he said, "what if I picked Djibril up from school this evening?"

"If you like," she said, with an undertone of disquiet in her bland, cold voice that immediately set his teeth on edge.

"It's been a hell of a while since I last picked him up from school, hasn't it? He'll be pleased at not having to catch the school bus for once."

"Oh, I don't know, but yes, if you like." Her voice was wary, constrained by calculation tinged with anxiety. "Make sure you get there early, otherwise by the time you arrive he'll already have got on the bus."

"Yes, yes."

. . . straight with himself, or at least if he had really wanted to be straight with himself, he had to admit he would not have believed in Fanta's sincerity even if he had suddenly noticed in her voice the honest, genuine tones of the past, those of the young woman with winged feet and passionate, focused aspirations whose determination and intelligence had already taken her from the small peanut stall which as a little girl she had set up every day in a Colobane street to the Lycée Mermoz where she taught French literature and prepared the children of diplomats and wealthy business people for the baccalaureate, this tall, upstanding woman with domed head and close-cropped hair who had looked him straight in the eye in a completely uninhibited, relaxed manner when, very unusually for him, he had on an impulse stroked lightly with the tip of his finger the delicate, quivering skin between her shoulder-blades, something which, never before, had he even . . .

"Fanta," he said, "is everything all right?"

"Yes," she said, cautiously, mechanically.

It was not true. He knew it, he could feel it.

He could not believe what she said any more.

He nonetheless persisted in asking questions which to his mind demanded honest answers – intimate questions, questions about feelings – as if the stubborn frequency with which he conducted these interrogations might one day wear down Fanta's current determination not to let anything slip and make her drop her guard.

"I'm taking Djibril to sleep at *maman*'s place tonight," he said abruptly.

"Oh no," she said, almost sobbed, unable to contain herself. Rudy felt pain gripping his heart for having made her so upset, but what else could he do?

Should he deprive his mother of the company of her only grandchild simply because Fanta could not stand being separated from him?

What else could he do?

"She's not had him to stay with her much for quite a while now," he said in a kindly, comforting tone which sounded in the earpiece so deceitful to him that, feeling embarrassed as if another person, who ought to feel ashamed at covering up his hypocrisy so badly, was speaking in his place, he moved the receiver away from his ear.

"She doesn't like Djibril!" Fanta said.

"What? You're completely wrong about that, she adores him."

He was speaking cheerfully and forcefully now, even though he did not feel remotely cheerful or forceful, not in the least bright-eyed-and-bushy-tailed, having emerged from the melancholy, depressing and painful dream (but a dream curiously not without a glint of hope) which every conversation with Fanta now resembled.

The sonorous shades of their cheerful prattle from times past floated around them.

He could discern their obscure cheeping and – he said to himself as his skull throbbed and the hair stuck to his forehead in the stifling heat of the telephone box – it made him as nostalgic as if he were by chance to hear a recording of the voices of dead friends, of old, loving, very dear friends.

"Oh *maman*'s god, oh good little father who's done so much for *maman* if she's to be believed, grant that Fanta . . ."

Even if he had never paid much attention to his mother's pious enthusiasms – greeting her assertions, prudent signs of the cross and muttered invocations with a permanently irritated, ironic smirk – he had retained, almost in spite of himself, as a result of hearing it said so often, that the moral rectitude of prayer was the necessary, if not sufficient, condition of its fulfilment.

In what he was asking for, where was the quality of honesty?

"*Maman*'s nice little god, compassionate father, I beg you . . ."

Where was it, his honesty, he wondered, being fully aware (or a second Rudy within him was: a younger, sterner, more scrupulous Rudy, a Rudy as yet unspoiled by setbacks, by lack of understanding and compassion and by the need to cobble together for himself good reasons and poor excuses), where was it, he wondered, his truth of soul, being well aware that, in announcing that he would take Djibril to his mother for the night, it was not *maman* he was thinking about, that concern for her pleasure and happiness was not uppermost in his thoughts, but solely his own peace of mind in thereby preventing Fanta . . .

Because, surely, she would never run away and leave the boy behind – or would she?

He could only judge from what she had done before, but if, the first time, she had taken Djibril with her, was it because Manille had asked her to?

But why would Manille have wanted to be saddled with the child if there had been any possibility that Fanta would agree to abandon Djibril to his father's custody?

No, no, she would not leave without Djibril. Besides, the boy was afraid of his father and Rudy, in a sense, was afraid of him too, because the child, his own son, did not like him, even if, in his young mind, he was unaware of the fact, and he did not like the house, his father's house . . .

A fresh surge of anger was welling up in Rudy, threatening to drown out all rational thought. He wanted to shout into the receiver: "I'll never forgive you for what you've done to me!"

He could just as well have shouted: "I love you so much, there's no-one else I love in the whole wide world, everything must go back to what it was before!"

"O.K., see you this evening," he said.

He hung up, downcast, exhausted and feeling stunned, as if – emerging from a long, melancholy, agonising dream – he had to adjust his consciousness to the ambient reality, a reality which for him, he thought, was frequently just an interminable, unchanging, cold nightmare; it seemed to him that he moved from one dream to another without ever finding the exit, an awakening which he modestly saw as putting in order, as organising rationally, the scattered elements of his existence.

He left the telephone box.

It was already the hottest hour of the morning.

A glance at his watch informed him that he would be even later than he had ever been before.

"So what?" he said to himself, annoyed, though, at feeling slightly anxious at the prospect of finding himself once again face to face with Manille.

If Manille had been able to show him not an iota of compassion, merely irritation and impatience, everything would have been much simpler.

Ought he not, Rudy, to detest Manille?

Was it not shameful and deeply regrettable that the kindness, the pity, as well as the arrogance (albeit barely perceptible in spite of everything) that he read in his boss's eyes prevented him feeling the hatred that any normal person – he said to himself – would have cultivated towards the man who . . .

He shook his head slowly, still dumbfounded, even though it had all happened two years earlier, at the memory, at the condemnation a normal man would have formulated in his mind. Oh, but he was only too well aware that he had not stayed there, at Manille's place, just biding his time, that he was not on the *qui-vive* all day long, awaiting the moment to bring down at last an avenging fist on Manille's head, and Manille was perfectly aware of it too, so that he had no fear of Rudy, had never feared him.

"So that's how it was, eh?" Rudy thought.

Was it admirable or was it degrading? How could one tell?

He thought he could smell the holm-oaks in the distance.

It was probably only the memory of the sourish scent of their tiny silky leaves, but he thought that if he breathed in gently he could indeed smell them. It cheered him up and made him almost happy to imagine himself over there, in the château, opening the shutters on a clear bright morning and sniffing his holm-oaks, smelling the sourish odour of the tiny silky leaves every one of which belonged to him, Rudy Descas – but he would never have scalped those poor old trees as that lot had dared to do, those Americans or Australians who had had the impertinence, according to *maman*, to consider themselves sufficiently French to believe that they were capable of producing the same excellent wine which . . .

The thought of his mother, of her pale, bitter face, put paid to his cheerfulness.

He was tempted to go back into the telephone box and ring Fanta again, not to check that she was still in the house ("Though come to think of it," he said at the same moment to himself, suddenly anxious and ill at ease), but to promise her that everything would be alright.

There, in the heat which was heavy with the smell of the

holm-oaks, he felt carried away by love and compassion.

Everything would be alright?

On the strength of the vision of himself opening the shutters in their bedroom on the first floor of the château?

No matter, he would have liked to talk to her, to inspire in her the confidence which filled his heart at this moment, as if, for once, the reality of existence coincided exactly with his daydreams, or was just about to do so.

He made as if to go back to the telephone box.

He was upset at the thought of getting back into the stifling Nevada with its vaguely doggy smell (it sometimes seemed to him that the vehicle's previous owners had used it as a kennel for their dog, many of whose hairs remained trapped in the felt of the seats).

Nevertheless he decided against ringing Fanta again.

He no longer had the time, did he?

And if, once again, she did not reply, what conclusions could he draw from that, and what good would it do?

And anyway he really no longer had the time.

But she would not run away without taking Djibril with her, and the child was out of reach for the moment, after all.

He cursed himself for working that out.

He almost felt then like defending Fanta against himself and his mean, calculating ways.

Oh, what could he do, since he loved her?

"What else can I do, dear God, good little father, *maman*'s good, kind little god?"

He was convinced that the shaky, flimsy, very flimsy, structure of his existence only just about held together because Fanta, after all, was present, and because she was present more like a small hen with clipped wings, unable to fly over the lowest fence, than she was like the brave independent human being whom he had met at the Lycée Mermoz. He had great difficulty putting up with that thought, it made him feel ashamed, and he only managed to countenance it because this dreary state of affairs was merely provisional in his eyes.

It was not just the lack of money – or was it?

To what extent did his monthly salary of a thousand euros make him less seductive than someone like Manille?

Yes, yes (standing all alone in the ten o'clock sun, near the scorching bonnet of his car, and shrugging impatiently), that was true to a large extent, certainly, but what he lacked above all was faith in his own talents, in his good fortune and in his eternal youth which once shone in the clear blue eyes he had inherited from *maman*, which made him push back, with a hand that was at once caressing and indifferent, the lock of fair hair on his forehead, and which . . .

All that he had well and truly lost, even though he was not old, even though in comparison with others he was still almost young, all that he no longer possessed since his return to France: all that must have played an essential part in making Fanta fall in love with him.

If only – he said to himself – he could slough off this harsh, depressing, painful, degrading nightmare and rediscover, even if it only meant moving from one dream to another, the vision of Fanta and himself, bathed in golden light, walking side by side in the streets of Colobane, their naked arms brushing against each other at every step, he, Rudy, tall and tanned, talking in his strong, cheerful voice, striving already, even though he was unaware of it, to ensnare in the web of his tender, flattering, bewitching words this young woman with the small shaven head, with the discreetly ironic, direct gaze, who had pulled herself up to the level of the Lycée Mermoz where she taught French literature to the children of army officers and prosperous business people; those adolescents had no idea, Rudy declaimed in his strong, cheerful voice, of the frightening determination it had required for this woman to be able to stand in front of them, this woman with the winged feet and the delicate quivering skin on her forehead, no idea of the time and trouble it took her to maintain the only two cotton skirts she possessed, one pink and the other white, always beautifully ironed, that she wore with a T-shirt top, between the straps of which the delicate skin of her back quivered as if two tiny wings . . .

He, Rudy Descas, had really been that charming, light-hearted, smooth-talking young man whom Fanta had eventually taken home, to the flat with green walls where they all lived.

He remembered how his heart had missed a beat when he entered the room suffused with shimmering, vaguely funereal light.

He had first climbed a cement staircase behind her and walked along a gallery off which doors with peeling paint opened.

Fanta had opened the last one and the greenish half-light, accentuated by the window-shutters, had seemed to engulf her.

He had seen nothing beyond the white blob of her skirt as she had entered the room before coming back and inviting him in, having checked, he had supposed, that the flat was in a fit state to be shown.

And he had moved forward, not without shyness and some embarrassment, but chiefly it was gratitude which suddenly rendered him speechless.

Because in the greenish half-light Fanta's calm expression said, here's where I live, this is my home.

Her expression, accepting the judgement of a foreigner with a white face (in that respect his tan made no difference!), blond fringe and smooth white hands on her well-kept but very humble home, accepted in advance its potential effects, the possible feelings of uneasiness or condescension.

Rudy could sense, could almost hear, how much this woman was aware of everything, how shrewd, lucid and immensely perceptive she was, but also how profoundly indifferent she was, through pride, to the opinion a man with such a white forehead, such white, smooth hands might have about her home.

She must have taken him, with his blond hair and fine words, for a wealthy, spoilt young man.

But she had invited him home and now, with a gesture and a word or two, she was introducing him to her uncle, to her aunt, to a neighbour and to other people as well, all of them gradually revealed by the pale light, sitting at the back of the room on chairs or threadbare velvet armchairs, silent, motionless, acknowledging Rudy with a vague nod, and he felt out of place and conspicuous because of the big hands he did not know what to do with, their pallor shining in the dim light as his white forehead and long, smooth forelock must have shone too.

He longed to fall at Fanta's feet and swear to her that he was not what he seemed — the type of man who, tanned and very sure of himself, spent every weekend at his Somone villa.

He longed to fall on his knees and embrace Fanta's slender legs and thank her and tell her how much love he felt for her for having allowed him to see what he had just seen: this austere room, these silent people who did not smile or pretend to be thrilled to meet him, this difficult, frugal life she led, about which people at the Lycée Mermoz, where she arrived every day on her winged feet, in her clean, starched pink skirt, or in her white one, probably knew nothing, as no doubt even less did the children of diplomats and the children of entrepreneurs who went water-skiing at Somone every weekend, that whole group of people, he longed to tell her, whom he could not abide even if occasionally he secretly envied them.

Oh, they certainly knew nothing about her or about the verdigris room with its heavenly glow.

The midday light now shone through the shutters on to the face of the aunt, on to the clasped hands of the uncle, both of whom seemed to be waiting for Rudy to leave so that they could go back to what they had been doing.

And he, Rudy, saw all that and did not know how to convey it to Fanta.

He contented himself – rather stupidly, he felt – with bowing to each person present, stretching his lips to form a little, quivering, gauche smile.

He knew at that moment, with a kind of surprised wonder, that he loved her, loved her infinitely.

Now he was opening the door of his car and slipping inside, holding his breath.

It was even hotter, stuffier inside the car than in the telephone box.

Was he right not to ring Fanta again?

And if she was trying, not to leave but, feeling utterly miserable because he had decided to take Djibril to spend the night at his mother's, trying to . . . ?

No, he could not bear even to think such a word.

"Oh, *maman*'s good little god, nice little father, help me to see things clearly!"

"Help us, dear God."

Could he not just – only for a minute – telephone her, was that not, in truth, perhaps what she was expecting him to do at this moment?

No, it's rather a case (a small sniggering voice murmured) that she no longer wishes to hear the sound of your voice until this evening, and what's more she understands that you feel guilty and are trying somehow to mend your ways whereas all you were after was to put an end to this habit of taking entirely upon your poor shoulders the blame for all the wrangling, since she no doubt doesn't respect you any the more for that and perhaps even despises you a little for losing your nerve after seeming tough, for seeking forgiveness and consolation from her after you had offended her by telling her, can you imagine that, to go back where she came from, can you really imagine that . . . ?

As he switched on the ignition he shook his head in a gesture of denial.

Such a thing he, Rudy Descas, just could not have said.

Just could not.

He could not restrain a dry little laugh.

Might he have meant, ha! ha! that she should go back to Manille?

He was sweating profusely.

The sweat was falling on the steering wheel and on his thighs.

When he tried to put the car into first gear, he could not, the lever had jammed.

The engine stalled.

He found himself once again wrapped in the silence that had been shattered briefly by the roar of the Nevada's engine, and he now saw himself as forming a necessary, incontestable and perfect part of this section of the countryside.

He was not being a nuisance or bothering anyone and no-one had any hold over him.

He leant back against the headrest.

Although he was still sweating, his heart beat less fiercely.

But he had to admit that Manille, in his rather discreet, provincial way, was a successful businessman, and that, even if he had never gone in for water-skiing or owned any other house than the big villa he had had built behind the firm's premises, his virile, if sober, rather elegant, reserved self-assurance, and the particular gentleness he possessed, that of someone who could afford to be gentle because nothing threatened or frightened him, could still attract an upset, confused woman with nothing to do all day, a woman who was lost, as Fanta was lost now.

It's strange, he said to himself, or perhaps it's the effect of love, that I can't forgive her, whereas with him, it's as if I understood him.

But stranger still, to tell the truth, it's her I understand, too, so much so that, were I a woman, I could imagine yielding joyfully and uncomplicatedly to Manille's straightforward charm – oh, how I understand her, and how I hold it against her.

But he was caught unawares by a feeling of panic, by a sort of hallucination, and his heart stood still as he tried to envisage Manille's bedroom, which he imagined was like the rest of the villa, vast and conventional, filled with the usual expensive trappings of contemporary interior design, and when he gently pushed open the door of this unfamiliar bedroom and saw on the huge bed, in a dazzling light, Fanta and Manille, Manille stretched out on Fanta, Rudy Descas's wife, Manille groaning softly while his powerful haunches, his centaur's buttocks, moved in a calm, slow rhythm which brought out the dimples in his hairy flesh, and his head rested on the neck of Fanta, Rudy Descas's own wife, the only woman Rudy Descas had ever truly loved in his whole life.

Or else, what he could see on this bed were the hindquarters of a no less vigorous man with a horse's head panting as he lay on top of Fanta – should he kill this monster, should he at least hate him?

And, under Manille's much more considerable bulk, of what

novel and mysterious nature could her sensations be, something he would never find out?

Rudy was a lean, delicate man, narrow-shouldered but robust, he liked to think, and Manille — but (he shook his head) he did not want to know anything about that.

And he shook his head again, alone at the wheel of his stationary vehicle, in the silence throbbing with heat, and he felt trapped, torn by the same deeply frustrating fear that had left him transfixed, mesmerised, capable only of a little, hideous, weird smile when someone or other (Madame Pulmaire, or *maman* perhaps), had in some drawing-room or other in a house he was visiting (so was it a client's, then?) revealed to him in a whisper what Fanta and Manille were up to, and this nasty suggestion had wiped off Rudy's face the silly smirk he could see in the mirror of the unknown drawing-room in which he stood with his legs apart, his eyes riveted now on the mirror in which he could see how foolish and bizarre he looked, but anything was preferable to the sight of that nasty mouth with its acid breath which took pleasure in shattering Rudy Descas's innocence, his lover's credulity, anything was preferable to the spiteful tone of impotent anger (well, it must have been *maman* because neither Madame Pulmaire nor a customer could have discussed the affair with so much animosity) demanding he take action and reject a woman like that.

What else could this indignant person, in a tone of sweet reasonableness, be suggesting (oh, it was certainly *maman*), except that any man with a shred of dignity left should not, could not, penetrate the very body in which there still reposed a sacred liquor, the centaur's sperm?

He could have answered, with a snigger, "No risk of that, I haven't been sleeping with Fanta for a long time, or rather she's not been sleeping with me."

But he could also have replied, with a cry of despair, "But it was you, *maman*, who got me taken on at Manille's, it was you who went and begged him to give me a job! Had it not been for that, he'd never have met her!"

But he had no recollection of having opened his own mouth, frozen as it was in a slack, feeble rictus.

He could see himself again, gazing at his own impassive face in the mirror, and just under it at the back of the head of this woman who was still talking, who was still trying to drown him in vile, sneaky appeals to his male honour, and had he not then thought that a simple blow to that head, with its short, dyed blond hair, would free him from this torment, had he not seen himself hitting *maman* to shut her up, shouting to her perhaps, just before she lost consciousness, "What do you know of honour, eh, and Dad, what did he know of it?"

But he did not wish to think about that any more.

It was humiliating and pointless and made you feel grubby as if you were emerging from a repetitive, interminable, stupid dream: you are only too familiar with every painful stage of it, but even while plunged in it you know that you are not going to be allowed to skip a single episode.

He did not wish to think about that any more.

He switched on the ignition again and put the car straight into second gear.

The engine protested and spluttered, then, slowly, the Nevada began to move forward, with jolts and moans from every section of its ancient carcase but, he said to himself with some satisfaction, rather pluckily for all that.

He would not think about that any more.

He lowered the window and, driving with one hand, let his left arm hang over the hot side of the car. He could occasionally hear the melting surface of the asphalt crackling under his tyres.

How he loved that sound!

He was now experiencing a gentle, delightful feeling of euphoria.

No, *maman*'s good little god, nice little father, he would not think about the mortifying past any more but only about making himself worthy of the love Fanta was going to feel for him again if he wished to make the effort, and hey, didn't he just, heaven, high, bright and scorching hot this morning, was his witness. Why, for once, shouldn't the best be there for the asking by Rudy Descas, the best and the most certain of the innumerable promises offered by the morning sun this fine spring morning?

He suddenly burst out laughing.

The sound of his own voice enchanted him.

After all, he thought, almost surprised, he was alive, still young, and in robust good health.

Gauquelan himself, that crook whose loathsome sculpture he was circling round at that moment (and today he found the strength not to look at it), that shamefully enriched artist, could he claim as much?

Certainly not.

Alive, alas yes, but the photo Rudy had seen in the paper showed a man with a rather puffy, scowling face, a balding forehead, a tuft of greying hair on top and, curiously, a gap in his front teeth, and Rudy had thought then, he now recalled with a slight feeling of shame, that a man who got paid a hundred thousand euros for a hideous piece of sculpture ought surely, before going in front of the camera, to have been in a position to get his teeth fixed.

The way Gauquelan was alive had nothing to do with his – Rudy's – impressive vitality which he – Rudy – felt throbbing in his every muscle as if he were a horse (or a centaur), a big, proud, young beast whose entire raison d'être consists in the mere fact of existing beautifully, and for whom none of those dreams that leave you with a clammy mouth and stale breath would ever prove invasive again, any more than they would for a horse (or a centaur).

Was *maman* alive?

After the roundabout, without intending to, he accelerated sharply.

He had no business thinking about his mother at that moment, nor about his father; his father was well and truly dead, and no-one would ever remotely have thought of comparing him to a horse (or a centaur) with rippling muscles under his damp skin – in the non-air-conditioned car Rudy's cheeks, neck and forehead were also damp, and in this reaction of his organism he accepted the effect of having evoked, however briefly and insignificantly, his long-dead father, and he recognized the terror and astonishment always provoked in him by the thought of that white-boned skeleton once named Abel Descas, with, Rudy imagined, its very white bones and the hole neatly drilled through its skull, lying in the hot sandy soil of the cemetery at Bel-Air.

He parked the Nevada in the car park of Manille & Co.

Before getting out he carefully mopped his face and neck with the towel which he kept on the back seat for the purpose and which had eventually absorbed the smell of the car.

Each time he promised himself he would change it, then forgot, and so his annoyance was intense when he reached for the towel and found this nauseating rag once again, because it seemed to him that this minor testimony to his own negligence, obliging him to wipe his face with a dubious piece of cloth, represented his whole current existence in its vaguely grimy disorder.

But this morning, just as he had not managed to suppress a reflex of irritation in wiping his face, he successfully forced himself to let his eyes wander over the different cars parked around him and evaluate them in the most neutral manner possible, without succumbing, as he usually did, to the bitter, violent feelings of envy that he found degrading.

So that's what my colleagues and customers drive in, he said calmly, almost ritually to himself, as he itemised the black and grey Audis, Mercedes and B.M.W.s which made the car park of a kitchen showroom on the outskirts of a small provincial town look like a grand hotel.

How do they manage to have so much money?

How are they able to extract from their hard-working existence the sums needed to buy such cars? I've not the slightest idea.

What's their fiddle, what's the knack they possess, what are the tricks of the trade? I'll never be able to make it out.

And other pointless questions like that swirled around in his furious mind as he slammed the door of the Nevada.

But he had been able, this morning, to resist the monotonous surge of covetousness.

With a light step he crossed the car park and dimly recalled feeling much the same during an earlier period in his life when he always walked like that, light of foot and at peace with himself – yes, always like that, and looking serene and benevolent – that was the face he always showed to the world.

It all seemed so distant to him that he almost doubted that he had been involved – he, Rudy Descas – and not his father or someone else he had dreamt about.

How long ago was all that?

He thought it must have been when he returned to Dakar alone, without his mother who had stayed in France, shortly before he met Fanta.

He thought too, with a start, because it was a detail he had forgotten, that for him, then, it used to seem natural to be inclined to be good and kind.

He stopped suddenly in the sun-drenched car park.

The smell of hot tar filled his nostrils.

He had quite a turn when he looked not at the sky but at the bitumen under his feet.

Had he really been that man who, light of foot and at peace with himself, strode along the calm streets of Le Plateau where he had rented a small flat, a man hardly different in appearance, with his blondness and pleasantly regular features, from the men with white faces whom he passed in the neighbourhood but whose business ambitions and frenetic activity he in no way shared?

Could he really have been that man, Rudy Descas, who aspired, calmly and clear-sightedly, to show himself good and just, and even more (oh, how that made him blush with surprise and embarrassment) to distinguish always between good and evil in himself, never preferring the latter even when it appeared under the mask of good as happened all too often here when one was a white man with well-filled pockets, and for very little could buy any kind of labour involving great patience and endurance?

He started walking again, slowly, towards the double glass doors of the building surmounted by the name Manille lit up in huge letters.

His legs had stiffened, as if suddenly robbed of the gift of lightness.

Because he wondered for the first time whether, in persuading Fanta to follow him to France, he had not knowingly looked the other way so as to give crime every latitude to take possession of him, and whether he had not savoured the feeling of acting badly without appearing to do so.

Until now he had only asked himself the question in pragmatic terms: had it been a good idea or a bad idea to bring Fanta here?

But oh no, it was not that, it was not that at all.

Put like that, the question was a ploy used by the crime comfortably installed in him.

And, in that radiant period of his life when every morning, with innocent heart, he left his small modern flat at Le Plateau, he was still able to recognise the bad impulses and fallacious thoughts that sometimes went through his mind and to shoo them away by thinking the opposite, and he was still able to find himself relieved and happy because of it, since he desired profoundly only one thing, to be capable of loving everything around him.

But now, now – the extent of his bitterness almost stunned him.

If he had been that man, what had happened to him, what had he done to find himself inhabiting the body of such an envious and brutal person whose disposition to universal love had shrunk around the single figure of Fanta?

Yes, truly, what had he done to himself to unload, now, all this untapped, importunate love upon a woman who had gradually become wearied by his incompetence, at an age, the mid-forties, when such faults (a certain lack of aptitude for sustained work, a tendency to entertain fantasies and to believe in the reality of what were only hazy projects) can no longer hope to meet with indulgence and understanding?

Not only, he said to himself as he pushed open the glass door through which, with a cowardly sense of relief, he could discern Manille's big shape, surrounded by a couple of people, customers probably, to whom Manille was presenting the main features of a showroom model of one of his kitchens, not only had he willingly connived in lies and corruption entering and taking possession of his soul, but on the pretext of loving her he had imprisoned Fanta in a fortress of dreary, cold love – for such was his love at present, distressing, everlasting, like a dream from which you struggle in vain to awake, a rather degrading and pointless dream – was not that how Fanta must be enduring it and was not that how, as a victim of such a love, he would himself experience it?

Once inside he walked purposefully towards the staff offices, even though he could not stop his upper lip trembling.

He knew that this *tic* made him look unpleasant, almost nasty, and that it was always fear that provoked it.

At such moments his lip curled back like a dog's.

And yet he had no need to worry about Manille. Really?

Out of the corner of his eye he watched the slow progress of the little group, having worked out that he would have reached the offices before Manille and his customers got close.

Afterwards, he said to himself, Manille would have forgotten seeing him arrive so late.

All he had to do was keep out of Manille's way for an hour or so and all would be well.

He had time to notice that, with his neatly ironed black T-shirt and well-cut pale jeans held up by a discreetly studded belt, Manille looked good this morning.

His thick grey hair was combed back, and his complexion was dark, almost golden.

Rudy could hear Manille's slightly husky voice as he opened and shut a cupboard door, and he was sure that the customers, a drably dressed middle-aged couple with thick legs, were without realising it succumbing to Manille's insistent charm as he fixed his dark eyes intently on theirs and seemed on the point of passing on an important piece of personal information or making a flattering comment which he was only holding back for fear of embarrassing them.

He never gave the impression, Rudy had often noticed, that he was trying to sell something.

Without seeming to make any effort in that direction he managed to create the illusion of a friendly, intimate relationship which would last well beyond the eventual sale of the kitchen, because that had merely been the fortuitous pretext for the birth of a friendship, and it often turned out that the tactic was quite sincere: Manille went on visiting his customers just for the pleasure of their company, and as they chatted he never forsook the tone of subdued, contained, delicate ardour that had led to the sale in the first place, so that, Rudy thought, the manner Manille adopted in overcoming a client's resistance ended up as his true way of speaking, the only one ever heard – that smooth, slightly hoarse timbre and that restrained fervour which, had he not mastered it, people must have thought, would have led him to sing their praises, to share secrets with them, even to hug them.

Rudy could not help admiring Manille even if he despised his trade.

How was it that he, Rudy, although taller, slimmer and younger than Manille, and dressed like his boss in jeans and T-shirt or in a short-sleeved top, and wearing the same sort of canvas shoes, always looked rather like an ageing hard-up adolescent: that Rudy just could not understand.

He would never possess Manille's relaxed elegance . . . No, he said to himself as he caught sight of his reflection in the second glass door, the one separating the showroom from the offices, no, don't even think about it.

He considered that he had a mean, crumpled, almost needy appearance.

Who could such a man, however kind, ever appeal to?

Where would people see in him his love of life and of others, even if he could find it again?

Where would people see it?

He had to admit that in someone like Manille, however hardened he was by a life in business, by the unremitting calculations and by the pragmatic manoeuvrings it required, and despite the *chic* sportswear and Chaumet watches and the villa at the back of the shop, despite, in a word, everything that had transformed Manille, a farm-labourer's son, into a banal provincial *parvenu*, the amiability, kindness and ability to show discreet compassion could be discerned at once in his gentle, modest look.

And then Rudy wondered for the first time if it had not been precisely that which had attracted Fanta and which he had long ago lost the talent for . . .

He went into the office and closed the door quietly behind him.

He felt himself blushing.

But it was certainly that, and even if the term was pompous, there was no other word for it: the talent for . . . forgiveness.

He had never thought, even in the depths of his anger and grief, after *maman* (yes?) had told him about the liaison between Fanta and Manille, he had never thought that it was Manille's wealth, and the respect and the power which went with it, that could have seduced Fanta.

He had never thought that.

Now – oh yes – he understood what it was all about, and he understood it in the light of what he no longer had, for he understood at last that he no longer had it, though he had unwittingly suffered because of it.

The talent for forgiveness.

He went to his desk and dropped down on his office chair.

Around him, in the big glass-walled room, all the desks were occupied.

"Ah, there you are!"

"Hi Rudy!"

He replied with a smile and a little wave of the hand.

On his cluttered desk, next to the keyboard, he saw a pile of leaflets.

"Your mother brought them a little while ago."

Cathie's voice, cordial but a shade anxious, reached him from the next desk and he knew that if he turned his head his eyes would meet hers, with their questioning, slightly perplexed look.

She would ask him in a low voice why he had arrived three-quarters of an hour late and perhaps, too, why he did not simply forbid his mother to set foot in Manille's workplace.

So he contrived to mumble an answer which meant he did not have to look her in the eye.

In the dazzling glare of the room the vivid pink of Cathie's blouse shone brightly around her.

Rudy could see it reflected in the white surface of his own desk.

He knew too that if he turned towards Cathie he would clearly see, beyond her small, pale face, on the other side of the picture window, Manille's villa, a big building with blue shutters, pale-pink roughcast walls and a roof of Provençal tiles, separated from the commercial premises by a simple lawn, and he could not help wondering, for the nth time, painfully and fruitlessly, whether Cathie and the others, Dominique, Fabrice and Nathalie, had watched Fanta's comings and goings at the boss's dream house, and noticed how many times she went indoors, and why he, Rudy, had never seen her there, although, during that terrible period when he "knew" without "really knowing" (he did not have to believe everything *maman* said, after all), he had never ceased glancing at the picture window, looking over the head of Cathie, who felt sorry for him and was sympathetic (so was everybody privy to his troubles?), at the villa's fussy double doors with their wrought-iron fittings.

How he had suffered then!

How ashamed, how violent he had felt!

All that was now long ago in the past, but he still could not speak to Cathie without feelings of rage boiling up in him as he glanced at Manille's house.

He suddenly felt like saying to her in a dry tone that would make her uncomfortable, "But that's pretty well the only consolation *maman*'s got left in life, dropping off right and left her bundles of pathetic leaflets in aid of poor cretins as lonely and as much at a loose end as herself, how do you expect me to tell her to stop coming here and, really, who's bothered by it, eh?"

But he said nothing.

He was conscious of the aura of fuchsia that surrounded her and it annoyed him, because he could not forget her presence.

He pushed to one side the packet of leaflets held together with a rubber band.

"They are in our midst."

The clumsy, almost laughable picture of an adult angel sitting down at table with members of an ecstatic family, and the angel's silly smirk.

"They are in our midst."

Such inanities stopped his mother from drowning in melancholy and anti-depressants and were, literally, her salvation.

He was outraged that an insignificant person like Cathie dared to suggest, with an air of seeking to be helpful, that he should deprive her of the pleasure of bringing her brochures to Manille's place.

What did she know of *maman*'s unhappy life?

"Hey, tell me, does Manille want my mother to stop coming here?" he asked suddenly.

He looked at Cathie, dazzled by the absurd intensity of her pink blouse. It was such an effort keeping his eyes fixed upon her face to thwart their tendency to wander beyond her skull that his head started aching violently.

Meanwhile he felt as if a hot poker was being pushed up his anus.

"Not at all," said Cathie. "I'm not even aware if he noticed your mother coming in."

She smiled, surprised he could think that.

Oh no, he thought, downcast, it's starting again.

He raised his buttocks feebly from the chair and balanced on the edge of the seat so that only the top of his thighs remained in contact with it.

But the mild relief he had hoped for failed to materialise.

He then heard, through the fog of pain that had suddenly enveloped him, Cathie's muffled voice.

"It's not like Manille to stop your mother coming, is it?"

Rudy could not now remember what he had said or what he had asked.

Ah, *maman*. It was not like Manille to show the slightest harshness, or to try and shoo away this ridiculous woman who really believed she could, with tracts written and printed in her living-room – tracts that swallowed up a not inconsiderable part of her meagre pension – convince kitchen salesmen of the presence of angels all about them.

At the very most he would . . .

That familiar itch, which had taken him by surprise, he was beginning to tame it in his mind.

He brought to bear all the old defence mechanisms (those he had not used in quite a while because for several months he had been left in peace by the problem), the most immediate of which consisted in directing his thoughts towards topics having no connection with his own body, or with any other body, real or otherwise, so that, quite naturally, he started thinking intensely about *maman*'s angels, and he reached out with his fingers to bring the packet of brochures nearer to him.

How would she answer the question whether angels suffered sometimes from piles?

Would she not be happy and flattered to see him asking, with apparent seriousness, to hear him broaching . . .

Stop, stop, he said to himself, in a panic. That was not at all what he ought to be concentrating on. The pain came back, more pressing, exasperating.

He had a terrible longing to scratch, no, to scrape off, to tear away, this goading, burning flesh.

He rubbed against the edge of the chair.

With a trembling finger he started up his computer.

Then he looked again at the picture of the angel, the clumsily drawn figure, the naïve décor sketched by *maman*, and suddenly he discerned beyond all possibility of error what his eyes had been content to skim over without any attempt at interpretation a few moments earlier.

As he had vaguely felt already, the three members of the small family seated at the table looked like Djibril, Fanta and Rudy, and only the artist's lack of skill shielded them somewhat from the risk of being recognised; but more than that, someone had afterwards attached to the angel a vigorous penis which was clearly visible under the table and seemed to emerge from a specially fitted pocket in the long white robe.

Rudy flicked through the packet of brochures.

The angel had only been ridiculed on the first leaflet.

He turned the packet over and pushed it towards a corner of his desk.

He glanced at Cathie.

At the same moment she raised her eyes and frowned anxiously.

"Anything wrong, Rudy?"

He grinned sardonically.

Oh, how it hurt, and how angry he felt at it hurting.

"Who put the brochures on my desk?" he said.

"I told you, your mother came in this morning."

"So it was she who put them there, in person?"

Cathie shrugged uncomprehendingly, slightly annoyed, and said: "I don't see who else it could have been."

"But you didn't see her?"

Cathie was smiling now, but coldly, conspicuously restraining her feelings of impatience.

"Listen, Rudy, I do know that your mother came in with her . . . sort of tracts, I caught sight of her in the lobby, but it so happens that I wasn't at my desk when she dropped them off."

He leapt off his chair, suddenly intoxicated with rage and pain.

But a small sad voice whispered inside him: "How can you hope to be good when you suffer the torments of the damned?" It was the voice of the calm, cheerful, seductive Rudy Descas that Rudy wanted so badly to be again, with the pitiless moral standards he set himself and the less stringent ones he applied to others.

And it was with terror and dread that he noticed Cathie flinch slightly as he approached her chair.

He felt the others around him watching him silently.

Had he become the sort of man feared by women and despised by other men, especially strong men capable of self-restraint, like Manille?

He suddenly felt terribly unhappy, craven, useless.

He grabbed the packet of brochures and flung it on Cathie's desk.

He hopped from one foot to the other, trying to calm the pain by rubbing his underpants against his inflamed skin.

"And that charming little joke, whose idea was that then?" he said, prodding the angel's penis with his finger.

Cathie glanced warily at the picture.

"No idea," she said.

He picked the packet up again and went back to his desk.

One of his male colleagues, at the back of the room, tut-tutted audibly.

"Hey! What's your problem?" Rudy said. "Go to hell!"

"Now you've gone too far, my lad," Cathie said drily.

"I just want my mother left out of it," Rudy said.

Because he was sticking to his guns that someone had wanted to humiliate *maman* by adding an obscene doodle to her drawing. Although he had always hated her sanctimonious propaganda and refused systematically to talk about it, the passionate assiduity with which she drafted and illustrated her messages, taking a lot of trouble to produce the best result that her meagre talent was capable of, laid an obligation upon him, he felt, to stand up for her.

As in those threatening, implacable, irresolvable dreams where a heavy, absurd and insurmountable obligation is laid upon you, no-one but he could defend that unreasonable woman, no-one but he could do it.

He recalled confusedly when and how that feeling of obligation arose, and the memory was so embarrassing that he blushed violently. At the same moment, a pain even sharper than before pierced his anus.

"They are amongst us, they are pure spirits, and even at table they address us in thought, just to ask us to pass the salt or the bread."

Who is your guardian angel, Rudy, what's his name and what is his position in the angel hierarchy?

Rudy's father had neglected his angel – treating his dog better – which is why, *maman* had hinted, he had had to endure such a sad end, because his angel had lost touch with him or had worn itself out looking for him in the dark shadows of pragmatism and indifference.

While all was going well for him Rudy's father had, out of spite or vanity, contrived to give his angel the slip. Ah, men can be so uppity!

So where – Rudy had wondered – where could the guardian angel of his father's business partner have been when he had been knocked unconscious and run over by Rudy's dad?

Had he – the partner – been a foolhardy man, someone too cocksure for his own good, a person who had delighted in giving his angel the slip? Or else did Africans in general have the misfortune to be poorly guarded, were their angels lazy and incompetent?

The dirty work of defending *maman*, no-one but he could do it, nobody else could . . .

"You need to get a grip, Rudy," Cathie said, in a tone of disappointment and reproach. "People haven't been attacking your mother."

"O.K., O.K.," he mumbled, unable to detach himself from his physical pain, so wrapped up in it that he could scarcely breathe.

"You need to get a grip," she said again, in a stubborn, monotonous voice.

"O.K., O.K.," he said, almost inaudibly.

"If you don't, Rudy, you'll land yourself in serious trouble. Monsieur Manille is beginning to get fed up, you know, and so are we. You must calm down and start doing your job."

"But who scribbled on my mother's drawing?" he said. "It's so . . . horrid!"

He heard the glass door open and, a few moments later, there was Manille standing in front of him with his fists on the desk as if he was restraining himself from leaping at Rudy, and yet his look was kindly, almost tender, but a bit weary.

And Rudy felt something sliding between them, as palpable as a thin sheet of rain. It was their mutual embarrassment, a mixture of shame and resentment shared equally, it seemed, by the two of them, Manille on the one hand, and himself, Rudy – who had the advantage of still having Fanta at his side whereas Manille had lost her – on the other.

But more recently Rudy had sensed something else, scarcely less embarrassing, but also more comforting, a remarkable, inexpressible communion born of an awareness of their having both loved the same woman at the same time.

He saw Manille's eyes focusing on *maman*'s drawing.

"You see that?" Rudy said in a shrill, febrile voice which echoed horribly in his ears.

Hearing that acrimonious tone, did Manille not wonder incredulously how it was that Fanta had finally preferred this narrow-hipped, gangling, ill, bitter man over him, how she could have gone back to Rudy Descas, who had long ago forfeited all honour and respect?

That was certainly, Rudy felt, precisely what he would think if he were in Manille's shoes.

Why had Fanta come back to him, in despair and completely numbed, as if, held captive in an implacable, irresolvable dream, she had inflicted upon herself the absurd obligation of spending the rest of her days in a house she disliked, beside a man whom she shunned and who had from the outset deceived her as to what he really was by passing himself off as a mild-mannered person of integrity though he had allowed untruth to take up residence in his heart?

Why, in fact, had she not stayed with Manille?

The latter gestured disdainfully at the packet of brochures as if to suggest that what he saw was of no importance.

"I'd like to know who played this dirty trick on my mother," Rudy said, panting slightly.

"It's not that serious," said Manille.

His breath smelt of coffee.

Rudy thought that nothing would have given him greater pleasure, at that moment, than a double espresso with sugar.

He wriggled about on his chair, gradually finding a rhythm which, without getting rid of the pain, helped bring some relief through well-managed scratching.

"It wouldn't be you, by any chance?" he asked as Manille was about to say something.

"If there's anyone I'll never make fun of, it's your mother," Manille said with a smile.

He took his hands off the desk and stuck his thumbs in his belt, a fine black leather strap with silver studs which seemed to Rudy to sum up Manille's personality, at once virile and held firmly in check.

"You perhaps don't remember, you were too small at the time," Manille said in a voice low enough for Rudy, alone, to be able to hear him, "but my recollection is clear. Your parents and mine were neighbours, we lived in the country, the back of beyond, and on Wednesdays my parents left me alone at home while they went to work, and they asked your mother to pop in from time to time to check that I was O.K. Well, your mother came as agreed and when she saw how sad and lonely I was, she took me back to your place, she gave me a big tea and I had a lovely afternoon. Unfortunately that all came to an end when you left for Africa. But whenever I meet your mother I always recall those happy times, so I'll never do anything, even behind her back, that could upset her, never."

"I see," said Rudy.

He affected a sneering tone, but he suddenly felt almost as jealous, wretched and disorientated as he had been when, no more than three or four years old, he had seen *maman* return every Wednesday with this bigger boy about whom he knew nothing and who – he had not realised until this moment – was none other than Manille. He had had to put up with the giant shadow of the boy towering above him, with his golden legs emerging from his shorts like two pillars barring his path towards *maman*. So it had been he, it was Manille!

He could not recall the boy's face, only the two strong legs at the level of his own face, and between them his mother's barely visible features.

So why had it always seemed that the atmosphere in the house changed dramatically upon the boy's entrance, that it became at once livelier and more highly charged, and that with barely-contained excitement, moving faster and speaking more rapidly, *maman* proposed, as if suddenly inspired, to make pancakes for tea? Why had it always seemed to him that this boy with the solid legs and deep voice relieved *maman* of the boredom which Rudy's simple presence failed to break and perhaps even accentuated and increased?

It was hard to escape from Rudy, and Rudy was sometimes a real drag, whereas, for the small neighbour of about nine or ten, who never asked for anything, *maman* was his salvation. She for her part failed to notice that Rudy had always before his eyes the boy's firm legs, and that those same legs seemed always to move at the same moment as Rudy did, thereby stopping him getting close to his mother.

Ah, so it was he, it was Manille!

Rudy, terribly shaken, was wriggling more and more on his chair.

The sunlight, still tinged with the shimmering glow of Cathie's pink blouse, shone directly on his face through the window.

He was hot, fearfully hot.

Manille seemed to be looking at him anxiously.

Was it not extraordinary that *maman* never reminded him of that period when a big, implacable, discreet boy filled the kitchen with his fateful presence every Wednesday afternoon? Was it not extraordinary that she had never told him that the lad was Manille?

Behind his back *maman* and Manille had both shared this secret memory – why, for God's sake?

Manille was talking to him.

Rudy could be in no doubt that Manille represented for his mother exactly the kind of son she would have liked to have, but was that a reason for . . .

Ah well, what did it matter, after all?

He tried to understand what Manille was saying to him in his subdued, mellow voice, but a violent feeling of injustice gripped him at the thought that Manille had always shielded *maman* and that she, for her part . . .

How hot he was!

Manille was so positioned that he was in shadow whereas Rudy was dazzled by the sun.

He then became aware that he was frantically rubbing his bottom against the chair and making it squeak, causing colleagues at the back of the room to turn round.

So what was Manille saying about that customer, Madame Menotti?

Without understanding exactly why, he had a sense of foreboding and unease at the mention of this customer's name, as if he were aware of having let her down while being unable to guess in what way.

He thought he had done with Madame Menotti and her pretentious kitchen, the design of which he had overseen from the outset, having sketched the plans himself, helped her choose the colour of the wood, and discussed at length with her the form the extractor-hood should take. When it finally occurred to him to wonder why Manille had entrusted the whole Menotti project to him, to someone as poorly qualified as Rudy was, he did not take long to find out: Madame Menotti had phoned him at home in the middle of the night to say she had awoken in a terrible fit of anguish – no, worse, in a hyperventilating fit such as she had never before experienced – at the thought that the whole design project was not at all to her liking and why could they not simply go back to the original idea and line the walls with the main elements, why could they not take back to the drawing-board the entire conception of this kitchen which, she admitted, spluttering with distress, she was not even sure she really wanted any more, sitting there in her nightie in her old, much-loved kitchen, why not draw a line under the whole thing, she felt so bad, so bad.

And it had taken Rudy a good hour to remind her precisely why she had gone to Manille in the first place: because she could no longer stand the ill-assorted old-fashioned furniture and fittings of her present kitchen; then, almost drunk with fatigue and boredom, he had assured her that her secret wish of seeing her life transformed, brightened up thanks to the installation of ingenious cupboards and a telescopic hood, was not an absurd hope – "Trust me, Madame Menotti," he had said.

He had hung up, exhausted, but too tense to be able to go back to sleep.

He had felt a spasm of hatred towards Madame Menotti, not because she had awoken him in the middle of the night but because she had envisaged quite simply cancelling weeks of tedious, disheartening work devoted to the attempt to adapt the woman's complicated, reckless desires to the limited budget at her disposal.

Oh, the time he had wasted in front of the computer, seeking ways of including an American worktop or a refuse bin that opened automatically into plans she had approved and then gone back on, oh, the disillusionment he had often felt at the realisation that he had to apply to such trivial matters nothing less than his whole intelligence, all his faculties of concentration and ingenuity!

It was at that point, perhaps – when he was offering Madame Menotti reassurances in the middle of the night – that, for the first time, certainly for the first time so acutely and painfully, he got the full measure of how far his world had collapsed.

He had gone over with Madame Menotti every aspect of the kitchen which he found grotesque, useless (built to receive each day many guests of refined taste, although she lived alone and, by her own admission, did not much like cooking) since that was his job, that was his life, and she could not imagine that he had aspired to a university chair or that at one time he had considered himself an expert on medieval literature, because nothing showed now of the fine erudition which he had once possessed and which was slowly fading, slowly disappearing under the ashes of the worries that continually plagued him.

Those that are in wedlock resemble the fish swimming freely in the vastness of the sea . . .

How could he extricate himself, he had wondered in despair,

coldly and lucidly, from this unending, pitiless dream that was his life?

. . . that comes and goes at will and comes and goes so much that eventually it encounters a creel . . .

"She's expecting you, go at once," said Manille.

Could he be referring to Fanta?

Rudy was sure of one thing, that if Fanta had stopped expecting him, her husband, she was not expecting Manille either. For some reason, Rudy did not know why, she had found Manille a big disappointment.

Manille turned on his heel.

"I've got to go to Madame Menotti's, is that it?" Rudy said.

Without looking back at him Manille nodded, then returned to the showroom where he had left his two customers sitting on bar stools, their fat legs hanging gauchely down on the ground, while he had gone to speak to Rudy.

From a distance the man smiled vaguely at Rudy.

He held his beret in his lap and Rudy could see, even at that distance, his bald pate shining over his pink forehead.

"They are in our midst!"

Might it be, he wondered, that this couple, interested in a complete period kitchen in dark wood fitted with wrought-iron cupboard handles and peppered with fake worm holes, formed part of the company of angels who, *maman* was certain, visited us regularly and whom we could recognise if (thanks to her brochures) our souls were made alert to their presence.

As Rudy smiled back, the man immediately looked away, inscrutable.

. . . in which there are several fish that have been caught by the bait within, having found it sweet of smell and good of taste, and when our fish sees it he tries hard to get inside . . .

Rudy got up and went over to Cathie's desk, putting on a jaunty air.

His anus was still burning terribly.

He picked up her phone. Cathie pursed her lips but said nothing.

As a junior salesperson he was not allowed a direct line.

He dialled his own number and let it ring a dozen or so times.

He suddenly felt his forehead and hands wet with sweat.

Fanta could not hear – or chose not to – or else, he thought, she could not answer because she was out or . . .

When he put down the phone his eyes met Cathie's. She was embarrassed, unsettled.

"It seems Madame Menotti wants to see me," he said cheerfully.

But he was in such pain that he felt his upper lip curling in the usual rictus. Unable to stand the burning itch any longer he scratched himself briefly, frenziedly, with one hand.

"I think that Madame Menotti is hopping mad, Rudy," Cathie said, rather regretfully, in a low voice.

"Oh, why?"

The old confused impression that he had fallen down on his duty of care towards Madame Menotti, not deliberately but through a culpable failure to pay close attention to the job, made his mouth suddenly feel dry.

So what had he done, or failed to do?

Madame Menotti, a lowly bank employee, did not have much money. She had taken out a loan of some twenty thousand euros to finance the purchase of this kitchen, and Rudy had had to juggle with different pieces of equipment taken from several models, some of them sale items, to meet the somewhat immodest requirements of this pragmatic woman who, though well-versed in money matters, suddenly pretended not to be able to grasp why the itemised list of the things she wanted added up to a lot more than the sum she had borrowed.

He had certainly had it up to here with that kitchen!

In many ways he had shown himself to be receptive, committed, on the ball.

And yet, once the whole order had been placed, a sort of unpleasant aftertaste and a threatening premonition had stayed with him . . . *and circles about so, that he finds the way through and goes inside, and trusts that he is in pleasaunce and delyte, as he trusts the others also to be, and once within he cannot go back* . . .

Oh God, what had he done now?

Since the start of his employment at Manille's four years ago (four years of his life!) he had no recollection of ever having done anything exactly as it should have been done.

Either through boredom or through resentment he had piled up mistakes and peccadilloes. Some customers, when they came back for a different purchase, recalled these lapses sufficiently well to tell Manille that this time they wanted nothing to do with Rudy Descas.

But in Madame Menotti's case he had gone to a lot of trouble.

"How's your wife?" Cathie said.

Startled, he blinked and wriggled helplessly.

"Fine, fine."

"And the little chap?"

"Djibril? Fine, yes, I think."

Now she seemed to be gazing at him with the same teasing, rather distant smile as the man with the beret shortly before.

He was seized with panic.

What was she smiling about in her reddish halo?

And once within he cannot go back.

"You've really no idea what Madame Menotti wants me for?" he said in an offhand way, knowing perfectly well that it was useless to pursue the matter but unable to make up his mind to leave without getting some light shed not only on Madame Menotti's concerns but on the incomprehensible trials of his own life, of his whole existence.

He cannot go back.

Cathie stared at her screen, conspicuously ignoring him.

It then struck him that once he had left the room he would not get back in, that he would not be allowed back in, and that people preferred, for a reason he could not discern, not to tell him so just yet – because they feared him, perhaps?

"I've done all I can for Madame Menotti, you know? Since I began working here I've never gone to so much trouble as I have over that blasted kitchen. I put in – unstintedly – hours of overtime."

He was calm and he could feel his face radiating with the warmth of his calm, light smile.

The sharp pain in his anus was also calming down.

Since Cathie went on stubbornly pretending to be unaware of his presence, and because he suddenly thought that if he did not come back to the office he would perhaps never see her again, he leaned down towards the tiny pink lobe of her almost translucent ear, and whispered, softly, calmly (as softly and calmly, he thought, as the young man he'd once been):

"I ought to do Manille in, don't you think?"

She moved her head sharply away from his.

"Rudy, just clear off!"

He raised his eyes and, through the picture window, looked once again at Manille's sunlit villa with its imposing, disproportionately large entrance bay, at this big low house very similar to those which rich business people built for themselves in the part of town known as Les Almadies, and indeed very comparable, he said to himself, his heart missing a beat, yes indeed, very comparable, to the villa built by his father Abel Descas who had chosen to have his shutters painted not in the Provençal blue now popular everywhere but in a dark red that reminded him of his Basque origins, not suspecting, how could he . . .

but he cannot go back

. . . that the slightly less red blood of his friend and partner would stain for ever the very white, porous stone he had chosen for the terrace.

Yes, Rudy thought, ambitious men like Manille or Abel Descas (whose strong legs, never obliged to bend gracefully at the knee, were firmly planted on the ground) built houses which looked alike because they were the same sort of men, even though Rudy's father would have laughed or rather taken umbrage at being compared to the owner of a kitchen dealership, he – Abel Descas – who early on had left his province, crossed Spain and a bit of the Mediterranean, then Morocco and Mauretania, before pulling up in his valiant old Ford on the banks of the Senegal river where – he straightaway said to himself, as he strove already to fashion his little family legend – he would found a holiday village the like of which the world had never seen.

Oh yes, Rudy thought, men of that sort, whose aims were pragmatic but just as ardent as any aspiration of the spirit, never felt that they had to struggle day after day against the icy blast of some endless, monotonous, subtly degrading dream.

Since he felt that Cathie was rigid with fear, her small immobile eyes striving desperately to avoid his own, he could not stop himself from adding, before moving away from her desk, in a slightly trembling voice,

"If you knew all the gentleness I've got stored up inside me!"

She gave an involuntary throaty gurgle.

But his father or Manille, although formidable in their different ways, were not the sort of men to make women afraid, whereas he, good God, how had he come to that?

He picked up his mother's brochures from his own desk, rolled them up and stuffed them in a trouser pocket.

He crossed the large sunlit room, aware that his colleagues were probably watching him go with relief, or contempt, or something else he could only guess at.

And yet, as he was approaching the glass door, his movements still affected by the sharp pain in his rectum, his thighs separated even though no excessive muscle pushed them away from each other (for he had slender, almost thin legs, and yet he was walking a bit like his father or Manille, men whose massive thighs forced their knees apart), he was amused at the thought that his colleagues had perhaps found in him their angel.

He moved forward, haloed in shimmering blondness, just as in the past when he left his little flat at Le Plateau and walked calmly down the hot avenue, serenely conscious of the solid decency of his heart and the unalloyed plenitude of his honour.

He would like to have shouted to his colleagues in a nice, kindly, charming, unaffectedly cheerful way: "I am the Minister my mother talked to you about!"

Had there not been a time, he remembered uneasily, when *maman* used to bleach the pale flaxen hair of her little Rudy so that he looked even blonder, almost white?

He remembered the unpleasant odour of the peroxide which ended up making him dazed and sleepy, sitting on a stool in the kitchen of the house where Manille had just informed him that he had spent so many Wednesdays, so Rudy must have been quite young when *maman* got it into her head thus to inflict on him the most conventional aspect of the angelic figure, because these sessions had been interrupted when they had left to join Rudy's father in Africa.

Perhaps, he said to himself, *maman* had thought that the natural blondness of Rudy's hair would be more than enough over there to establish him as a seraph, or else she had not dared to carry on with the bleaching in the presence of her husband who, with incredulous, derisive bluntness, had dumped his own guardian angel and, to get rid of him, had galloped off even further into the shadows of his cynical calculations, of his more or less secret, more or less lawful, schemes and dodges.

"I'm your messenger from the order of Thrones!" he wanted to shout out, but refrained, not wishing to look at his colleagues.

Suddenly, it pleased him to think that they would perhaps at that precise moment welcome a revelation like that as they saw him pass by in front of them with his rather stiff walk and his legs bizarrely spread, but for all that haloed with a fearsome, luminous majesty and sunny brilliance.

He had not been able to protect Fanta.

He had claimed to be the guardian, in France, of her social fragility, but he had let her down.

He pushed the door open and entered the showroom.

Manille's two customers were now at the stage of choosing the stools for the breakfast bar where, Rudy was ready to bet, they were never going to eat, which they would never lean their elbows on as they drank a cup of coffee, preferring the little impractical table they had always used till then. He knew they would find a way, surreptitiously, of bringing the table back into the brand new kitchen which Manille would have built for them, and when their children visited them and in their astonishment got almost cross with them for reinstalling their greasy old table, its grooves filled with crumbs, at the end of the breakfast bar, blocking access to the fridge, they would, thought Rudy, argue in self-justification that it was only temporary and that they would get rid of their dear table once they found the small piece of furniture which, whenever they got back from the shops and wanted to put their bags and boxes down, they still lacked.

Manille was getting them to feel the brown leatherette covers of a pair of dark wooden stools.

He stood beside them, infinitely patient, never pressing, never in a hurry to move on.

The man heard Rudy's footsteps from afar and looked up.

Deeply moved, Rudy thought he gazed at him more insistently than usual, with an affable, friendly look.

Rudy had the impression that the man was making as if to raise his beret in greeting.

And whereas he would normally have been worried and embarrassed by a gesture like that and by such an insistent gaze, fearing some unpleasantness to come, he told himself cheerfully that the man might simply have seen him somewhere before.

I am the spirit of the order of Dominations!

Yes, the chap had perhaps seen one of *maman*'s tracts and, watching the haloed Rudy pass by, his heart had evidently been touched by a feeling of beatitude.

"Art thou the one that is to take care of me?" his look seemed to ask.

How to answer that?

Rudy smiled broadly, something he normally avoided because he was aware that rapture, like fear, caused his lips to twist and made him look nasty.

He mouthed, looking the bloke straight in the eye: "I am the little Master of the Virtues!"

He hurried out of the showroom.

He was overcome by the heat in the car park. It brought him back down to earth.

Not, he mumbled, that anyone could reproach him with having knowingly abandoned Fanta to her exiled state, and as for the fact that she did not have the precise qualifications to teach in France, that was not his fault.

And yet what never left him was the certainty that he had deceived her in bringing her here, since he had turned his face away from hers and spurned the mission, implicitly accepted when they were still abroad, of watching over her.

The thing was, he was then emerging from a mortifying experience!

What a thrashing he had received, what a thrashing!

It sometimes seemed to him that he was still affected by it whenever he raised his arms, but especially when a smell of hot fuel oil arose from the baking asphalt of Manille's car park. Then with painful clarity he saw himself again lying prone on a similar bitumen surface softened by the heat, his back and shoulders crushed by sharp knees, his face swollen as he struggled to get up, to avoid all contact with the dusty, sticky tar.

Years later, such a vision still made him blush with shame and astonishment.

But now he felt, for the first time, how automatic that reaction was becoming.

He breathed in deeply, soaking up the acrid smell.

He realised then that the opprobrium had left him.

Yes, it was certainly he whom teenagers from the Lycée Mermoz had beaten up before hurling him to the ground, crushing his chest against the asphalt and ending up pushing his face, which he had tried to keep clear of the ground, against the surface of the court-yard. It was indeed his cheek that would now always bear the fine scars, it was his shoulders that still hurt slightly, and yet the shame no longer clung to him, not that he could or would pass it on to someone else, but rather because he felt he had accepted it and that now he had the chance of freeing himself of it, as from a continual, unending, cold, terrifying dream to which you submit, grinning and bearing it, in the knowledge that you are now going to be able to break loose from it.

He, Rudy Descas, sometime literature teacher at the Lycée Mermoz and medieval specialist, no longer formed one body with the infamy he had suffered.

He had lost all honour and dignity and had returned to France dragging Fanta with him, knowing that the withering effect of his experience would pursue him because he had internalised it and had convinced himself that it was no more than that, while hating it and fighting against it.

And now that he was starting to accept it, he felt a great weight had been taken off his shoulders.

Now he could calmly and quietly go over in his mind the images of that violent humiliation – and the humiliation no longer bore much relation to himself as he was at the present moment, standing in the warm, dry air; and the burden that had weighed his heart down and filled his chest with a dense, oppressive mass he now saw leaving him, dissolving, as he remembered clearly the faces of the three boys who had assaulted him and could even still smell on his nape the slightly sour breath (fear? excitement?) of the one who had held him down – the three faces, oh so dusky and so beautiful in their unblemished youth, which only the day before in class had looked up at him like the others with a concentrated, innocent air as they listened to him talking about Rutebeuf.

He saw their faces again without it upsetting him.

He thought, "Well, I wonder what they're doing now, those three?"

He began walking towards his car, putting each foot down firmly for the sheer pleasure of feeling the stickiness of the tar and hearing it detach itself with a tiny sound like a kiss.

He saw it all again without it upsetting him.

How hot it was!

The pins-and-needles in his anus were active once more.

Yes, he saw it all again and . . .

"What happiness," he said to himself.

He scratched himself, not without pleasure, aware that the itching would no longer precipitate him into the same abyss of anger and despair, that he no longer had any reason to consider these ordinary evils as a punishment or an illustration of his inferiority.

He was now capable of . . .

He laid his fingers on the red-hot handle of the car door.

He did not take them off straightaway.

It burned him and it was not pleasant, but he seemed in contrast to perceive more clearly the new lightness of his spirit, the weight lifted from his chest and the freeing of his heart.

"Let off at last!" he said to himself.

How was that?

How could that be?

He gazed for a long time about him at the big black or grey cars of his colleagues and at the road in the front of the car park lined with warehouses and villas. He raised his head to expose his face to the infernal sun.

"Free at last!"

Very well, he could go the whole hog despite the slight blush of embarrassment which he felt on the forehead he was proffering to the sky, he could perfectly well go the whole hog and test his new-found freedom by acknowledging, for the first time, that the three teenagers had not attacked him.

What remained within him of the old Rudy Descas objected.

But he held fast, even if the start of a panic attack, a feeling of helplessness, now made him shiver.

He opened the car door and flopped onto the seat.

It was stifling inside the vehicle.

He tried however to take in a big lungful of this overcooked air to calm himself down and banish the fear, the awful fear which was creeping up on him at the thought that, if he admitted that the boys had not attacked him, he also had to concede that it was he, Rudy Descas, literature teacher at the Lycée Mermoz in Dakar, who had hurled himself on one of them, leading to the two others coming to their friend's aid.

True?

Yes, that was what must really have happened, eh, Rudy?

His eyes began to fill with acid tears.

He had worked so hard at persuading himself of the contrary that he was no longer sure what was true and what was not.

He was no longer sure.

He reached behind him, grabbed his old towel and dabbed his eyes.

But could he glimpse the truth and not be afflicted by it?

Under the midday sun stretched the sizzling tar of the *lycée*'s vast courtyard.

Rudy Descas was leaving the premises, happy and nimble of foot, a young teacher loved by his pupils and by his colleagues who included his wife Fanta, and he had no need then – Rudy said to himself without bitterness – to believe that he was a minister of the deity's wishes to feel himself haloed with benevolence and an air of subtle triumph and refined ambition.

The tar was clinging slightly to the soles of his loafers.

The contact had filled him with joy and he was still smiling to himself as he passed through the school gate. This smile had spread like an involuntary gesture of benediction towards the three teenagers who were waiting in the meagre shade of a mango tree, their faces shining in the midday sun.

The three were all pupils of his.

Rudy Descas knew them well.

He felt a particular affection for them because they were black and came from modest backgrounds. One of them, he understood, was the son of a fisherman at Dara Salam, the village where Rudy and his parents had once lived.

Sitting in his car on Manille's car park Rudy remembered what he always used to feel at that time, whenever his gaze fell on the fisherman's son: an exaggerated, resolute, anxious friendship which bore no relationship to the boy's particular qualities and which could suddenly turn to hatred without Rudy's realising it, or even understanding that hatred, and no longer friendship, was what he actually felt for his pupil.

For the boy's face forced him to think of Dara Salam.

Horror-struck, he struggled against any vision of Dara Salam.

And this struggle mutated into a disproportionate affection for the teenager, an affection that was probably hatred.

But under the full midday sun of this unchanging, sweltering day in the dry season, as he was leaving the *lycée* happy and at peace with himself, his smile had enveloped the three boys equally, had flowed towards them, replete, impersonal, with all the exquisiteness of an unction.

Had the fisherman's son suddenly managed to guess that Rudy Descas's extreme kindness towards him was but a desperate way of containing the antagonism his Dara Salam face inspired in his teacher?

Was it that – a barely concealed hatred – which the teacher's smile obviously conveyed in the off-white glare of the midday sun?

The hot air quivered.

No puff of wind shook the grey leaves of the mango tree.

Rudy Descas felt so lucky, so flourishing, in those days.

Little Djibril had been born two years earlier. He was a smiling, voluble child. His forehead was not marked with a puzzled frown. Unlike later on . . . when he felt afraid of his father and uncomfortable in his presence.

Rudy had applied for a teaching post at a foreign university and his final interview with the head of the department of medieval literatures had gone splendidly. He had had no doubt about the outcome, so much so that he had already, out of sheer vanity, phoned his mother to tell her he had got the job.

Your son, the guardian of your middle years, a university teacher with a doctorate in literature.

Yes, life was good.

Even if it was not in Fanta's nature to say so, he was sure she loved him, and through him the life they had made together in the fine apartment they had recently rented at Le Plateau.

He occasionally felt that Fanta loved Djibril even more than she loved him – that she loved the child with a similar, but much stronger love – whereas he had believed that her love for him would merely be different in kind, and that he would not lose by it.

Now he thought he had lost out, that she had rather drifted away from him.

But it scarcely mattered.

He then became so concerned about Fanta's wellbeing that he

accepted, even was pleased, that she was happy, even if it was rather at his expense.

So, yes, in this perfect life, it was only the memories of Dara Salam, which he had to struggle with every time he saw the teenager, that foreshadowed possible disaster ahead.

The young man had emerged from the shade of the mango tree, slowly, with an effort, as if obliged to confront Rudy's fearsome smile.

In a calm, clear, decisive manner, he shouted:

"Son of a murderer!"

And Rudy had said to himself later – and now on Manille's car park was once again saying to himself – that he had been stabbed, literally, not just by what had been said but by the calm self-assurance in the voice of the boy, who had not had the finesse, had not even taken the trouble, to insult him.

Without meaning to, the fisherman's son had uttered nothing but the plain and simple truth, because that was what it was: the truth. Perhaps it was only the teacher's smile, a false, suave smile, full of fear and hatred, that had allowed the truth to come out.

Rudy had dropped his briefcase.

Without knowing or understanding what he was going to do, he had grabbed the boy by the throat.

Rudy had been deeply shaken to feel under his thumbs the warm, moist, ringed tube of the boy's windpipe. He remembered that more vividly than anything else, and as he had squeezed the boy's throat he recalled thinking only of the tender flesh of little Djibril, his son, whom he bathed every evening.

He turned his hands over without thinking and looked at them.

He seemed to feel again at the tips of his fingers, on the fleshy part of the first phalanxes, that sensation of soft resistance which made him giddy, and the mobile, firm bump of the boy's Adam's apple that, seething with exultant, self-intoxicating fury, he had pressed so hard.

It was the first time in his life that he had been beset by such a fit of anger, the first time he had hurled himself at anyone, and it was as if he was at last discovering his true nature, what he was made of and what gave him pleasure.

He had heard himself groaning, gasping from the effort – unless it was the boy's grunts that he mistook for his own.

He had pushed the teenager into the *lycée* courtyard, still clutching his throat, which he was squeezing with all his strength.

The young man had begun to sweat profusely.

Enough, enough of being nice, repeated a small, ferocious, triumphant voice in Rudy's head.

What had he said, the bastard?

"What's that you said, eh? Son of a murderer? Very well, so let's be true to our blood, eh?"

Were they of the same nature, the blood of his father's partner that had stained for ever the fine porous stone of the terrace, and Abel Descas's own blood splashing the wall of his cell in Reubeuss prison, and the blood of this boy, the son of the Dara Salam fisherman, that would inevitably pour from his skull if Rudy managed to knock him over in the courtyard and then hit his head against the ground?

"Bastard," he had said, without being able to understand clearly why he was insulting the person who was giving him so much physical pleasure.

A violent pain shot through his back and shoulders.

He had felt the neck soaked in sweat slipping through his fingers.

First his knees, then his chest, had hit the ground hard, taking his breath away.

He had tried keeping his head as far off the ground as possible until it was forced by someone's hand down onto it, grazing his cheek and forehead against the tiny stones in the asphalt.

He had heard the boys panting and hurling abuse at him.

Their voices were feverish, ruffled, but without venom, as if the words hurled at him formed part of the treatment they were compelled, though his fault, to mete out.

They were now wondering what to do with him, their literature teacher, whom they were kneeing hard in the back, not grasping, Rudy realised, quite how much they were hurting him.

Were they afraid, if they let him go, that he would attack them again?

He had tried to mumble that it was over, that they had nothing to fear from him.

He succeeded only in dribbling on the asphalt.

His lips, crushed against the ground, had, in trying to move, got badly scraped.

Rudy switched on the ignition, put the car into reverse, and the old Nevada, chugging and smoking, moved out.

And whereas, for the past four years, he had been studiously cultivating the theory of the profound cruelty of the three boys who, just for the hell of it, had sadistically attacked him, he now knew that it had all been a lie – oh, he had always known it but refused to acknowledge it, and now he was refusing no longer, remembering the kindness, embarrassment and astonishment he had picked up from what the teenagers were saying as they held him down, unwittingly causing him a degree of pain he would never completely recover from, because they were searching for a way out of the situation that safeguarded their and their teacher's dignity and security, showing no desire for vengeance nor any wish to give him a hard time, despite the fear and suffering he had caused the boy from Dara Salam.

He had understood – listening to them as they talked nervously, with stupefaction but not rancour, above him – that they fully realised, with their adolescent good sense, that their teacher had probably lost the plot, even if, coming from that particular teacher, it greatly surprised them.

Whereas he, Rudy, hated the boy from Dara Salam.

Whereas he had hated, up to that moment in Manille's car park, the three pupils whom, in his heart, he had held responsible for his forced return to the Gironde, for his troubles, for all his misfortunes.

There could be no doubt, he said to himself as he drove out of the car park and onto the road, that anger, mythification, and a generalised feeling of resentment had taken hold of him at that moment – when he had chosen to believe himself the boys' victim rather than looking the facts in the face; that he had long harboured feelings of hatred, wrapped up in an outward show of smiling friendship, that stemmed directly from Dara Salam, where Abel Descas had murdered his business partner.

Oh yes: no doubt, he said to himself, his present state of *dis*grace stemmed from that, from his cowardice, from his smug self-pity.

He went back the way he had come an hour earlier, but at the roundabout he went a little further around the statue before turning into a wide road bordered by high banks, at the end of which stood Madame Menotti's house.

Just as he was wondering if it would be all right to ask Madame Menotti if he could use her telephone to try and get in touch with Fanta (what was she doing, good God, what was she thinking?), he saw right in front of him the pale breast and vast brown wings of a low-flying buzzard.

He took his foot off the accelerator.

The buzzard flew straight at the windscreen.

It gripped the windscreen-wipers with its claws. It rammed its abdomen against the windscreen.

Rudy shouted in surprise and braked sharply.

The buzzard did not move.

With its wings spread out along the windscreen, its head turned to one side, it glared at him with its horridly severe yellow eye.

Rudy hooted.

The buzzard's whole breast shuddered. It seemed to be tightening its grip on the windscreen-wipers and, still looking coldly and accusingly at Rudy, it gave out a screech like an angry cat.

Slowly, he got out of the car.

He left the door open, not daring to go near the bird which had moved its head slightly to be able to continue watching him, and was now staring at him stubbornly, icily, with its other eye.

And, melting with anxious tenderness, Rudy thought: "*Maman*'s good little god, nice little father, please grant that nothing's happened to Fanta."

He stretched out a slightly shaking hand towards the buzzard.

It let go of the windscreen-wipers and screeched again, angrily, in a cry of irreversible condemnation, and flew off, its heavy wings flapping as it went.

As it rose above Rudy's head one of its claws grazed his forehead in passing.

He could feel a heavy wing-beat against his hair.

He flung himself back into the car and slammed the door.

He was panting so hard that for a moment he thought the

sound was being uttered by someone else – but no, these panicky, bewildered, hissing gasps were coming from his own mouth.

He grabbed the towel on the back seat and wiped his forehead.

Then he gazed for a long time, vacantly, at the bloodstained towel.

How was he going to convince Fanta that he now saw their situation in a new light?

How could he make her understand that, whatever he had said to her this morning (if indeed those grotesque words he was not sure of remembering had truly passed his lips), he was a changed man, and that, in the heart of this changed man, anger and falsehood no longer had a place?

Probing the wound on his forehead carefully with his finger, he said to himself fearfully: "There was no longer any need, Fanta, to send me that avenging bird – really there wasn't . . ."

Stunned, he set off again, driving with one hand, and with the other, unable to stop himself, fingering the crescent-shaped scratch on his forehead.

"It's not fair," he kept saying mechanically to himself, "it's really not fair."

A little further on he stopped in front of Madame Menotti's house.

The road was lined with modest farmhouses which wealthy couples had bought and restored, eager to conceal the buildings' humble origins (short roof, low ceilings, narrow windows) with much lavish, meticulous interior decoration, or at least to make them seem as if they too were the result of a deliberate choice, just like the copper piping, Moroccan floor tiles and the vast bathtub set into the floor.

Rudy had realised that Madame Menotti's modest income scarcely made it possible for her outlay ever to match her neighbours' luxurious, finicky extravagance, and that, for her, a new kitchen would remain the only manifestation of a sudden mad longing for comfort and for the chance to show off.

He had also noted, with considerable anxiety and annoyance, that there was a realm in which Madame Menotti was able largely to make up for her relative poverty. Within himself he referred to it as "wreaking big, blustering havoc."

He got out of the car.

He saw at once that Madame Menotti's wild, destructive, ham-fisted wilfulness had dealt a mortal blow to an old wisteria root, thick as a tree trunk, which had been planted near the front door probably half a century earlier.

The first time Rudy had come to the house, thick bunches of sweet-smelling mauve flowers were hanging under the gutters, above the door and windows, clinging to a wire that the former owners had strung along the front of the building.

He had stood on tiptoe to sniff the flowers, deeply moved, enchanted by so much beauty and scent offered for nothing, and he had then congratulated Madame Menotti on the luxuriance of her wisteria which reminded him, he said – oh yes, he, who never spoke of his past life, had let that slip – of the blossom of the frangipani trees in Dara Salam.

He had seen Madame Menotti purse her lips in a mixture of scepticism and vague annoyance – just like, he had said to himself, a mother with divided loyalties being complimented on the child whom she did not care for.

In a tone of dry condescension she had complained about having to sweep up the leaves in autumn: so much dead foliage, so many shrivelled petals.

She had shown Rudy how, at the corner of the house, she had already dealt with an enormous bignonia that had had the nerve to let the wild entanglement of its orange flowers climb all over the grey roughcast walls.

The slender branches, the glossy leaves, the strong roots, the dead corollas, all lay on the ground waiting to be thrown on the bonfire, and Madame Menotti, as the heroine of a battle she had won hands down, had pointed to it proudly and scornfully.

Crestfallen, Rudy had followed her in a tour round the garden. There was nothing but the pathetic remnants of a struggle that had been as absurd, as ferocious as it had been reckless.

Madame Menotti wanted to clean everything up, make the place tidy and lay down a lawn. She had taken out her destructive frenzy on the hornbeam hedge (scalped), on the old walnut tree (sawn off at the root), and on the many rosebushes (dug up). After thinking better of it, she had replanted the rosebushes elsewhere; now they were dying.

Madame Menotti still pressed on, satisfied that her acts of vandalism had established her proprietary rights. Seeing her fat bottom wobble as she moved between two piles of hundred-year-old box which she had uprooted, Rudy had felt that, for her, it was as if nothing demonstrated her omnipotence better than the destruction of the patient labour, of the memorials to the delicate, simple taste of all those numberless ghosts who had preceded her in that house and who had planted, sown, and arranged the vegetation in the garden.

And he was now discovering that Madame Menotti had cut down the wisteria.

He was not surprised. He was devastated.

The little house stood there, austere, stripped bare, sadly reduced to the mediocrity, which the leaves had concealed, of the materials used in building it.

Of the magnificent plant only a short stump remained.

Rudy walked slowly towards the garden gate.

He looked at the bare façade and sobbed.

Madame Menotti had opened her door when she heard the car approaching. She found Rudy standing at the gate, his cheeks wet with tears.

She was wearing a purple track suit.

She had short grey hair and glasses with thick black plastic frames that made her look perpetually cross. When she took them off, Rudy had already noticed, her face was that of a helpless, lost woman.

"You had no right to do that!" he said.

"Do what?" Madame Menotti looked exasperated.

Then he felt in his mouth again that taste of iron, that vague taste of blood which welled up in his throat whenever he thought of Madame Menotti and of what he still had to do despite all he had already done and which for some obscure reason, perhaps through lassitude, he had failed to do and then forgotten about.

He now recalled only the lapse, not what the lapse had involved.

"The wisteria!" he said. "It wasn't yours!"

"It wasn't mine?" Madame Menotti said.

"It belonged . . . to itself, to everybody."

His words were distorted and his voice faded away in embarrassment as he realised how futile his protest was.

It was too late, too late, in any case.

Ought he not to have attempted to save such an admirable wisteria?

How could he have imagined that Madame Menotti would spare it?

Once he had witnessed her brutality towards a nature that in her eyes represented the enemy and the threat of invasion, how could he have turned his back on the wisteria whose death sentence had been pronounced the moment she had complained of the chore of sweeping up dead leaves?

He opened the gate and climbed up a few steps to her door.

The house now stood isolated in the middle of its grassy plot. The sun beat down on Madame Menotti.

The wisteria had given gentle shade to this same terrace, to these same concrete steps, recalled Rudy, grief-stricken, and had there not also been, in the corner, a large bay tree which smelt of spices in the warm air?

Gone, the bay-tree, like everything else.

"Monsieur Descas, you're an incompetent, you're a monster."

His eyes still damp with tears, but indifferent to what she might be thinking (it was as if shame could no longer reach him however hard it tried), he met Madame Menotti's scandalised gaze.

He realised that she had gone well beyond the stage of indignation, that she was now close to despair and to a sort of intoxication, wandering in a turbid zone in which the slightest hitch must seem to her like a deliberate act of aggression.

He realised too that she was absolutely sincere, in her way.

In him, a vague feeling of pity was now vying with a sense of grievance. He suddenly felt downcast and very tired.

Once again his anus was itching painfully. Thinking with weary diffidence about the demise of the wisteria and making no attempt to spare Madame Menotti's blushes or his own, he scratched himself fiercely, vigorously, through the thickness of his jeans.

Madame Menotti appeared not to notice.

She now seemed to hesitate between the need to bring him in (he was getting an inkling as to the nature of the problem, as to what she held against him) and an almost equally strong desire never to have anything to do with him again.

Finally she turned on her heels and gestured to him brusquely to follow her.

She was so upset, he could see her shoulders quivering.

It was the first time he had been back to the house since he had come to measure up for the kitchen several months earlier.

Then, as he crossed the hall and the dining room behind her, a painful process of realisation began. He felt an icy grip in the pit of his stomach as the dimensions of the problem became clearer to him. Then the brutal truth hit him.

He stopped in the kitchen doorway.

Horror-struck, he had difficulty restraining a hysterical fit of the giggles.

Without realising it he started scratching himself frantically whilst Madame Menotti flopped on to a chair that was still wrapped in plastic.

She kept savagely pushing her glasses up her nose, to no purpose.

Her knee was quivering uncontrollably.

"Oh my God, oh my God," Rudy said.

He felt himself blushing furiously with humiliation.

How, after so much hard work, had he managed to get his sums so badly wrong?

He knew he was not very good at it, but when it came to designing the kind of kitchens he despised he had secretly taken pride in his deficiencies, so much so that his arrogance had prevented him noticeably improving his skills.

He simply did not wish to be good at the job.

It had seemed to him that his bloody-mindedness was a bulwark shielding from complete disintegration the erudition he had acquired in his former life: those rare, those subtle pieces of knowledge which he had not had the strength, courage or desire to cultivate and sustain and which were gradually losing their preciseness and solidity.

But such an error as this was merely ridiculous, pitiful, and in no way a credit to the refined man he considered himself to have been; no, in no way, he thought, aghast.

He moved forward cautiously.

His eyes met Madame Menotti's and he remembered the wisteria. Still bearing a grudge, he looked away. Madame Menotti's gaze now appeared to be drained of the scandalised hatred he had seen earlier, but he refused to meet it, thinking "I refuse to communicate with her, if that's what she expects."

Because he had the impression she felt now a kind of impersonal dismay that was a plea for help and support, as if they were both looking at the consequences of an act of madness committed by someone else.

He then dared to venture towards the middle of the room, towards the square worktop with its marble and slate surface containing a vast hob surmounted by a bell-shaped hood, the centrepiece of this petrified, intimidating spectacle which had come to represent for Madame Menotti the essence of the concept "kitchen".

The worktop was in place and the hood was attached to the ceiling.

But the hob was not under the hood but well to the side. Rudy understood at once that if one tried to move the worktop in order to position the hob correctly, it would be impossible to move around it easily.

In making those calculations where he had been called upon to invest all his intelligence and mental stamina, he had simply proved incapable of determining precisely the relative positions of a four-burner hob and its hood.

"They're going to give you the sack, at Manille's," Madame Menotti said in a flat tone of voice.

"I fear so," said Rudy.

"I was due to invite a few friends in to see the kitchen tomorrow, now I'll have to cancel everything."

"Yes, that would be better," said Rudy.

Exhausted, he drew up a chair that was still in its packaging and flopped on to it.

How was he going to manage to persuade himself that getting the sack from Manille's was not a disaster?

What would become of the three of them?

He felt all the more inept because, had he had the guts to probe the diffuse, troubling, submerged awareness he had had for a while of a particular form of indiscretion towards Madame Menotti, he could have pulled back in time to correct the mistake before building work began.

But he had simply suppressed that awareness so as not to be troubled by it, in much the same way, he thought, as he had buried, far out of reach until today, the truth about the Dara Salam boy, the whole Dara Salam saga.

What would become of the three of them if he lost his job?

"And yet I knew it," he said, "I knew I'd made a mistake!"

"Ah yes?" said Madame Menotti.

"Yes, yes . . . I should have . . . dared to face up to the fact . . . to the possibility that I'd made a mistake, but I chose to close my eyes to it."

He looked at Madame Menotti, who took off her glasses and wiped them on her T-shirt, and he noticed that her face was calm, as if, everything having been said about the affair, there was no reason to go on feeling so cross about it.

He also noticed that the woman had fine features which were

usually hidden behind her heavy glasses.

What would become of them?

His mortgage payments amounted to five hundred euros a month. What was going to happen to the house, to their family life?

"Would you like a cup of coffee?" Madame Menotti said.

Somewhat surprised, he nodded.

He remembered the pleasant smell of coffee on Manille's breath.

"I've been dying for a coffee for ages," he said, his eyes following Madame Menotti as she hauled herself to her feet, grabbed a coffee-pot, filled it with water and then perched on the edge of the new worktop to pour a measure of coffee into the filter.

"All the same," he could not help saying, "that wisteria can't have been bothering you, it was so beautiful."

Absorbed by what she was doing, Madame Menotti did not turn round or attempt an answer.

Her trainers dangled above the floor.

He suddenly remembered other feet not touching the ground or scarcely appearing to touch it, the swift, indefatigable feet of Fanta flying above the pavements of Dakar, and he said to himself, "I cut that wisteria down," and, with bitter sweat pouring down his face, went on to add, "That's the wisteria I cut down, it wasn't bothering me and it was so beautiful," and he left unsaid the harsh things he had been intending to say to Madame Menotti about the wisteria she had cut off at the root.

A cold, bitter sweat was pouring down his face.

Nevertheless it seemed to him, in the light of what he was now prepared to admit to himself, that he was beginning to emerge from an old dream, from the old and unbearable dream in which, whatever he was able to say, whatever he was able to do . . .

"Here's your coffee," Madame Menotti said.

She poured some out for herself and went back to sit on her chair. The plastic covering squeaked every time she moved.

They sipped their coffee in silence, and Rudy felt good and at peace with himself. Although he realised that, objectively speaking, his situation had never been so distressing, the cold, bitter sweat was drying on his forehead.

"I won't find work around here," he said calmly, as if he were talking about someone else.

And Madame Menotti replied in the same calm, detached tone of voice, licking her lips to show she had finished her coffee and greatly enjoyed it, "No, there's not much chance of finding work around here."

Slightly embarrassed, he said: "May I use your telephone?"

She led him into her sitting-room and pointed to the telephone on a pedestal table.

She kept pushing her glasses up her nose to little effect, but otherwise remained motionless by his side, not so much to keep an eye on him, he gathered, but so as not to be left alone in her bungled kitchen.

"You don't have a mobile telephone?"

"No," he replied, "it was too expensive."

Shame dealt a blow against the still tender carapace of his lucidity and self-esteem, but he felt that its attacks were routine and that it was his duty not to give in to them, not to wallow in the paradoxical comfort of such a familiar sensation.

"It was really too expensive," he said, "and it was something I could do without."

"You did the right thing then."

"Like your kitchen," he said, "too expensive and something you could have done without."

Gazing rather sadly before her, she said nothing.

For Madame Menotti it was still too soon, he felt, and it was more than she was capable of, to give up the hopes of happiness, frivolity, consistency and peace enshrined in the supposed perfection of a kitchen from Manille's.

Besides, was it not what he had implicitly promised her, when she had telephoned in distress one night and when he had felt her resolution flagging, and he had pointed out that she had no chance of enjoying an enviably harmonious and well-ordered existence in an old kitchen with unmatching furniture?

He dialled his own number again.

He let it ring for a long time, so long indeed that if Fanta had picked up the telephone at that point he would have felt more anxiety than relief.

Next to the telephone was the local directory. To while away the time he picked it up, thumbed through it with one hand and deliberately went straight to the name of Gauquelan, the sculptor, and with a touch of unease noted that he lived not far away, in a new development occupied by wealthy former city-dwellers who, like Madame Menotti's neighbours and to a lesser extent Madame Menotti herself, had bought rural properties which, at great expense, they were doing up to live in.

Later, as he waited on the doorstep to say goodbye to Madame Menotti, he thought he could smell the wisteria.

He stood there in the harsh glare of the sun. The heavy, intoxicating scent of the mauve clusters into which, drunk with gratitude, he had plunged his nose a few weeks earlier, now crept up on him once again, and he was deeply moved.

The scent probably came, he said to himself, from the pathetic heap of wisteria by the side of the house. It was spreading its fragrance for one last time. Was it not, in its own way, saying: "You've done nothing, you've never tried doing anything for me, and now it's too late and I'm dying, slowly decomposing in my perfume."

He was overwhelmed with feelings of resentment.

To hide them he lowered his head and stuck his hands in his back pockets.

From one of them he pulled out a brochure of *maman*'s and brusquely handed it to Madame Menotti.

"They're amongst us," she read aloud. Puzzled, she asked "Who are 'they'?"

"Oh, the angels," Rudy said with feigned nonchalance.

She sniggered and screwed up the brochure without opening it.

Feeling hurt on *maman*'s behalf and sensing his anger rising again within him, he went quickly down the steps and, almost running, returned to his car.

He drove slowly, aimlessly, thinking there was no point in setting foot in Manille's place again, now that his goose was thoroughly cooked.

A feeling of pique still made it painful for him to think about his failure, because he would have loved to walk out of Manille's place and slam the door behind him rather than find himself sacked for a gross error of calculation on a project to which he had given so much of himself, but the dread inspired by the vision of his future was softened by a realisation that there was nothing that could be done about it, that it was all in the order of things.

He ought not to crawl before Manille.

His head was spinning a little.

How had he managed to put up with such a life for four years? It was only an academic question, he realised, a purely formal, pretended bafflement, because he knew very well, in truth, how people put up with long years of a petty existence.

What he did not know, rather, was how he could have not put up with those bitter, pathetic years – what kind of man would he have been, what kind of man would he have become, what would have happened had he not put up with such mediocrity?

Would it have been a good thing or would he have fallen even lower than now?

And what would he have done with himself?

Oh no, it was not difficult to get used to living with self-disgust, bitterness and disorder.

He had even got used to a state of permanent, barely contained fury, he had even managed to get used, willy-nilly, to his frosty, tense relations with Fanta and the child.

At the thought that he was going to have to look quite differently at his domestic situation he felt dizzy again, and although he had long aspired to rediscover the love and tenderness they had known together before they had left for France, he felt obscurely anxious. Was Fanta going to recognise him in what he had become, was she too weary, too mistrustful and too sceptical to meet him at the point he thought he had arrived at?

You've come too late and I'm dying.

Where could she be at this precise moment?

Much as he longed to rejoin Fanta, he was afraid of going back home.

There was no need, Fanta, to send me that horrid avenging bird.

A voice kept cawing in his head: You've come too late, I'm dying, my feet are cut off, I've fallen on the floor of your hostile house, you've come too late.

He was hungry now and Madame Menotti's coffee had made him terribly thirsty.

He was driving slowly with all the windows down along the quiet little road, between the thuja hedges and white fences beyond which occasionally shimmered the bluish water of a swimming pool.

He had left Madame Menotti's area behind and, noting that the neighbourhood he was now in consisted of even larger houses that had been more luxuriously and more recently restored, he thought he had lied to himself once more in affecting to drive aimlessly; he was annoyed to think that he, Rudy Descas, ought to have owned up to wanting to prowl around Gauquelan's place ever since he had seen the sculptor's address in Madame Menotti's sitting-room, and ought no doubt to own up to having wanted to do it for a quite a while, ever since he had read that the municipality had awarded Gauquelan more than a hundred thousand euros for the statue – whose face so closely resembled Rudy's – that had been installed on the roundabout.

Tortured by heat and thirst, he wondered if he was not being cast back into the dangerous eddies of that tiresome, monotonous, degrading dream which left such a bitter aftertaste and from which by sheer force of will he was just beginning to extricate himself.

Should he not forget Gauquelan, the man who had inspired in him so much unjust, spiteful, uncalled-for rage?

Of course he should, and that was certainly what he was going to do – stop thinking that the man was in some mysterious, symbolic way responsible for Rudy's rotten luck, that he had secretly taken advantage of Rudy's innocence to prosper while he, Rudy . . .

Yes, it was absurd, but merely thinking about it made him gloomy and irritable.

He could see again the photo in the local paper of this Gauquelan, with his missing tooth, fat face and smug expression, and to Rudy it seemed unquestionable that the man had robbed him of something, just like all those clever, cynical people who benefit from the inability of the Rudy Descases of this world to grab their share at fortune's great bun-fight.

That pathetic artist, Gauquelan, had succeeded because Rudy was stagnating in poverty. In Rudy's eyes it was no coincidence: he could not shake off the notion that there was a link here of cause and effect.

The other man was growing fat at his expense.

The idea drove him mad.

What's more . . .

He managed a smile, he forced himself to smile, even though his dry lips were stuck together. How thirsty he was!

What's more . . . it might have been silly, but that was the way it was, it had the perfect luminosity of unprovable truths: while Rudy's little soul was fluttering around unsuspectingly the other had grabbed hold of it to create his despicable work, the statue of a man who looked like Rudy even down to his pose of angry, terrified submission.

Yes, it drove him mad to think that, although they had never met, Gauquelan had made use of him, that people like him exploited for their own benefit the trustfulness, ignorance and weakness of those who failed to take steps to cloister their conscience.

He pulled up in front of a brand-new, black, wrought-iron gate with tips of gold. Feeling a little giddy, he said to himself that this was where Gauquelan lived, in that big house built of exposed stone blocks freshly scrubbed and pointed.

The tiled roof was new and the windows and shutters gleamed with white paint. On the wide terrace a set of pale wooden table and chairs stood in the shade of a yellow parasol.

It was impossible, Rudy painfully thought, to be unhappy in a house like that.

How he would love to live there with Fanta and the child!

The gate was purely emblematic since – and this was a detail that Rudy found particularly impressive – it defended nothing: on both sides of the twin stone pillars there was a gap before the privet hedge began, and it was easy to pass through it.

He got out of the car and closed the door gently.

He slipped through the gap and strode quickly to the terrace. Total silence.

These houses had huge garages, so how could you tell whether anyone was in? Where Rudy or *maman* lived, a car parked outside proved beyond doubt that the owner was at home.

Bending low, he went round to the back of the house where he found a door that he supposed opened on to the kitchen.

He pressed the door handle down, as if, he thought, he was letting himself in to his own house.

The door opened and he went in, closing it normally behind him.

He stopped, nevertheless, on the *qui-vive*.

Then, reassured, he helped himself to a bottle of water on the surface, checked it was unopened, and drank it all even though the water was barely chill.

As he drank, he let his eyes wander over Gauquelan's large kitchen.

He noticed at once that it could not have come from Manille's, which offered nothing half as sumptuous, and that irritated him; it was as if, by ordering a kitchen from a more upmarket competitor, Gauquelan had chosen this way of further humiliating him.

Nevertheless, as a connoisseur, he judged it to be a really fine kitchen, far more sophisticated, indeed, than anything he could have designed.

The centrepiece was an oval worktop in pink marble. It rested on a succession of white cupboards that curved elegantly, following the line of the marble above.

Hanging over the whole was a glass cube, probably the hood. It seemed to hold up supported solely by the miracle of its own refinement.

The floor, paved in traditional style with reddish sandstone flags, shone discreetly in the bright room. It looked as if it had been waxed and polished many times.

Yes, what a marvellous kitchen, he thought in a rage, built to cater every day for a large family gathered around slow-cooked food – and it seemed to him he could almost hear a beef stew simmering on the magnificent stove, an eight-burner professional job in shining white enamel.

And yet the installation seemed never to have been used.

The marble surface was dusty, and apart from the bottle of water and a plate of bananas, there was nothing to indicate that anyone cooked or ate under the varnished beams of this big room.

Rudy crossed the kitchen and went into the hall, conscious of the lightness and suppleness of his refreshed, invincible self.

The air-conditioning bolstered his self-assurance, because he had stopped sweating heavily.

He felt on his chest and back the cotton of his almost-dry shirt.

Oh, he said to himself in surprise, I'm not afraid of anything now.

He stopped in the doorway of the lounge, which was situated opposite the kitchen on the other side of the hall.

He could hear, clearly, the sound of snoring.

Tilting his head forward, he could see an armchair. Sitting in it was a fat elderly man whom he recognised as the Gauquelan of the newspaper photo.

With one cheek resting on the wing of the armchair, the man was snoring softly.

His hands rested palm-upwards on his thighs in an attitude of confidence and abandon.

His half-open lips produced the occasional bubble of saliva which burst when he next breathed out.

Wasn't he grotesque, Rudy, panting slightly, said to himself.

Snoozing peacefully like that whilst . . .

Whilst what? He wondered, almost suffocated by a malicious, dizzying sense of joy.

Whilst in his undefended house his light-footed murderer prowled around him?

A murderer with a heart full of hatred?

He felt himself thinking clearly, rapidly.

In one of the drawers (fully opening with built-in shock-absorbers) of that perfect kitchen there would no doubt be found a set of butcher's knives, the most fearsome of which could strike at Gauquelan's heart – piercing the thick skin, the muscle, the layer of hard dense fat like that round a rabbit's small heart, thought Rudy, who occasionally bought from Madame Pulmaire at a knock-down price one of the large rabbits which she kept in cages scarcely bigger than themselves and which he was obliged to skin and gut himself though he loathed doing it.

He was going to return to the kitchen, get that fantastic knife and plunge it into Gauquelan's heart.

How calm, strong and purposeful he felt! How he loved the feeling!

But then what?

Who would be able to link him to Gauquelan?

He alone was privy to the reasons he had for cursing the Gauquelans of this world.

He thought of his old Nevada parked in front of the house and stifled a giggle.

His ghastly car would give him away at once, but it was pretty unlikely that, in this neighbourhood, and at this hour, anyone would have noticed it.

And even if they had . . .

He feared nothing now.

He looked hard at Gauquelan. From the lounge door he watched this man sleeping – a man who was able, quite brazenly, to make a lot of money – and whose fat hands lay limply, trustingly on his thighs.

Rudy's anus began itching again. He scratched himself mechanically.

His father, Abel Descas, had been in the habit of taking a siesta in the big, shady living room of the house at Dara Salam, and he used to sit in his wicker chair just like Gauquelan in his low armchair – abandoned, confident, unaware of the crimes being dreamt up around him and of the crimes about to be hatched in his temporarily abandoned, confident mind.

On his trousers Rudy wiped his hands: they had suddenly started sweating.

If his father's business partner Salif had taken advantage of Abel's siesta – of his afternoon nap and of his abandonment, his confidence – to stab him, Salif would no doubt still be alive, even today, and Abel's death would have changed nothing as far as Abel's mortal fate was concerned, since he (Abel) had killed himself a few weeks after Salif's murder.

Salif, Rudy recalled, had been a tall, slender man of slow, careful movements.

Had he, Salif, stood on the threshold of the big, shady room and gazed at Abel asleep, thinking that, plunged in the strange dreams of the afternoon, Abel knew nothing of the crimes being dreamt up around him?

Had Salif so hated Rudy's father that, despite the hands turned palms upwards on the thighs, he had wished to kill him, or had he felt for Abel an affection that was in no way belied by his attempts at swindling him? Were these two tendencies – affection and treachery – present simultaneously in Salif's mind and intentions, but kept distinct, so that the one never interfered with the other?

Rudy had no privileged insight into what his father's partner Salif felt about Abel, and did not know if Salif had really tried to cheat or whether Abel had mistakenly jumped to that conclusion, but now Rudy's thoughts were, despite himself, going back to the time when his father used to take a nap in the wicker chair. Rudy's thighs were getting damp and his trousers were clinging to them, and the itch was back with a vengeance. Feeling confused, angry and upset, he was starting to wriggle once more, clenching and un-clenching his buttocks.

Gauquelan had not stirred.

When he woke up and rubbed together those hands no longer innocent and abandoned but impatient and eager to return to that contemptible *métier* of his that paid so well and, when he labori-ously hauled himself out of his dark green crushed-velvet armchair and raised his cold devious eyes, he saw Rudy Descas standing in the doorway, would he realise that his death – his brutal, misunderstood death – had been dreamt up by this stranger, or would he think, rather, that he was looking at the unexpected face of a friend, and could he take that look of hatred for one of benevolence?

There must have been an afternoon, Rudy thought in a kind of panic, when his father had awoken from his siesta and from a pos-sibly recurrent, cold, monotonous dream, had rubbed his eyes and face with hands that were no longer trusting but active and busy, had hauled himself from his wicker chair with the hefty suppleness of the trim, muscular man he was, and had left the dark shady room in the quiet house for Salif's office, a bungalow not far away. He was, perhaps, still letting float hazily through his mind the vestiges of a painful, vaguely degrading dream in which his partner was trying to rob him by drawing up artificially inflated estimates for the construction of the holiday village Abel was planning. Perhaps as he walked towards Salif's bungalow he had not shaken off the mistaken belief fostered in some dreams that the Africans around him had but one aim, to diddle him, even though, like Salif, they felt real affection for him, because those two tendencies – friendship and deception – cohabited independently, without blending, in their minds and in their intentions.

Rudy knew he had been somewhere on the property that afternoon when his father, perhaps carried away by the illusory certainty of a humiliating dream, had struck Salif in front of the bungalow.

He knew too that he had been about eight or nine at the time, and that during the three years after he and his mother had rejoined Abel in Dara Salam, a single fear occasionally tempered the plenitude of his happiness – a fear *maman* assured him was groundless – that of having perhaps one day to return to France, to the little house where, every Wednesday, a tall lad with straight, smooth legs like young beech trunks had monopolised *maman*'s attention, laughter and love and whose mere, adorable, presence had transformed Rudy, aged five, into a nonentity.

On the other hand what he was not able to work out, was . . .

Without thinking he stepped into the living room and moved towards Gauquelan.

He could now hear the sound of his own heavy breathing, to which the other man's snoring seemed to reply with discreet solicitude, as if to encourage him to calm down, to breathe more softly.

What he was not yet able to work out was whether he had been present at the row between his father and Salif, or whether *maman* had told him about it so graphically that he had later believed that he had seen it with his own eyes.

But how and why, then – since she had not been there – could his mother have described so vividly what she had been told by other people?

Rudy did not have to close his eyes to see, as if he were still there or as if he had never been there, his father shouting something at Salif, then, without giving the other man a chance to reply, hitting him hard in the face and knocking him down.

Abel Descas had been a strong man, with big broad hands that, however gentle, trusting and abandoned they appeared when he was asleep, were used to handling tools, lifting heavy loads and carrying sacks of cement, so that with a single blow of his fist he had been able to knock Salif down.

But had Rudy really seen the tall, slim body of his father's partner bite the dust, or had he only imagined (or dreamt about) the almost comic way Salif had been flung backwards by the force of the blow?

Suddenly he could not bear not knowing any longer.

He looked at Gauquelan's hands and fat neck, telling himself that if he took it into his head to strangle the man it would be difficult, through so much flabby skin and flesh, to feel the rings of his windpipe under his thumbs.

And he said to himself that, like him, his father must sometimes have enjoyed his fits of hot, all-enveloping, intoxicating fury, but he also said to himself that it had been pitiless self-control rather than rage that had been the driving force in Abel when he had got into his 4 × 4 parked near the bungalow and slowly, calmly, as if setting off on an errand to the village, had directed its huge wheels at Salif's body, at the unconscious form of his partner and friend whose mind had never confused affection and a possible taste for embezzlement, and who, therefore, if he had cheated Abel, had not harmed the friend or even the notion of friendship, but merely, perhaps, a simple, neutral image of a colleague, a blank face.

Still gazing at Gauquelan, Rudy stepped backwards, over the doorway to the lounge, and stopped once more in the hall.

He covered his mouth with his hand, licked his palm, and nibbled it.

He wanted to snigger, to howl, to shout insults.

What could he do to find out?

What would need to happen for him to be able to find out at last?

"Oh God, oh God," he kept repeating, "*Maman*'s kind, sweet little god, how can I find out, how can I get to understand?"

For what did his mother herself, who was not there, know with certainty about Rudy's presence or absence that afternoon in front of the bungalow when Abel, as calmly as if he were setting off to get bread in the village, had driven over Salif's head?

Was it possible that she had told Rudy about the short, sharp sound, like that of a big insect being squashed, which Salif's skull had made as it was crushed by the wheel of the 4×4, and that Rudy had later dreamt about it to the point where he believed he had heard it himself?

Maman was quite capable, he said to himself, of having described such a sound and of having told him about Salif's blood flowing in the dust, reaching the first flagstones of the terrace and staining the porous stone for ever.

She was well capable of that, he said to himself.

But had she done so?

He scratched himself frantically but to no avail.

With his eyes wide open he could clearly see the courtyard in front of the corrugated-iron and wooden bungalow, the white paving of the narrow terrace, and his father's big grey vehicle crushing Salif's head in the thick, heavy silence of a hot, white afternoon, and, panting with sorrow and disbelief, he could clearly see, down to the last detail, the scene in which the colours and sounds never varied, but he was also capable of seeing in his mind's eye this unchanging scene from different angles as if he had been present in several places at once.

And in his heart of hearts he knew what his father's intentions had been.

Because, afterwards, Abel had denied deliberately running Salif over; he had invoked jitteriness and irritation to explain the accident and his crazy driving, claiming that he had got into the car with the sole idea of going for a drive to calm himself down.

Rudy knew it was nothing of the sort.

He had always known that his father had tried to blot the whole thing out and convince himself that he had never wanted to give the *coup de grâce* in such an ignoble fashion to his partner and friend who in his heart never mixed . . .

He knew that in getting into the car and switching on the ignition Abel had wanted to take revenge on Salif and sustain the pleasurable feeling of exultant rage by pulverising the man he had knocked to the ground; Rudy knew it as well as – or even better than – if he had felt it himself, because he had no need, to save his skin, to try and argue the toss.

So why was he so sure?

Was it because he had been there and seen the way the car moved and realised that it was a furious, passionate, focused act of will that was directing the vehicle at Salif's head?

Rudy ran through the kitchen and out of the back door, straight to the gate, and hurled himself through the gap in the hedge.

His shirt caught on the thorns. He pulled it roughly away.

Only when he was sitting in the Nevada again did he dare take breath.

He gripped the steering wheel and lowered his head on to it.

Groaning softly, hiccupping and choking back his saliva, he said "What the hell, what the hell!"

Because that was not the issue, was it?

How could he have allowed himself to be blinded by the notion that the fundamental question was finding out whether, on that terrible afternoon, he had been present or not?

Because that was not the issue.

It now seemed to him that fretting about this so much was just a distraction, albeit a painful one, a way of concealing the insidious progression of untruthfulness, criminality, perverse enjoyment and insanity.

Trembling, he set off and at the next junction turned right, to get away from Gauquelan's house as quickly as possible.

Why did he have, for better or for worse, to be so like his father?

Who expected that of him?

He could still see, from where he had stood in the doorway, Gauquelan's sleeping face and defenceless hands, while his own face had been misleadingly composed, and he could recall his deceptively calm thoughts as he wondered in which drawer he would find the most suitable weapon for killing Gauquelan with a single blow – he, Rudy, with his aspirations to pity and goodness, standing in the doorway of this stranger's living room and, under the tranquil and gentle facade of a cultivated person, planning an act which, from the point of view of pity and goodness, was inexcusable.

His teeth were chattering.

Who would ever have expected him to be as violent and abject a man as his father, and what did he have to do with Abel Descas anyway?

He, Rudy, had been a specialist in medieval literature and a competent teacher.

The very thought of building a holiday village to make money filled him with embarrassment and loathing.

So – clinging to the steering-wheel and aware of driving carelessly and too fast along a country road far from Gauquelan's neighbourhood – what inheritance did he feel he had to own up to?

And why would it have been necessary to stop Gauquelan getting out of his armchair after he had brought up to his face hands suddenly no longer vulnerable and childlike . . .

Oh, thought Rudy as he threw the car around the bends, it was not Gauquelan who should for ever have been prevented from awakening from his siesta, his head filled with deceitful dreams that rubbing his eyes did not dispel, but rather Rudy's father, a man with murderous tendencies firmly, fanatically rooted in a heart where friendship and anger, affection for others and the need to destroy them, were constantly rubbing shoulders.

And was it not that man's worthy son who had taken pleasure in throttling the Dara Salam boy and then – just now – in spying on a stranger deep in sleep?

Overcome with self-loathing, Rudy recalled having wept over the murdered wisteria, just as his father had revealed a touching streak of sentimentality about animals, occasionally talking at mealtimes of becoming a vegetarian, and making a show of blocking his ears to the death-cries of the chickens his mother regularly slaughtered at the back of the house.

On entering a village he slowed down and pulled up outside a grocer's he knew slightly.

A bell tinkled as he opened the glass door.

The smell of cold meat, bread and confectionery in the window made him realise how hungry he was.

Sounds of shouting and laughter on television filtered through a curtain made of plastic strips which separated the shop from the grocer's living room. The sounds grew louder as the woman slipped through the curtain, parting the strips as little as possible to stop flies coming in.

Rudy cleared his throat.

The woman waited, her head slightly turned to one side towards the back room so that she could go on listening to the programme.

In a hoarse voice he asked for a *baguette* and a slice of ham.

Deftly, confidently and (he thought, mechanically) with un-washed hands, she lifted up the shiny ham, placed it on the machine, cut a slice, popped it on the scales, then took a limp-looking *baguette* from a large paper bag on the floor, felt it, dropped it back in again and picked up another.

Despite the precision of her movements he noticed her absent look, the way she kept an ear cocked towards the sound coming from the television, even though no word was audible, as if she could follow the programme by the varying intensity of the noises and clamour.

"Four euros sixty," she said without looking at him.

This provincial France he knew so well suddenly made him feel weary, oh yes – he reflected – terribly weary of poor-quality bread lying on the floor, of pale, damp ham, of hands like hers handling food and coins, bread and banknotes, in succession.

Those hands, indifferent to bread getting dirty, did they some-times, he wondered, lie abandoned, fragile, palms upward?

Then his feeling of disgust faded.

But there remained in his heart the nostalgic pang he felt whenever he remembered, from those long years spent at Dara Salam, and later at Le Plateau in the capital, that he had never felt the slightest repugnance when the hands of people serving him there touched meat and coins at the same time.

Indeed he had never felt any revulsion at anything, as if his joy, his well-being, his gratitude for the place had sterilised everyday actions with a purifying fire.

Whereas here, in his own country . . .

As he left the shop he could hear behind him the swishing of the plastic curtain and the tinkling of the bell, then the heavy silence of midday and the thick, dry heat enveloped him.

The pavements on either side of the road were narrow, and the greyish houses all had their shutters closed.

He got back into the car.

It was so hot inside he felt slightly faint.

The inside of his head felt hot and flabby. It was not an entirely disagreeable sensation, and its effects in no way resembled the furnace that was raging inside his skull when, stretched out on the ground in the *lycée* courtyard, his face pressed against the asphalt, he had felt alarmed unskilled hands trying gingerly and laboriously to lift him up, first by the armpits and then by the waist as he said to himself confusedly, "But I'm not all that heavy," until he realised that the delicate hands belonged to the terrified head of the *lycée*, Madame Plat.

Then, despite the shooting pain in his shoulders, he had tried to help her, and he had felt embarrassed for the two of them, as if Madame Plat had caught him in a moment of intimacy that nothing in their relationship ever justified their sharing.

The three boys were standing there, erect, in a group, silently and calmly, as if waiting for justice to be done, so sure of their case that they felt in no hurry to explain themselves.

Rudy's eyes had met those of the Dara Salam boy, who had gazed back with a look of cold, neutral, indifference.

He had gently touched his Adam's apple as if to signify, no doubt, that he was still very badly hurt.

"Do you want me to call the nurse?" Madame Plat had asked. Rudy had said no.

And although it was so hot inside his head that he had not been able, before uttering them, to ascertain precisely what words were going to pass his lips, he had embarked on a passionate, confused speech that was aimed at completely exonerating the boys.

Puzzled and mistrustful, Madame Plat looked hard at Rudy's bloody temple and cheek.

She was a youngish unstuffy woman with whom he had always got on.

She was now looking at him suspiciously and somewhat fearfully. Rudy was starting to feel, as he talked on, that his panicky defence of the three boys was working in his disfavour as much as theirs, and that Madame Plat was beginning to sense between all four a dubious, incomprehensible complicity or, worse still, a reaction of terror on his part to pupils whose vengeance he had reason to fear.

By this point Rudy had already lost sight of what had really happened.

Earlier, in Manille's car park, he had been willing to embrace the truth, but now he was no longer aware of it.

Thus, in clearing the boys of all responsibility in provoking the confrontation, he was convinced he had been lying. 'It was they who attacked me', he thought to himself, because his fingers had already forgotten the warm neck of the Dara Salam boy, and what he had been saying to Madame Plat – through fear or through shame at seeming to be a victim – was the opposite of the truth.

Later, in Madame Plat's office, he would stick to his guns: the boys had flung him to the ground because he had deliberately, foolishly insulted them.

"It's not true, it's not true," he had thought, "I've never hurt a fly," and his head was aching terribly and his shoulders were hurting dreadfully.

"But why did they do that? What did you say to them?" Madame Plat had asked, all at sea.

He had said nothing.

She had asked him again.

He had still said nothing.

When he did say something, it was to affirm that the boys had been right to beat him up, because what he had shouted at them was unforgiveable.

The boys, when questioned in their turn, had said nothing. No-one said anything about Monsieur Descas hurling himself at the Dara Salam boy.

Only Rudy's version of the story had been retained, namely that he had said a vile thing to the boys and had brought a brutal reaction upon himself.

Madame Plat had advised Rudy to take sick leave.

His case was considered by a disciplinary panel and, as if coming from nowhere, the insult "nigger swine" was considered as the one he had allegedly hurled at the three boys.

Someone had remembered that, twenty-five years earlier, Rudy's father had humiliated and murdered his African business partner.

The disciplinary panel had therefore decided to suspend Rudy.

He was panting, as if he had been hit.

He could now, for the first time, remember that period, he could remember the smell of tar and the pressure of his fingers on the boy's windpipe, but the old pain was stirring.

As he awaited the verdict of the disciplinary panel, he had spent a month in the flat at Le Plateau.

He had begun to hate that pretty three-room apartment in a newly built block of flats that ran along an avenue shaded by flame trees.

He only went out to take his son for walks and to shop as close to home as possible, convinced that everyone was aware of his fall from grace and was laughing at him.

Was it at that point too, he wondered, that he had begun to dislike the child in a way he had never owned up to and would indeed have hotly denied?

He set off and drove to the edge of the village.

He parked on a dirt track between two fields of maize, and without getting out, began devouring the bread and ham, biting first one and then the other.

Although the ham was watery and tasteless and the *baguette* limp, it was so good to be eating something at last that his eyes filled with tears.

But why, oh why, had he never been able to feel for Djibril the manifest, strong, joyous, proud love that it seemed to him other fathers felt towards their children?

He had always made an effort to love his son, and those efforts, previously masked by his eagerness to please and the limited amount of time he spent with the child, had been laid bare during the long weeks he spent shut up in the flat.

He would have preferred then to hide away from everybody, but Djibril was there, always there, a witness to Rudy's downfall, to his degradation and the nullification of everything he had done to make himself a man whom people loved and respected.

That the boy was only two made no difference.

This little angel had become his fearsome, watchful guardian, the silent, mocking judge of his fall from grace.

Rudy screwed up the ham wrapping-paper, tossed it in the back and ate the rest of the bread.

Then he got out of the car and went towards the first row in the maize field to urinate.

Hearing a wing beat, the gentle flutter of feathers in the warm, still air above his head, he looked up.

As if on cue, the buzzard dived towards him.

He raised his arms to protect his head.

Just before touching him the buzzard swerved away, shrieking with rage.

Rudy jumped in the car, reversed out of the dirt track and drove slowly down the road.

Although when he had finished eating he had been ready to go back home and see Fanta, he was now gripped with fear and resentment so he deliberately went in the other direction

The idea crossed his mind that the bird had perhaps been trying to tell him that he should indeed go back home as quickly as possible, but he rejected it, convinced deep down that the angry buzzard was, on the contrary, indicating that he should stay well away.

He felt his head throbbing.

"What for, Fanta, what for?" he said.

Because was he not, in a sense, now worthier of being loved than he had been that morning?

And from the lofty position whence she was able to launch an attack bird that enjoyed her complete support, could she not understand that?

Just as he would never again say those absurd, cruel things he had uttered only in the white heat of anger, just as he would no longer let himself be prey to a particular kind of humiliating, impotent, comforting rage, so he would never try again to charm Fanta with seductive, deceitful phrases, because the comments he had made in the flat at Le Plateau had not been intended to get at some truth or other but only to drag her back to France with him even at the risk (which he did not think of at the time, almost did not care about) of her own downfall and the collapse of her legitimate ambitions.

He recalled the gentle, persuasive tones he had managed to give his voice, he who, after a month spent alone with Djibril, spoke only in a sort of hesitant croak. Even when Fanta came home in the evening he felt too weary to utter more than a few words.

With subdued joy at being back once more with her child, she took over with unobtrusive vivacity from Rudy, even though they both knew that he had not had to do very much, and she busied herself so energetically with the toddler that Rudy could pretend there was no opportunity to talk because the situation did not lend itself to it.

He was relieved about that, and would go out and lean on the balcony, watching the sun set over the peaceful avenue.

Big grey or black cars were bringing home businessmen and diplomats who would pass a few servant-girls returning on foot carrying plastic bags, and those women who did not pad wearily along flew above the pavement in the same way as Fanta still did, seeming not to touch the ground but merely to use it as a springboard.

Then, sitting on opposite sides of the table, they would eat the meal Rudy had prepared and, since by then Djibril had been put to bed, their feigned wish to listen to the news on the radio meant that they did not have to speak to each other.

He would gaze furtively at her sometimes: at her small, shaven head, the harmonious roundness of her skull, the casual grace of her movements, her long slender hands which, at rest, hung at right angles to a wrist that was so slender it looked as if it would snap easily, and her serious, thoughtful, conscientious air.

He was overwhelmed with love for her, but he felt too tired and depressed to show it.

Perhaps obscurely, too, he held it against her for bringing home with her the hurly-burly of her day and images of a *lycée* he was no longer in touch with, and for being able to move freely in a milieu from which he had been excluded.

Perhaps, obscurely, he was insanely jealous.

Early on in his period of suspension, when he was supposed to be on sick leave only, he used to listen glumly to titbits of news she thought would be of interest to him, about colleagues and pupils and this and that; he had got into the habit of leaving the room at that point, interrupting her by this evasion as effectively as if he had hit her in the mouth.

Was it not to avoid doing precisely that, that he would walk out of the room?

But once he had been informed of the panel's verdict – dismissal from his post and withdrawal of his teacher's certificate – he had recovered the gift of smooth talking and put it at the service of his unhappiness, dishonesty, underhandedness and envy.

He had assured her that it was only in France that they had a future, and that through her marriage to him she was lucky to be able to go and live there.

As for what she would do there, no problem: he would make it his business to get her a job in a middle school or a *lycée*.

He knew nothing was less likely, and yet his tone became all the more eloquent as he started to get assailed by doubts, and Fanta, who was naturally honest, never suspected anything, the more, perhaps, because he had reverted to the young man in love, the fiancé with the cheerful, tanned face and pale blond forelock which he tossed back with a puff of breath or jerk of the head, and if Fanta knew various people whose faces were adept at dissimulating lies and whom therefore she would not have trusted, she could not see what might lie behind that loving, tanned, open face, that eye so limpid and pale that it was unlikely anything could be concealed by it.

They had spent long days visiting members of Fanta's extended family.

Rudy had stayed on the threshold of the green-walled apartment where, a few years earlier, he had first met the uncle and aunt who had raised Fanta.

His excuse for not going in was that he felt unwell, but in truth he could not bear looking those two old people in the eye, not because he feared that the lying mask on his face would be torn off but rather because he was afraid of betraying himself and – standing in that greenish-blue room beside Fanta who was talking in proud, confident, determined tones about all the good things that awaited them over there – of being tempted to drop everything, of saying to her, "Oh, they won't give you a teaching job in France," and of telling her at last about the crime Abel Descas had committed long ago and how he had died, about why the boys had thrown him, Rudy, to the ground, because Fanta, not believing he had insulted the pupils in the way people said, must have thought he had disrespected them in some way.

He had stayed put, not daring to go into the flat.

He had not run away, he just had not gone inside.

He had been content to defend his interests while avoiding any risk of letting the cat out of the bag.

Feeling very tired all of a sudden, he turned off the road into a plantation of poplars.

He parked on a grassy track where the last row of poplars gave way to a wood.

He was so hot in the car he thought he would faint.

The ham and soft white bread lay heavily on his stomach.

He got out of the car and threw himself on the grass.

The earth was cool and smelt of damp clay.

Drunk with happiness, he rolled around a bit.

Then he stretched out and lay on his back with his arms crossed above his head, and turning his face towards the sun screwed up his eyes and looked at the poplars' white trunks and their tiny silvery leaves turning reddish between his eyelids.

"There was no need, Fanta . . ."

It was at first only a black spot amongst others high above him in the milky sky. Then he heard and recognised its bitter, aggressive shriek and, when he saw it diving towards him, realised it had recognised him, too.

He leapt to his feet, jumped in the car and slammed the door just as the buzzard landed on the roof.

He could hear its claws scraping on the metal.

He switched on the ignition and rammed the gear-lever into reverse.

He saw the buzzard fly off and land on one of the middle branches of a poplar. Rigid and erect, it looked at him askance, its mottled eye full of menace.

He did a three-point turn and drove away along the track as fast as he could.

The heat was stifling. He was in anguish.

Was he ever now, he wondered, was he ever now going to be able to get out of his car without that vindictive bird pursuing him relentlessly over his old misdeeds?

And what would have happened if he had not been made aware, precisely on this day, of his past misdemeanours?

Would the buzzard have appeared, would it have manifested itself?

It's very unfair, he said to himself, on the brink of tears.

When he arrived at the little school, the children were coming out of their classrooms, which were all situated on the ground floor.

One after the other each door was flung wide and, as if they had been pressed up against it to force it open, the children tumbled out on to the playground, staggering a little, looking rather frantic as they blinked against the golden light of the late afternoon.

Rudy got out of the car and looked up at the sky.

Reassured for the time being, he went up to the gate.

In the midst of the children who, at a distance, all seemed to look so alike that they could not be told apart but formed a mass made up of the same individual multiplied bizarrely many times over, he recognised Djibril, even though, with his chestnut hair, gaily coloured T-shirt and trainers, he differed little from the rest. That child was, of all the others, his child, and he recognised him at once.

He said: "Hey, Djibril!"

The boy stopped in his tracks and his wide-open, laughing mouth closed at once.

Feeling hurt and uneasy, Rudy saw his son's lively, mobile features freeze with anxiety the moment he caught sight of the man standing behind the gate and all hope that it was not his father's voice evaporated.

Rudy waved to him.

At the same time he scrutinised the sky and tried above the noises in the playground to catch the sound of a possible curse.

Djibril stared at him.

He turned round deliberately and began to run.

Rudy called out to him again, but the boy paid him no more attention than if he had seen a stranger behind the gate. He was now at the far end of the playground, immersed in a ball game that was unfamiliar to Rudy.

Ought he not to know the games his son played?

Rudy thought that he could go into the playground like any other father, walk over to his son, seize him crossly by the arm and take him to the car.

But apart from the fact that he was afraid Djibril might start crying – something he wished at all costs to avoid – he was fearful of embarking on the wide open space of the playground.

If the buzzard arrived, doleful, pitiless, where would he hide?

He went and sat in the Nevada.

He saw the school bus arrive and the children line up in the playground ready to get in.

As Djibril was leaving the playground Rudy jumped out of the car and trotted up to the bus.

"Come on, Djibril!" he said in a tone that was both cheery and insistent. "It's Dad who's taking him home today," he said to the woman in charge of supervising the children on the bus. He ought to know her, he thought, at least by sight, but it was the first time he had fetched Djibril from school.

The boy left the group and followed Rudy. He kept his head down as if he were ashamed. He looked at nothing and no-one, and his manner was falsely casual.

He held the straps on his schoolbag at the armpits and Rudy noticed that his hands were trembling slightly.

Rudy was about to put his arm round Djibril's shoulder in a gesture he never normally went in for. He had to think it before doing so in order, paradoxically, to make it look as natural as possible. Then, beside the acacias which lined the road, he saw a brown shape out of the corner of his eye.

Turning his head gingerly he looked at the calm, watchful buzzard perched at the top of one of the trees.

Frozen with terror he forgot to embrace Djibril. His arms hung stiffly and gauchely down his sides.

It took a lot of effort to get to the car. He threw himself in with a groan. "What do you want with me, what can you possibly want with me?" he wondered.

The child got in the back and slammed the door with studied brusqueness.

"Why did you come and fetch me?" he said. Rudy sensed that he was on the brink of tears and did not answer straightaway.

Through the car window he gazed at the buzzard, uncertain as to whether it had seen him.

His heart was beating less fiercely now.

He drove off slowly so as not to attract the buzzard's attention. Perhaps it had learned to recognise the sound of the Nevada's engine.

When they were out of sight of the school, driving with his left hand, he turned round to face his son.

The child was frowning, anxiously and uncomprehendingly.

It made him look so much like Fanta whenever she dropped her mask of indifference and revealed what she commonly felt – anxiety and incomprehension – about her husband and their life in France, that Rudy was momentarily annoyed with the boy and felt welling up within himself again the old dark, aggressive emotions towards Djibril – as if the son had never had any aim other than to be his father's judge – emotions which had burgeoned in him when, suspended from his post at the *lycée*, he had spent a month of mortification, indignity and bitter regret in the child's company.

It seemed to him now that, whatever he did, his son would blame him and be terribly afraid of him.

"I felt like coming to fetch you from school today, that's all," he said in his most amiable voice.

"And Mummy?" the boy almost shouted.

"What about Mummy?"

"Is she O.K.?"

"Yes, yes, she's fine."

Still a bit suspicious, Djibril nonetheless relaxed a little.

So as not to betray his own feelings Rudy now looked straight ahead.

What did he know about how Fanta was at the moment?

"We're going to your grandmother's," he said. "You can spend the night there. It's been quite a while since you last saw her, hasn't it? Is that O.K. by you?"

Djibril grunted.

Choking suddenly with emotion, Rudy realised that the child was so relieved by his assurances about Fanta that all the rest – what was going to happen to him personally – was merely of secondary importance.

"Mummy's O.K., you're quite sure?" the boy asked again.

Rudy nodded without looking round.

In the rear-view mirror he could see the little pale brown face with its coal-black eyes, its flat nose and quivering nostrils like a heifer's, its thick lips, and he recognised all that and said to himself: "That's my son, Djibril," and although that statement failed to resonate, although it seemed to sink within him like a stone, he was beginning to see, to take measure of both the innocence and the independence of the boy whose thoughts and intentions bore no relation to his own, and who inhabited a whole intimate, secret world in which Rudy had no place.

The meaning of Djibril's existence did not boil down to condemning his father – or did it?

Oh, that death sentence which the two-year-old child with the stern look had seemed to pass upon his father: a man so debased, and held in such contempt!

But the person he saw in the rear-view mirror was but a pensive – and for the moment pacified – schoolboy who at that moment was enjoying childhood reveries far removed from Rudy's preoccupations: it was his son, Djibril, and he was only seven.

"Tell me, are you hungry?" Just hearing himself ask this in a voice choked with emotion made Rudy embarrassed.

Like Fanta, Djibril took time weighing his response.

Not, Rudy imagined, to work out what he really wanted but to avoid laying himself open to anything that might be misinterpreted, as if everything he said could later be used in evidence against him.

How did we get to this point?

What sort of man am I, to make them tread so carefully with me?

Feeling demoralised, he did not repeat his question and Djibril remained silent.

His inscrutable face had a serious look.

Rudy felt a great awkwardness between them.

What should he say?

What did other fathers say to their seven-year-olds?

It was so long, so long, since they had been alone together.

Was it necessary to talk?

Did other fathers find it necessary?

"What was that game you were playing just now in school?"

"What was . . . ?" the child repeated after a few seconds.

"You know, when you were playing with a ball. It's not a game I know."

Djibril's eyes darted anxiously, hesitantly, to right and left.

His mouth was half open.

He is wondering "Why this sudden, unusual curiosity?" and since he cannot work it out, he is looking for the best strategy to adopt, for the best way to find out what lies behind my question.

"It's just a game," the child said slowly, in a low voice.

"But what do you have to do? What are the rules?"

Rudy was trying to make his voice sound kindly and unthreatening.

He lifted himself up to smile into the rear-view mirror.

But the child now seemed terror-struck.

He is so scared he cannot think straight.

"I don't know the rules!" Djibril almost shouted. "It's just a game, that's all there is to it."

"O.K., O.K., no problem. Anyway, you were enjoying yourself, weren't you?"

The child, still not looking any less anxious, mumbled something that Rudy did not catch.

Rudy felt that his son was looking a bit of a booby. That annoyed and upset him.

Why was the child incapable of understanding that his father was only trying to get closer to him? Why did he not make the effort to meet his father half way? And the high intelligence that Rudy had, perhaps smugly, always credited him with, did it still exist, had it ever existed?

Or else, finding little stimulation at the village school where the teachers were narrow-minded and hardly up to much – at least that was what, deep down, Rudy felt – and held in check at home by the atmosphere of sadness, resentment and dread that prevailed there, the boy's intelligence had shrivelled and withered, so that without it Djibril, his son, would be just like so many other children: not very interesting . . .

Rudy felt no particular hostility towards mediocre children, but he saw no reason to love them and did not think it likely he ever would.

He was sliding into a state of bitter affliction.

He was powerless to offer his son unconditional love, so that must mean he did not love him. He needed good reasons to love. So was that what fatherly love amounted to? He had never heard it said that such love depended on the qualities a child might possess or not possess.

He looked at Djibril in the rear-view mirror again; he looked at him intensely, passionately, on the *qui-vive* for any sign of paternal feeling stirring within himself.

It was his son, Djibril; he would recognise him even in the midst of other children.

By force of habit?

His heart was just a muddy pool into which, with a ghastly hissing sound, everything was slipping.

Rudy's mother lived in a tiny, low-roofed, square house in a new housing development at the end of a village consisting of only one street.

When she had returned to France with Rudy just after Abel's death she had gone back to live in their old house deep in the countryside, and Rudy had had to become a boarder at the nearest secondary school.

He had gone to university in Bordeaux (he remembered the infinite desolation of the grey streets, the campus located far away in the dreary suburbs), and it was to the same old, isolated house that he occasionally went when visiting his mother.

Then, after taking his finals, he had gone back to Africa and was appointed to a teaching post at the Lycée Mermoz.

When after his sacking he had returned to France under a cloud five years before with Fanta and Djibril in tow, he had found that his mother had left her house to move into that little villa with tiny square windows and a roof that, like a lowering forehead, made the whole place look mulish and stupid.

How ill at ease he had felt from the word go in this neighbour-hood of houses that all looked alike, built on bare rectangular plots, now naively graced with tufts of pampas grass and a few replanted Christmas trees!

He had had the impression that in moving there *maman* was not only submitting to, but ratifying, even anticipating in a smug, rather nasty way, the acknowledgement of absolute failure which, at the end of her life, a supreme authority would be handing down.

Rudy had been burning to ask her: was it really necessary to advertise her ruination in that manner? Had not her existence in the countryside been more dignified?

But as always with *maman*, he had said nothing.

His own situation seemed hardly brilliant, either!

Besides he had soon realised that she liked the neighbourhood and that its large captive female audience made it much easier than before to shift her stock of angelic brochures.

She had made friends with women the very sight of whom filled Rudy with embarrassment and sadness.

Their bodies and faces bore all the signs of a brutal, terrible life (scars, bruises, skin turned purple through alcohol addiction). They were for the most part unemployed and willingly opened their door to *maman* who tried to help them determine the name of their soul's guardian and then track it down – the angel none of them had ever seen and who had never come to their aid because it had never been correctly invoked.

Oh well, Rudy had finally said to himself, not without bitterness, *maman* was perfectly at home in her unlovely housing estate.

He wandered round a bit in the development, lost as usual (that happened every time he visited), going up and down the same streets without realising it.

His mother's pocket handkerchief of a garden was one of the few not littered with plastic toys, bits of furniture and parts of motor vehicles.

The yellowish grass was overgrown because *maman* – completely taken up with her proselytising – claimed she had no time to mow the lawn.

Djibril got out of the car very reluctantly, leaving his schoolbag on the back seat. Rudy, getting out in his turn, grabbed it.

He could see from the terrified look on the boy's face that he had just realised that his father was going to leave without him.

But he has to see his grandmother from time to time, Rudy thought, very upset.

How distant, now, seemed the morning of this very same day when, informing Fanta he would collect Djibril and take him to spend the night at his grandmother's, it had dawned on him that he had not so much wanted to give *maman* a nice surprise as to stop Fanta leaving him!

Because why otherwise would he suddenly get it into his head to try and please *maman* in that way?

Even if he could not agree with Fanta when she claimed that his grandmother did not love Djibril – because that would be to make the mistake of looking upon *maman* as an ordinary person who simply loved someone or did not love them – it seemed obvious to Rudy that ever since the child was born, ever since his mother, leaning over his cot, had examined his physical characteristics and found that he in no way corresponded – never had any hope of corresponding – to her idea of a divine messenger, and so had never really taken the trouble to bond with the child: it seemed obvious to Rudy that it was this attitude – benign indifference – which Fanta had taken for hostility.

Rudy put his hand on Djibril's shoulder.

He could feel the little, pointed bones.

Djibril let his head fall against his father's stomach. Rudy ran his fingers through the boy's silky curls, feeling the beautifully smooth, perfect, miraculous skull.

His eyes suddenly filled with sharp tears.

Then he heard a cry above them, a single angry, threatening shriek.

He took his hand away and pushed Djibril towards the garden gate, so brusquely that the boy stumbled.

Rudy steadied him, gripping him tightly, and they crossed the overgrown lawn to the front door. Rudy thought he looked as if he were dragging the child along against his will.

But, terrified and distraught, not daring to look up at the sky, he had no intention of letting go.

But, moaning, Djibril shook himself loose. Rudy did not try to stop him.

The child looked at him in fear and bafflement.

Rudy forced himself to smile and banged on the door.

If the buzzard were going to swoop down on Rudy before *maman* opened the door, what would become of his attempts at restoring his honour?

Oh, all would be lost then!

The door opened almost at once.

Rudy dragged Djibril inside and closed the door.

"Well, well," said *maman* in a cheery voice, "what a surprise!"

"I've brought Djibril to see you," Rudy murmured, still in a state of shock.

There was no need to do that, Fanta, there was no need to do that now . . .

Maman stooped down towards Djibril's face, looked at him closely and kissed the boy's forehead.

Ill at ease, Djibril wriggled.

She stood up next to kiss Rudy, and he felt from the quivering of her mouth that she was happy and excited.

That made him slightly anxious.

He guessed that her cheery feverishness was due not to their presence but to something which had happened before their arrival and which their visit was in no way going to disturb, because they were negligible, superfluous beside this mysterious source of exultation.

He felt jealous about that, both for himself and for Djibril.

He placed his two hands heavily on his son's shoulders.

"I thought you'd be pleased to keep him for the night."

"Ah!"

Nodding gently, *maman* folded her arms, and her searching gaze played on the child's features again as if trying to estimate his worth.

"You could have warned me, but all right, it'll be O.K."

Rudy remarked with some displeasure that she seemed particularly young and amiable today. Her short hair had been freshly dyed, a nice ash-blonde colour.

Her powdered, very pale skin was stretched over her cheekbones.

She was wearing jeans and a pink polo shirt, and when she turned round to go into the kitchen, Rudy saw that the jeans were quite tight and hugged her narrow hips, her small buttocks and her slender knees.

In the tiny kitchen which was all dark wood, a boy was sitting at the narrow table having his tea.

He was dipping into a glass of milk a shortbread biscuit which Rudy recognised as being like those *maman* made for special occasions.

He was about Djibril's age.

He was a beautiful child with pale eyes and fair curly hair.

Rudy nearly retched.

He had in his mouth the taste of ham and soft white bread.

"There, you sit down here," *maman* said to Djibril, pointing to the other chair in front of the small table. "Are you hungry?"

She asked that with an air of hoping that his reply would be in the negative. Djibril shook his head. He also declined her invitation to sit down.

"It's a little neighbour, I've got a new friend," said *maman*.

The blond child did not look at anyone.

Self-assured, self-confident, he was eating happily, diligently, his lips wet with milk.

Rudy felt certain, at that moment, that there was no other explanation for his mother's eager bliss, for the hard sheen of happiness on her face, than the presence in her kitchen of this boy feasting on the shortbread she had baked for him.

No, there was no other cause for the quivering of her lips and trembling of her skin but the boy himself.

It was equally clear to him that he would not leave Djibril with her, not that evening nor any other evening, and having decided this, he felt immensely relieved.

Holding his son close he whispered in his ear, "We're both going home, you're not staying here, O.K.?"

Then, since Djibril was probably hungry and, for such a short time, might just as well be seated at *maman*'s table, Rudy pulled up a chair for him and poured him a glass of milk.

"Come," *maman* said to Rudy, "I've got something to show you."

He followed her into the living room filled with heavy, useless furniture, to get round which only narrow corridors with complicated angles were provided.

"What do you think?" asked *maman* in a tone of false detachment.

He could hear her voice trembling with desire, impatience and delight.

"I use him as a model, he is an excellent sitter. I won't let go of him."

She let out a brief, shrill laugh.

"In any case, no-one takes care of him at home. Good heavens, he's so beautiful, don't you think?"

From the table covered in pens, paper and brochures tied together with string, she picked up a sheet of paper which she showed to Rudy.

It was the sketch for a more developed drawing.

Clad in a white robe, *maman*'s little neighbour was shown flying above an adult group frozen in what was presumably intended to look like an attitude of fear or ignorance. The execution was clumsy.

In a strained, sharp but delighted tone she explained: "He's there, above them, and they've not yet recognised him, it has not yet been granted to them to see the light, but in the next drawing they will be enlightened and their eyes will be opened and the angel will be able to take his place amongst them."

Rudy was overwhelmed by a feeling of weary disgust.

She's stark, staring mad, and in the most ridiculous way imaginable, and I can't and shouldn't cover up for her any longer. Poor little Djibril! We'll never set foot in here again.

Rudy thought his mother had read his mind because at that moment she smiled tenderly at him, stroked his cheek and patted the back of his head with her cold, damp hand. Rudy found that rather disagreeable.

Since she was short, he could see her fairly heavy breasts revealed by the plunging neckline of her polo shirt. They appeared swollen with milk or with desire.

He looked aside and backed away to get her to remove her hand.

She only talks to me about boring things that get on my nerves, but the things I still want to know she won't, off her own bat, ever tell me, because long ago she lost interest in all that.

"Did anyone ever find out," he said stiffly slowly, "who provided my father with a gun?"

She stiffened momentarily with surprise, but that was perceptible only during the time it took her to put the sketch down and turn towards him. Her dry lips parted slightly in an annoyed, pinched smile.

"That's all over and done with," she said.

"Did anyone find out?"

She sighed ostentatiously, coquettishly, annoyed at his insistence.

She flopped down in an armchair and seemed almost to disappear in the folds of the flabby, disproportionate, over-the-top, pinkish leatherette upholstery.

"No, obviously, no-one ever found out, I'm not even sure if an investigation was ever carried out, you know the country, you know how things were. When all's said and done, what does it matter? You can get hold of anything in prison as long as you've got the wherewithal to pay for it."

Maman's voice once again took on that bitter, rancorous, flat, stubborn tone which Rudy had heard ever since she had returned to France some thirty years earlier, and which her passion for angels and the almost professional way she diffused her propaganda about them had made her gradually forsake.

He heard it again, intact, unaltered, as if the memory of that time had to be accompanied by the voice and feelings associated with it.

"Your father had the wherewithal to pay, it wasn't a problem. He hadn't been in Reubeuss six weeks before he'd found a way of getting hold of a revolver; as you're well aware he knew how things were done, he knew the right people, he knew the country. He'd decided he preferred to die rather than rot in Reubeuss and endure a trial which he knew was bound to lead to his conviction."

"He'd told you that? That he preferred to die?"

"Well, not in so many words, but there are ways of implying such things. At the time, even so, I'd never have imagined he'd go that far: have a gun delivered to his cell, so to speak. No, I'd never have imagined that."

And, as always, his mother's voice was contaminated by that sullen, bitter, vaguely whining tone which used to upset Rudy so in the past, causing him to feel guilty for not succeeding in making her happy merely by his kindly, considerate presence at her side, by the mere fact that he existed, the only child of this obscure woman.

"There were no individual cells, not even cells for six or seven people, he was in a room with sixty other men and it was so hot – or so he told me when I went to visit him – that he was half-fainting most of the time. I did what I could, I tried to get to know his guardian angel, but faced with his ill-will, his negative attitude, his disbelief, what could I hope to achieve?"

Rudy wanted to ask – nearly did ask – "Was I there when my father ran his 4 × 4 over Salif? Did I actually see that?"

But a deep reluctance, a vivid burning feeling of hatred, stopped him uttering these words.

How he loathed his father for making him formulate such terrible questions in his mind.

It seemed to him that whatever had in reality occurred between Salif and his father that afternoon, his father was at least guilty of having made it possible for such words to stick to him, albeit in the shape of a question.

Nevertheless, filled with disgust, he did not put that question.

It was his mother who started speaking about his father again, perhaps because she had sensed how much spite and disapproval had been conveyed by her silence.

"He had convinced himself that he was done for," she continued in her caustic, plaintive, monotonous voice, "that the police investigation, or whatever it was, considered him guilty as hell and so wouldn't be impartial, whereas it could already be proved that this chap Salif had indeed swindled him, I could see that straight away when I went through your father's papers. It was after all something that justified, I don't mean the blows and the rest, but the anger, the altercation, because this Salif, when all's said and done, he was supposed to be your father's best friend out there, it was your father who'd given him board and lodging and taken him on as his business partner, and there Salif goes and starts doing the one thing Abel couldn't forgive or even understand: cheating him outrageously, without batting an eyelid, without there being any hint of a problem between them, without Salif's smiling attitude or friendly voice changing in any way whenever they met. All that could have been said at the trial. I went through every estimate Salif had drawn up, for bricklaying, joinery and plumbing, and I went to see the contractors and lo and behold! they were all one way or another hand-in-glove with Salif or with Salif's wife and God knows who else, it stuck out a mile that they were inflated, those estimates, and that Salif had got it all worked out, how he was going to be able to line his own pocket along the way. I could never understand how Abel could trust that chap so blindly, you have to watch your back constantly over there, people are out to cheat you the whole time. Friendship, that doesn't exist over there. They may believe in God, but angels, they despise them, find them funny. When you went back there to try and make a living, I knew it wouldn't work out, I was certain of it, and as you can see, it didn't work out."

"If it didn't work out," said Rudy, "it was because of my father, not the country."

She sniggered triumphantly, acrimoniously.

"That's what you think. You're too white and too blond, they would have taken you for a ride, they would have done everything to destroy you. Even love, that doesn't exist over there. Your wife, she married you out of self-interest. They don't know what love is, all they think about is money and status."

He left the room and returned to the kitchen. He felt that his anger had been assuaged, almost eliminated, by his intoxicating, invigorating decision never to visit *maman* again, thinking, she can come if she feels like it, thinking too, the Manille Kitchen Company, that's all over and done with, what joy, and he felt young, light as a bird, in the way he had not since the time he had first met Fanta and walked down the Boulevard de la République in the warm, pale, dazzling morning light, simply, clearly aware of his own honesty and goodness.

Slumped on his chair, Djibril had not touched his milk or short-bread.

The other boy was still eating with concentration and delight. Djibril looked at him with glum alarm.

"You see, he wasn't hungry," *maman* said as she walked in.

Outside, as they moved towards the car, Rudy put his arm round Djibril and wondered if he had not glimpsed on the ground, just in front of the Nevada, an indistinct lump of something that had no reason to be there.

But the thought was so fleeting and superficial and, besides, he was so proud and happy to be taking Djibril home to Fanta, that he forgot what his eyes had perhaps seen almost at the same time as he had wondered if his eyes had seen anything.

He let Djibril in and dropped the schoolbag at his feet, and for the first time in ages – Rudy thought disconcertedly – the child shot him a big wide smile.

He got in himself and started the engine.

"Home," he said with gusto.

The car moved forward.

It passed over a big, soft, dense object which threw it slightly off balance.

"What was that?" asked Djibril.

After a few yards Rudy pulled up.

"Oh my God, oh my God, oh my God," he said.

The child had turned and was looking out of the rear window. "We've run a bird over," he said in his clear voice.

"It's nothing," Rudy said. "It doesn't matter now."

COUNTERPOINT

Waking from her daily siesta, emerging from hazy, satisfied dreams, Madame Pulmaire gazed for a moment at her hands resting contentedly on her thighs then looked towards the living-room window opposite her armchair and saw on the other side of the hedge her neighbour's long neck and small delicate head which seemed to emerge from the bay-tree like a miraculous branch, an unlikely sucker looking at Madame Pulmaire's garden with big wide eyes and with lips parted in a big, calm smile that greatly surprised Madame Pulmaire because she could not remember ever seeing Fanta look happy. Hesitantly, shyly, she raised a rather stiff, withered hand flecked with liver-spots, and moved it slowly from right to left. And the young woman on the other side of the hedge, the strange neighbour called Fanta who had only ever looked at Madame Pulmaire with a blank expression, raised her hand too. She waved to Madame Pulmaire, she waved to her slowly, deliberately, purposefully.

THREE

WHEN HER HUSBAND'S PARENTS AND SISTERS TOLD HER WHAT WAS expected of her, what she was going to have to do, Khady knew already.

She had not known what form their wish to get rid of her would take, but that the day would come when she would be ordered to leave, that she had known or gathered or felt (that is to say, silent understanding and feelings never revealed had gradually melted into knowledge and certainty) from the earliest months of her settling in with her husband's family following his death.

She remembered her three years of marriage not as a time of serenity, because the longing, the terrible desire for a child, had made of each month a frantic climb towards a possible benediction, then, when her period came, a collapse followed by gloomy despondency before hope returned and, with it, the gradual, dazzling, breathless ascent day after day, right up to the cruel moment when a barely perceptible pain in her lower abdomen let her know that it had not worked this time – no, those years had truly been neither calm nor happy, because Khady never did become pregnant.

But she thought of herself as a taut, strong cord, vibrating in the restricted, impassioned space of this waiting game.

It seemed to her that she had not been able to concentrate on anything, throughout those three years, other than on the rhythmic alternation of hope and disillusionment, so that disillusionment – provoked by a twinge in her groin – might quickly be followed by the stubborn, almost ridiculous surge of hope regained.

"It'll perhaps be next month," she would say to her husband.

And, careful not to show his own disappointment, he would reply in a kindly way: "Yes, for sure."

Because that husband of hers had been such a nice man.

In their life together he had given her full latitude to become that desperately taut cord which vibrated with every emotion, and he had surrounded her with kindness and had always spoken to her with prudence and tact, exactly as if, busy with creating a new life, she needed to be surrounded by an atmosphere of silent deference in order to be able to perfect her art and give shape to her obsession.

Never once had he complained about the all-pervasive presence in their life of that baby which was never conceived.

He had played his part with a degree of self-denial, she said to herself later.

Would he not have been within his rights to complain about the lack of consideration with which, at night, she pulled him towards her or pushed him away, depending on whether she thought her husband's semen would at that moment be of use or not, about the way, during her safe period, she did not beat about the bush in making it clear that she did not wish to make love, as if the expenditure of useless energy could damage the only project she then cared about, as if her husband's seed constituted a unique, precious reserve of which she was the keeper and which should never be drawn upon in the pursuit of mere pleasure?

He had never complained.

At the time she had not seen how noble his behaviour was because she would not have understood that he could complain about – or even simply fail to accept as legitimate, obligatory and exalting – the ascetic self-denial (ascetic in a sense, though their tally of sexual acts was impressive) to which this wild urge to procreate subjected them.

No, certainly she would not have understood that at the time.

It was only after the death of her husband, of the peaceable, kindly man she had been married to for three years, that she was able to appreciate his forbearance. That only happened once her obsession had left her and she had become herself again, rediscovering the person she had been before her marriage, the woman who had been able to measure the qualities of devotion and gallantry which her man possessed in abundance.

She then felt great unhappiness, remorse, hatred almost, about her lunatic desire to get pregnant that had blinded her to everything else, in particular her husband's illness.

Because surely he must have been ill for some time to die so suddenly, early one pale morning during the rainy season? He had scarcely got out of bed that day to open as usual the little *café* they ran in a lane in the *medina*.

He had got up and then, with a sort of choking sigh, almost a restrained sob, a sound as discreet as the man himself, he had collapsed in a heap at the foot of the bed.

Still in bed and barely awake, Khady had not at first imagined that her husband was dead, no, not for a second.

For a long time she would be angry with herself over the thought that had flashed through her mind – oh, a year or more later, she was, in truth, still angry with herself – over the thought that wouldn't it just be their rotten luck if he fell ill at that precise moment, because she had had her period a good two weeks earlier, and her breasts felt slightly harder and more sensitive than usual, so she supposed she was fertile, but if this man was so out-of-sorts as to be incapable of making love to her that evening, what a mess, what a waste of time, what a horrid let-down!

She had got up in her turn and gone over to him, and when she had realised he was no longer breathing but just lying there inert, hunched up, his knees almost touching his chin, with one arm trapped under his head and with one innocent, vulnerable hand lying flat, palm upwards, on the floor, looking, she had said to herself, like the child he must have been, small and brave, never contrary but open and straightforward, solitary and secretive under a sociable exterior, she had seized his open palm and pressed it to her lips, tortured at the sight of so much decency in a human being. But even then stupefied grief was battling it out in her heart with a still-unattenuated, still-undeflated feeling of exultation that enveloped her at the thought that she was ovulating, and at the same moment as she was running to get help, diving into the house next door, with tears she was unaware of pouring down her cheeks, that part of herself which was still obsessed with pregnancy was beginning to wonder feverishly what man could, just this once, replace her husband to avoid losing the chance of getting pregnant this month and of breaking the exhausting cycle of hope and despair which, even as she ran shouting that her husband was dead, she saw looming, were she forced to pass up this opportunity.

And it was beginning to dawn on her that this fertile period would be wasted, and the following months too, and huge disappointment – a feeling that she had put up with all that hope and despair for three whole years to no purpose – polluted her grief at this man's death with an almost rancorous bitterness.

Could he not have waited for two or three days?

Khady still, now, reproached herself with having entertained such thoughts.

After her husband's death the owner of the *café* threw her out to make way for another couple, and Khady had had no choice but to go and live with her husband's family.

Her own parents had handed her over to be brought up by her grandmother, long since dead, and after seeing them during her childhood at rare intervals only, Khady had finally lost touch with them altogether.

And although she had grown up to be a tall, well-built, slender young woman with a smooth oval face and delicate features, although she had lived for three years with this man who had always spoken to her kindly, and although she had been able, in the *café*, to command respect with an attitude that was unconsciously haughty, reserved, a touch cold and had therefore discouraged ribald comments about her infertility – despite such major pluses, her lonely, anxious childhood, and later her vain efforts to get pregnant, which, even though they had kept her in a state of intense, almost fanatical emotion, had dealt barely perceptible but fatal blows to her precarious self-assurance: it had all prepared her to find it not at all abnormal to be humiliated.

So that, when she found herself living with in-laws who could not forgive her for having no means of support and no dowry, who despised her openly and angrily for having failed to conceive, she willingly became a poor, self-effacing creature who entertained only vague impersonal thoughts and inconsistent, whitish dreams, in the shadow of which she wandered about vacantly, mechanically, dragging her feet with indifference and, she believed, hardly suffering at all.

She lived in a three-room run-down house with her husband's parents, two of her sisters-in-law and the young children of one of them.

Behind the house there was a back-yard of beaten earth shared with the neighbours.

Khady avoided going into the yard because she feared getting sarcastic remarks thrown at her about her worthlessness and the absurdity of her existence as a penniless, childless widow, and when she had to go there to peel the vegetables or prepare the fish she huddled so closely inside her batik, with only her quick hands and high cheekbones showing, that people soon stopped paying her any attention and forgot all about her, as if this silent, uninteresting heap no longer merited a rude or jeering remark.

Without pausing in her work she would slide into a kind of mental stupor which stopped her understanding what was going on around her.

She then felt almost happy.

She seemed to be in a blank, light sleep that was free of both joy and anguish.

Early every morning she would leave the house with her sisters-in-law. All three carried on their heads the plastic bowls of various sizes which they would sell in the market.

There they found their usual pitch. Khady would squat a little to one side of the two others who pretended not to notice her presence and, responding with three or four raised fingers when asked the price of the bowls, she stayed there for hours on end, motionless in the noisy bustle of the market which made her slightly dizzy and helped her sink back into a state of torpor shot through with pleasing, unthreatening, whitish dreams like long veils flapping in the wind on which there appeared from time to time the blurred face of her husband smiling his everlasting kindly smile, or, less often, the features of the grandmother who had brought her up and sheltered her and who had been able to see, even while treating her harshly, that she was a special little girl with her own attributes, not just any child.

So much so that she had always been conscious of her uniqueness and aware, in a manner that could neither be proved nor disproved, that she, Khady Demba, was strictly irreplaceable, even though her parents had abandoned her and her grandmother had only taken her in because there had not been a choice, and even though no being on earth needed her or wanted her around.

She was happy to be Khady, there had never been any dubious chink between herself and the implacable reality of the person called Khady Demba.

She had even happened on occasion to feel proud of being Khady because – she had often thought with some amazement – children whose lives seemed happy, who every day got generous helpings of chicken or fish and wore clothes to school that were not stained or torn, such children were no more human than Khady Demba who only managed to get a minuscule helping of the good things in life.

Even now that was something she never doubted: that she was indivisible and precious and could only ever be herself.

She just felt tired of existence and weary of all the humiliation she had to undergo, even if it did not cause her any real pain.

All the time they were sitting together at their stall her husband's sisters never once spoke to her.

On the way back from the market they were still quivering with pleasure, as if all the feverish, impassioned hubbub of the crowd still filled them with excitement and they had to shake it off before getting home, and they never stopped plaguing, shoving and pinching Khady, irritated and titillated by the impregnable firmness of her body, the cold scowl on her face, knowing or surmising that she would blot everything out as soon as they began tormenting her, knowing or surmising that the most cutting remarks were transformed in her mind into reddish veils which started to get muddled up fleetingly and partially with the others, her pallid beneficent dreams – knowing it, surmising it and feeling silently irritated by it.

Khady sometimes stepped quickly aside or began walking at a discouragingly slow pace, and the two sisters soon started losing interest in her.

On one occasion, one of them shouted, "What's the matter with you, cat's got your tongue?" when she turned round and noticed the lengthening distance between themselves and Khady.

And Khady could not prevent her mind taking that in. The expression surprised her by revealing what, without realising it, she already knew: that she had not opened her mouth in a very long time.

The chattering in her dreams, made up vaguely of the voice of her husband, her own and that of a few nameless people from the past, had given her the impression that she did speak from time to time.

She was seized with a sudden panic: if she forgot how words were formed and uttered, what kind of future, even a tiresome one, could she expect?

She sank back into numb indifference.

But she made no effort to say anything, fearing that she might not succeed and that a strange, disturbing sound would reach her ears.

When her parents-in-law – backed up by their two daughters who, for once, were content to listen in silence – told Khady she had to go, they did not expect her to reply because they were not asking her a question but giving her an order and, although her apathy was now being tempered by anxiety, Khady said nothing, asked nothing, believing perhaps that, by so doing, she avoided the risk of their intentions concerning her person acquiring greater precision, of her departure becoming a reality, as if, she would later tell herself, her husband's parents had the slightest need to hear any words of hers in answer to theirs in order to reassure themselves about the reality and validity of what they were proposing.

No, they had no need to hear anything she might have to say, none whatever. Khady knew that for them she simply did not exist.

Because their only son had married her against their wishes, because she had not produced a child and because she enjoyed no one's protection, they had tacitly, naturally, without hatred or ulterior motive, separated her from the human community, and their hard, narrow, old people's eyes made no distinction between the shape called Khady and the innumerable forms of animals and things which also inhabit the world.

Khady knew they were wrong but she had no way of telling them so other than by being there and looking obviously like them. But she knew that would not be enough and she had ceased being concerned to prove to them that she was human.

So she listened in silence, focusing on the patterned skirts worn by her two sisters-in-law sitting on each side of their parents on the old sofa, their hands lying palm upward on their thighs and marked by an artless fragility which was not in the women's nature but which all of a sudden presaged their death – which unveiled and looked ahead to the innocent vulnerability of their faces when dead – and those defenceless hands were so similar to those of her husband, their brother, after his life had suddenly left him that Khady felt a lump in her throat.

Her mother-in-law's voice – dry, monotonous, threatening – was still spelling out what must have been, Khady thought distantly, a number of disagreeable recommendations, but she was no longer making any effort to understand.

She barely heard about someone called Fanta, a cousin who had married a white man and was now living in France.

She opened her mind once again to the insipid pipe dreams which had stood in for thoughts ever since she first came to live with these people, forgetting, indeed being quite incapable of remembering, that she had been terrified a few moments earlier of having to leave, not that she wished to stay (she wished for nothing) but because she had felt that those dreams would not survive such a radical change in her situation, that she would have to reflect, undertake things, make a number of decisions (including about where to go), and that, in her languid condition, nothing was more terrifying than that.

Grey snakes on a yellow ground biting their tails, and cheery women's faces, brown on a red ground above the inscription "Year of the African Woman", adorned the cloth from which the sisters had made themselves skirts; the snakes and faces, multiplied several times, were monstrously crushed by the folds of the fabric, and they danced in a cruel ring within her head, supplanting the kind, nebulous face of her husband.

It seemed to Khady that the two sisters, whom she normally avoided looking at, were gazing at her derisively.

One of them straightened her skirt without taking her eyes off Khady, and her hands, smoothing the fabric insistently, seemed to Khady as dangerous, provocative and indecipherable as they had appeared helpless and artless when upturned and at rest earlier.

Khady was hugely relieved when, with a wave of her hand, her mother-in-law indicated that she was done and that Khady could leave the room.

She had no idea what had just been said to her about the cir-cumstances of her departure – when she was to leave, where she should go, what for, or how? – and since in the following few days no-one spoke to her again or paid her any attention and she went to market as usual, the worrying possibility of her world being turned upside down got confused in her mind with the memory of the printed snakes and faces, took on their phantasmagorical and absurd character and slid into the oblivion to which all useless dreams are consigned.

One evening her mother-in-law prodded her in the back.

"Get your things," she said.

And since she was afraid Khady would take what did not belong to her, she herself spread out on the floor of their shared bedroom one of Khady's batiks, put on it the only other batik she possessed, an old faded blue T-shirt and a piece of bread wrapped in newspaper.

She folded the batik carefully and tied the four corners together.

Then slowly, with an air of solemnity full of pique and regret, she drew a wad of banknotes from her bra, and (aware that Khady did not own a bra?) sliding her fingers roughly under the belt of the batik, slipped them in the top of Khady's panties, tucking the money between the elastic and the skin which she scratched with her yellow nails.

She added a piece of paper folded in four which contained, she said, the cousin's address.

"When you get over there, to Fanta's, you'll send us money. Fanta must be wealthy now, she's a teacher."

Khady lay down on the mattress she shared with her sister-in-law's children.

She was so terrified she felt sick.

She closed her eyes and tried to call to mind the chalky, shimmering dreams that protected her from intolerable contact with a reality of which, thanks to her anxious, grief-stricken heart filled with remorse and doubt, she was herself part. She tried desperately to detach herself from the feeble, timorous person she was, but her dreams that night could not cope with the intrusions of existence.

Khady was left in a *tête-à-tête* with her terrors, and no attempt at indifference could free her from them.

Her mother-in-law came to fetch her at dawn, silently indicating to her to get up.

Khady stepped over her sisters-in-law lying on the second mattress, and although she had no wish to hear their harsh, mocking voices or see their pitiless eyes shining in the grey light of dawn, it seemed to her a bad omen that the two women were pretending to be asleep at the moment of her departure into the unknown.

Was it because they were sure of never seeing Khady again that they chose to avoid the trouble of looking at her, of raising a hand, of lifting a kindly, angelic palm towards her to say goodbye?

That was it, no doubt: Khady was walking towards her death, and so, swayed by the very understandable fear of getting involved in some way in her fate, they chose to have nothing further to do with her.

Khady stifled a moan.

In the street a man was waiting for her.

He was dressed in western clothes: jeans and a check shirt. Although the sun had barely risen he wore gleaming sunglasses, so that when tiny, anxious Khady, holding her bundle pressed against her chest, was pushed towards him by her jumpy, irritated, impatient mother-in-law, she could not tell whether he was looking at her, but she could see herself reflected in the twin mirrors of his glasses.

She noticed his habit of biting his lower lip, so that the lower part of his face was constantly moving, like the jaw of a rodent.

Her mother-in-law quickly put a few banknotes in his hand and he stuffed them in his pocket without looking at them.

"You mustn't come back here," she murmured in Khady's ear.

"You must send us some money as soon as you get over there. If you don't make it, you mustn't come back here."

Khady made as if to clutch the old woman's arm but she slipped quickly inside the house and shut the door behind her.

"It's this way, follow me," the man said in a low, flat tone.

He started down the road without bothering to make sure Khady was behind him, as if, she said to herself as she followed in his footsteps, tottering clumsily in her pink plastic flip-flops while he seemed to leap along on the light thick soles of his trainers, he did not doubt for a second that it was very much in her interest to accompany him, or as if, having been paid in full, he could not care less what she did.

Such lack of concern about her Khady found somewhat reassuring.

As soon as she stopped thinking about that, taking care not to get left behind or lose one of her flip-flops, she found that her mind was being invaded by the usual fog, this time shot through not with the dead faces of her husband or grandmother but with the images she saw as she followed in the man's footsteps along streets that she could not recall ever having been in before, although, she suddenly thought, she could have walked through them in her usual stupor and mental prostration without remembering it – whereas it seemed to her that, this morning, the most humble scenes along the way were delicately insisting on being frozen in a kind of back-projection behind the screen of her dreams.

Now that she found herself cast into the unknown, could it be that she had been wrenched from her dangerous torpor and was willy-nilly being protected?

What surprised her more was the twinge of grief she felt on seeing a pregnant woman sitting under a mango tree feeding a small child boiled rice.

She had not felt for a long while – not since she had gone to live with her husband's family and everything had frozen inside her – that great distress at not having had a baby, that immense, bitter grief which was unconnected with any reflex of shame *vis-à-vis* her entourage.

And now she was gazing at the woman instead of merely glancing at her, unable to take her eyes off that swollen belly and the smeared lips of the little boy, and thinking sadly, "Won't I, Khady, ever have a child?" She was however less sad than surprised at being sad, at identifying the feeling which shook, in an obscure, almost gentle way, a part of herself that had got accustomed to being merely lethargic or terrified.

She hurried on because the man in front of her was walking quickly.

A young woman who could have been her, Khady, in her previous life, came out on to the pavement and lifted off the wooden panel that covered the only window of her drinks stall, and on seeing that long, slender body, narrow at the hips and the shoulder with a barely perceptible waist but one as dense and vigorous in its slimness as the body of a snake, Khady recognised a shape very like her own, and she was made aware of the action of her muscles in enabling her to move so quickly, of their vigour and unfailing presence which she had forgotten, of the whole of her young body which she no longer paid the slightest attention to but which she remembered and found again in the bearing of this unknown young woman who was now lining up on the counter the fizzy-drink bottles she was about to sell and who, with her calm, focused, reserved air could have been her, Khady, in an earlier life.

The man was now leading her down the Avenue de l'Indépendance.

Schoolboys in blue shorts and white tops were moving slowly

along the pavement, holding pieces of bread which they bit into from time to time, scattering crumbs as they went, with the crows hot on their heels.

Khady hurried, caught up with her guide and began trotting in order to stay alongside him, her flip-flops making such a racket on the asphalt that the suspicious crows flew away.

"We're nearly there," the man said in a neutral tone of voice, less to reassure or encourage Khady as to forestall a possible question.

She wondered then if he was embarrassed to be seen walking alongside this woman with her faded batik, short unadorned hair and feet white with dust, whereas he, with his fitted shirt, sunglasses and green trainers obviously took particular pride in his appearance and cared what people thought of him.

He crossed the avenue, turned into the Boulevard de la République and walked down towards the sea.

Khady could see crows and gulls flying in the soft pale-blue sky. She was aware of watching them in their flight and was surprised, almost fearful, of this awareness, saying to herself, not clearly but limply and confusedly, her thoughts still impeded by the fog of her dreams, It's a while since I've been this way, to the sea-shore where her grandmother sent her when she was a child to buy fish from the boats that had just landed their catch.

She then felt so completely sure of the indisputable fact that the thin, valiant little girl haggling fiercely over the price of mullet and the woman she now was, accompanying a stranger towards a similar shore, were one and the same person with a unique, coherent destiny, that she was moved and felt satisfied and fulfilled. Her eyes were pricking, and she forgot the uncertainty of her situation, or rather its precariousness no longer appeared so serious in the light of the dazzling radiance of such a truth.

She felt the ghost of a smile playing on her lips.

Hello Khady, she said to herself.

She remembered how much, as a little girl, she had liked her own company, and that whenever she felt lonely it was never when she was by herself but when she was surrounded by other children or by members of the numerous families where she had been employed as a servant.

She remembered too that her husband, a kindly, placid, taciturn and slightly withdrawn character, had given her the reassuring impression that she had no need to give up her solitude, that he did not expect her to, any more than he imagined that she would attempt to draw him out of himself.

And for the first time perhaps since his death, as she half-walked, half-ran along the boulevard, gripping the end of her flip-flops with her toes to stop them falling off, as she felt on her forehead the still gentle heat of the blue sky, as she heard the shrieking of the crows in their fury at being always hungry and as she saw at the edge of her field of vision the innumerable dark specks in their jerking whirls, for the first time in a very long while she missed her husband, precisely because of the kind of man he had been.

She felt a knot in her chest.

Because that was such a new sensation for her.

This pain was very far from the breathtaking disillusionment and profound grudge she had felt when confronted by that unexpected death with the certainty that she would never have a child any time soon, and when confronted so cruelly, too, with the evidence that she had gone to all that trouble for nothing. This pain was very far, too, from the no less bitter regret at having forfeited an existence that suited her perfectly. This feeling of hurt over her loss took her by surprise and upset her, and with her free hand (the other gripping her bundle) she struck her chest between her breasts with little taps as if to make herself believe that she suffered from a form of physical imperfection.

But that was it all right: she wanted her husband to be there – or simply to be somewhere in that vast country of which she only knew this town (even only a small part of this town), a country the limits, extent and shape of which she had merely the vaguest notion. She just wanted her husband to be there so that she could remember his smooth, dark, calm features and feel secure in the knowledge of that face remaining unchanged, warm and animated, swaying somewhere on earth, a heavy flower on its stalk in time with her own face, which she now turned mechanically towards that of the stranger, the unknown, disdainful face twitching disconcertingly ("That's where the car will pick people up, it'll be here soon"). Khady could not fail to acknowledge its living presence next to her own, she could feel its heat close to her cheek and smell the light odour of sweat it exuded, whereas what her husband's face might look like now she had no idea and could not even imagine.

That beloved face, she would have put up with never seeing it again if she had been sure that, even far removed from her, it was intact, warm and damp with sweat.

But the thought that it would exist for ever only in the memory of a handful of people suddenly filled her with sadness and pity for her husband, and although she ached and kept hitting her chest, she could not help feeling lucky.

The man had stopped at the bottom of the boulevard near a small group of people laden with packages.

Khady put her bundle down and sat upon it.

She let her body relax and wiggled her toes on the thin plastic sole of her flip-flops.

She had pulled her batik almost up to the knee to let the sun play on her dry, cracked and dusty legs.

She did not care that she did not matter to anyone or that no-one gave her a single thought.

She was herself, she was calm, she was alive, she was still young, and she was in excellent health; every fibre in her body was savouring the kindly warmth of the early morning sun and her twitching nostrils gratefully sniffed the salty air blowing in off the sea which she could not observe but could hear just at the bottom of the boulevard like a surge of blue-green radiance in the morning light, like the glint of bronze against the soft blue of the sky.

She half-closed her eyes, leaving only a slit through which she could watch the man assigned to be her guide pacing nervously up and down.

To be her guide to where?

She would never dare ask him; in any case she did not want to know, not yet anyway, because, she wondered, what would her poor brain do with the information, knowing as it did so little of the world, knowing only a small number of names, names of things in everyday use but not the names of what cannot be seen, used, or comprehended.

Whenever memories of the school to which her grandmother had briefly sent her insinuated themselves into her dreams, it was all noise, confusion, jibes and scuffles and a few vague images of a bony, mistrustful girl quick to scratch the face of anyone who attacked her, who, squatting on the tiled floor because there were not enough chairs, could hear (but could not tell apart) the rapid, dry, impatient, cross words of a teacher who luckily did not pay the slightest attention to her, whose perpetually scandalised look (or look of someone perpetually on the *qui-vive* for something to be scandalised by) passed over the girl without seeing her; and if the girl was happy to be left in peace she was not in the least afraid of that woman or of the other children, and if she put up with harassment she was not, for all that, cowed by anyone.

Khady smiled inwardly. That small, cussed girl was her.

She touched her right ear mechanically and smiled again on feeling the two separate parts of the lobe: a child had jumped on her in class and torn off her earring.

Oh no, she had never learnt or understood anything at school.

She would simply let the litany of indistinguishable words, uttered in a toneless voice by the woman with the unlovely face and annoyed expression, wash over her. She had no idea of what sort of things the words referred to; she was aware that they involved a language, French, which she could understand and even speak a little but could not recognise it in the woman's rapid, irascible delivery. Meanwhile part of her remained constantly on the alert as she kept an eye open for the group of other children who might at any moment launch a surprise attack and kick or slap her when the teacher turned round to face the blackboard.

That was why, today, she knew of existence only what she had lived though.

She therefore preferred that the man imposed on her as her guide or companion or protector did not inflict on her ignorant mind – were she to ask him where they were going – the vain torment of a word it could not possibly recognise, since she was well aware that her fate was linked to the obscure, even bizarre and quite unmemorisable name.

It was not that her fate bothered her all that much, no, but why spoil this brand-new, life-enhancing feeling of pleasure at the warm atmosphere and slight odour of fermentation, or healthy rot, rising from the pavement on which her feet were resting contentedly and her body was relaxing in that state of complete immobility which it knew so well how to attain – why risk spoiling all that for no good reason?

The people around her were doing much the same as they waited, sitting on large tartan plastic bags or cardboard boxes tied with string, and although Khady looked straight in front of her through half-closed eyelids, she could tell from the absence of vibration, from a certain stagnant quality of the air around her, that the man – shepherd or jailer or protector or secret caster of evil spells – was the only one fidgeting, pacing feverishly up and down the sandy, uneven pavement, bouncing and hopping about involuntarily in his green trainers exactly like (Khady thought) the black and white crows nearby, black crows with broad white collars, whose brother he perhaps was, subtly changed into a man in order to steal Khady.

Her impassivity was disrupted by a shudder of dread.

Later, after it turned so hot that Khady had wrapped herself in the batik packed the night before and the small group of individuals had become a turbulent crowd, the man suddenly grabbed her by the arm, pulled her to her feet and pushed her into the back of a car already occupied by several others, then jumped in himself protesting loudly, scornfully and indignantly; it seemed to Khady, that he was furious at finding so many people in the car, that he had been assured it would not be so, and that he had even paid for it not to be so.

Ill at ease, she stopped listening, feeling the hot anger of this man against her thigh and his anxious, exasperated quivering.

Was he hiding behind his gleaming lenses the small, hard, round, staring eyes of the crows, was he concealing under his check shirt, curiously buttoned up at the neck, that band of whitish feathers they all wore?

She shot him a sideways glance as the car started moving slowly and with difficulty out of the square that was now filled with minibuses and other big, heavy vehicles like theirs into which there clambered, or tried to clamber, large numbers of people whose words and sometimes shouts and cries mingled with the aggressive shrieks of the black and white crows flying low over the roadway; she looked at the man's mouth which never stopped twitching and at the feverish quivering of his neck, and she thought then that the crows opened and closed their black beaks ceaselessly in much the same way, that their black and white breasts – black trimmed with white – jerked rhythmically in a similar fashion, as if life was so fragile that it had to indicate, or warn, how delicate and vulnerable it was.

She would not have put a question to him for all the world.

Because what she was afraid of now was not that he would say something which bore no relation to the little she knew, but that, on the contrary, he would remind her of his fellow crows and conjure up the dark, far-off place he was perhaps returning to, taking her with him: she, Khady, who had not earned enough in the family to pay for her food and who was being got rid of in this way, but, oh, were the banknotes tucked in the elastic of her knickers intended to pay for her passage to that undoubtedly baleful, terrible place?

Drawn back into the evanescent disorder into which she had previously been plunged, but without the gentle slowness that had protected her, she was on the verge of a panic attack.

What was she supposed to think, what was she failing to understand?

How was she to interpret the clues to her misfortune?

She vaguely remembered a story her grandmother used to tell about a snake, a violent and invisible creature that had several times tried to carry off the grandmother, and a neighbour had managed to kill it even though it could not be seen, but she was unable to recall anything being said about crows, and that frightened her.

Should she have remembered something?

Had she already, in the past, been put on her guard?

She tried to move away a little from her companion by pressing up against the two old women on her left, but the one closest to her elbowed her meaningfully in the ribs without looking at her.

Khady then tried to make herself as small as possible by hugging her bundle tight.

She stared at the folds on the back of the shaven head of the driver and tried to not to think about anything, just allowing herself to note that she was now hungry and thirsty, reflecting longingly on the piece of bread her mother-in-law had packed, feeling its hard edges against her chest, her head swaying from left to right as she was thrown about roughly by the car jumping up and down as it now drove along a wide, badly rutted road that Khady could see rapidly unfolding between the head of the driver and that of the front-seat passenger: something that was soothing, when viewed through the cracked windscreen, despite the jolts.

The road was lined by breeze-block houses with corrugated iron roofs in front of which small white hens were pecking and lively children were playing, houses and children such as Khady had dreamt of having with her husband (he of the kindly face): a house of well-laid cement blocks and with a shiny roof, a tiny, clean yard and bright-eyed children with healthy skin, her children who would romp about at the roadside without a care in the world although it seemed to Khady that the bonnet of the car was going to gobble them up as it swallowed the fast, wide, rutted road.

Something in her wanted to shout a warning to them about the danger and to beg the driver not to devour her children — they had all inherited her husband's kindly face — but the moment the words were on the point of being uttered she held them back, feeling horribly ashamed and frustrated because she was becoming aware

that her children were only crows with unkempt plumage pecking in front of the houses and, as the cars passed by, sometimes
grumpily flying off, black and white and quarrelsome, towards the
low branches of a kapok tree, and what would people say if she got
it into her head to try and protect her crow-children, she who by
chance still had the face and name of Khady Demba and would
keep her human features as long as she was in that car and kept
staring at the fat shaven nape of the driver and thus stayed out of
the clutches of this man, this ferocious light-footed bird, what
would people say about Khady Demba, Khady Demba?

She jumped violently as the man gripped her shoulder.

Already outside the car himself, he pulled her towards him to
make her get down, whilst the women pushed her out forcibly (one
of them was complaining that their door was jammed).

Khady stumbled out, still half-asleep, leaving the stuffy heat of
the car for the suffocating humidity of a place which, if it did not
remind her of anywhere in particular, was not unlike the neighbourhood she had been living in, with sandy streets and pink or
pale-blue or roughcast walls, so that she began to lose her fear of
having been brought to the crows' lair.

The man gestured impatiently to her to follow him.

Khady looked quickly around her.

Stalls lined the little square where the car had parked in the
middle of others very like it, long, badly dented vehicles, and a
crowd of men and women was moving between the cars haggling
over fares.

Khady noticed in a corner the two letters W.C. painted on a wall.

She pointed them out to the man who had turned round to
make sure she was still there, then ran to relieve herself.

When she came out of the latrines, he had disappeared.

She stopped exactly where he had stood a few moments before.

She undid her bundle carefully, tore off a piece of bread and began eating it slowly.

She let each mouthful dissolve slowly on her tongue because she wanted to savour it fully. It was stale, so rather bland and tasteless, but she enjoyed eating it. At the same time, her eyes darted from one end of the square to the other, trying to see the man who held her fate in his hands.

Because now that the crows could no longer be seen anywhere (only pigeons and grey sparrows flitting here and there) she was much less afraid of a possible family connection between the crows and the man she was with than of being abandoned there: she, Khady Demba, who had no idea where she was and did not want to ask.

The sky was dull and overcast.

From the dimmed brilliance of the light and the low position of the pink halo behind the pale grey of the sky, Khady guessed with some surprise that night was drawing in, so that they had been driving for several hours.

Suddenly the man was standing in front of her again.

He thrust a bottle of fizzy orange towards her.

"Come on, come on," he said in an urgent, edgy tone of voice, and Khady, her flip-flops scraping along the dusty ground, began trotting behind him again, drinking with big gulps straight from the bottle and briefly taking in, in a state of focused, lucid terror, the distant smells of putrefaction blowing in from the sea and the crumbling facades, such as she had never seen before, of enormous houses with sagging balconies graced with dilapidated columns which seemed, in the fading light and violet dusk, to take on the look of very old bones propping up the ravaged body of some large animal. Then the faint smell of rotting fish became more insistent as the man turned towards one of those half-collapsed monsters, pushed a door open and let Khady into a courtyard where she saw nothing at first but a pile of sacks and bundles scarcely darker than the violet dusk of the fading day.

The man whispered to her to sit down but Khady remained standing close to the door they had just come through, not because she wanted to disobey him but rather because in the terrible effort which she was making, within the constraints of the scanty means at her disposal and the diminished reference points in her possession, to force her untamed, volatile, timorous mind to note and attempt to interpret what her eyes were taking in – in that terrible effort of will and intelligence her body had frozen, her legs had stiffened and her knees had been transformed into two tight balls as hard and inflexible as the knots on a stick.

Between herself and the other people there was one simple connection: they all found themselves huddled together in the same place at the same time.

But what was the nature of – and what was the reason for – that connection, and was the situation a good one for them and for her, and how would she be able to recognise a bad situation, and could she freely dispose of her person?

That she was capable of formulating such questions in her mind surprised and troubled her.

Her laboriously searching mind was suffering from being subjected to reflection in this way, but the progression within her of that hard work did not displease her, indeed she found it fascinating.

The man did not insist on her sitting down.

She could smell the chalybeate odour of his sweat and feel, too, the almost electrical vibrations of his anxious excitement.

For the first time he took off his sunglasses.

In the semi-darkness his pitch-black eyes seemed very round and shiny.

Khady was gripped again by her old fear that the man had something to do with crows.

She glanced at the blurred group of packages and of people sitting or lying amongst them. She would scarcely have been surprised to see wings flapping there, recognisable in the dark by their white fringes, or hear wings fringed with white beating against invisible sides. She felt then that in this very fear of hers an escape was being plotted: her mind's attempt to flee towards the pallid, dreamy, solitary lands she had just left – only that very morning in fact – and she forced herself to suppress her anxiety and to concentrate on the immediate reality of the imminent threat she discerned in the man's gleaming eyes, in the voracious hiss of his voice asking for, indeed demanding, money.

"Pay me now, you have to pay me!"

Khady suddenly realised that he might be attributing her motionlessness, her lack of reaction, to an unwillingness to give him what he wanted, so she softened her stance and facial expression and opened her mouth in a kind of conciliatory smile which he probably could not see in the dark.

As if from a great distance she could hear herself cawing – and was it not a bit as if she were imitating the man's voice?

"Pay you? Why must I pay you?"

"I brought you here, it was agreed!"

Abruptly turning her back on him she slid her hand along her belly, felt around and pulled out five warm, damp banknotes, so soft and worn that they looked like bits of rag.

She spun round and shoved the notes into the man's hand.

He counted them without looking at them.

Satisfied, he muttered something to himself and stuffed the notes in the pocket of his jeans. Seeing him so easily placated, Khady regretted at once having given him so much.

She felt obscurely that she would have been ready now to ask him, not the name of the town he had brought her to nor the name of the place they found themselves in, but the reason for their journey – that she would now have been in a position to listen to what he had to say in order to try and learn something, but she was loath to speak to him again, to hear her own voice and then his, heavy with the grating sound of his throat being cleared, that reminded her of the cry of the ferocious black-and-white birds with the white wingtips.

But he had already turned on his heel and left the courtyard.

And though she had not known all day whether he was her fearsome jailer or her benevolent guardian angel, though she had feared looking him in the eye, his disappearance blocked the calm, studious, rapt flow of her newly channelled, submissive thinking, and Khady slipped back into the anguished misty vagueness of her monotonous daydreams.

She slid to the ground and curled up on her bundle.

She lay prostrate, neither awake nor half-asleep, and was almost unaware of what was going on around her. In the depths of an inertia interspersed with occasional jolts of anxiety she was conscious only of feeling hot, hungry and thirsty. Then a sudden commotion made her lift her head and start to get up.

In response, Khady hurriedly thought, to the entrance of a small group of men, all the people in the courtyard had stood up.

There was much whispering amongst the previously silent crowd.

The darkness was heavy and deep.

As she crouched Khady could feel the sweat running down her arms, between her breasts and at the back of her knees.

She heard short, deliberately stifled shouts coming from the three or four men who had just entered, and although she had not grasped what they were saying, either because she was too far away or because they were speaking a language she was not familiar with, Khady understood, from the busy, preoccupied, muffled rustling which ran through the crowd, that what the people in the court-yard had been waiting for was now at last taking place.

Her head was buzzing.

She picked up her bundle and, a little unsteadily, followed the slow procession to the door.

Hardly had they reached the sandy street, dimly lit by a thin crescent moon, than silence fell once again on the group walking slowly in a spontaneously organised, discreet line behind the men whose arrival had put an end to the long wait in the courtyard, because even the small children, strapped to their mothers' backs, were quiet.

Dogs were howling in the distance.

Apart from the rustling of people's clothes and the noise of their flip-flops scraping on the sand, that was the only sound to be heard in the darkness.

The last houses disappeared.

She then felt her thin plastic soles sinking into deep sand, still warm on the surface and cold underneath. It slowed everyone down: they were inconvenienced by the mass of fine sand which filled their slippers and flip-flops and suddenly froze their toes and ankles, while their foreheads were still pouring with sweat.

She was aware, too, almost in advance, almost before it hap-pened, of an end to the tacit, prudent hush that had prevailed in the street, and she guessed, from an imperceptible quiver, from a more pronounced sound of breathing running though the moving, undulating crowd, that the danger, whatever it was, of being heard and noticed, had passed, or else perhaps the tension had reached such a point now they were approaching the sea that the need for restraint could be set aside and forgotten.

Shouts broke out. All Khady could distinguish was a change of tone, to one of considerable anguish.

One child started to cry, then another.

The men in front leading the group halted and shouted orders in a feverish, menacing tone of voice.

They had switched on torches which they shone in people's faces as if they were looking for someone in particular.

Then, illuminated by the sudden flashes of harsh white light, Khady was able to see, fugitively, fragmentarily, the dazzled, half-closed eyes and individual faces of those who until then had seemed to form an undifferentiated mass.

They were all more or less young, like her.

One man with a calm, rather sad air made her think fleetingly of her husband.

The beam of light flashed across her own face and she thought, "Yes, me, Khady Demba", still happy to utter her name silently and to feel it in such harmony with the precise, satisfying image she had of her own features and of the Khady heart that dwelt within her to which no-one but herself had access.

But she was afraid now.

She could hear the waves crashing close by, and out to sea she could see other lights, less harsh, yellower, bobbing up and down.

Yes, she was very afraid.

With an effort of memory that made her dizzy she tried frantic-ally to connect what she was seeing and hearing — flickering lights, the roar of the surf, men and women assembled on the beach — to something she had heard in her husband's family, at the market, in the yard of the house where she had been living, and even before that, in the little *café* she ran where she thought of nothing all day but of the child she so longed to conceive.

It seemed to her she ought to have been able to remember snatches of conversation or the odd word heard on the radio, things caught on the wing and stored vaguely in her mind along with other information lacking in interest at the time but not without the potential one day of acquiring it – it seemed to her that, without paying attention to the subject at a certain stage in her life or thinking it important, she had known what such a combination of elements (night, flickering lamps, cold sand, anxious faces) signified, and it seemed to her that she still knew, but that the stubborn sluggishness of her mind blocked access to a zone of scanty, disorderly knowledge to which possibly, certainly, the scene before her was in some way connected.

Oh, she was very afraid.

She felt as if she had been prodded in the back and was being pushed forward by the abrupt surge of the group towards the sound of crashing waves.

The men with torches were getting more and more jumpy and were shouting more and more insistently as people got nearer the sea.

Khady felt her flip-flops getting submerged in the water.

She now clearly saw lights moving in front of her and realised that they must come from lamps hanging on the bow of a boat. Then, as if she had had to grasp what it was all about before being able to see it, she made out the shape of a large craft not unlike those she had waited to land when, as a little girl, she had been sent by her grandmother to buy fish on the beach.

The people in front of her went into the water, holding their bundles above their heads, then climbed into the boat, helped up by those already there whom Khady could make out in the yellowish, fragile, swaying lights, their faces calm and preoccupied, before she too moved forward awkwardly in the cold sea, throwing her bundle in and letting herself be pulled up into the boat.

The bottom was filled with water.

Gripping her bundle, she crouched on one of the sides.

A doubtful, putrid smell rose from the wood.

There she remained, stunned and dazed. Such a large number of people were still climbing into the boat that she was afraid of being squashed or suffocated.

She staggered to her feet.

Seized with terror, she was panting.

She pulled up her wet batik, put a leg over the edge of the boat, grabbed her bundle and lifted the other leg.

She felt a terrible pain in her right calf.

She jumped into the water.

She waded back to the beach and began running along the sand. It got increasingly darker as she left the boat behind.

Although her calf hurt a great deal and her heart was beating so fast that she felt sick, she was filled with delirious, fervent, savage joy at realising, clearly and indubitably, that she had just done something that *she* had resolved to do, once she had decided – very quickly – how vitally important it was for her to leave the boat.

She realised, too, that such a thing had never happened before: making a decision, quite independently, about something which mattered to *her*. Her marriage, for instance: because it represented a way of cutting loose from her grandmother, she had been only too eager to accept when this quiet, gentle man – a neighbour at the time – had asked her for her hand. It certainly had not been – she thought as she ran, gasping for breath – because she thought that her life was her own and that it involved choices which she, Khady Demba, was free to make, oh, certainly not. It was *she* who had been chosen: by a man who had turned out fortunately to be a good husband. But she had not known it then: at the time she had just felt grateful, relieved, to have been chosen.

Exhausted, she collapsed in the sand.

She was barefoot: her flip-flops had remained in the water or perhaps at the bottom of the boat.

She touched her injured calf and felt blood running from her torn flesh.

She told herself she must have caught her leg on a nail as she leapt out of the boat.

It was so dark she could not see the blood on her hand even when holding it close to her eyes.

She rubbed sand on her fingers for a long while.

What on the other hand she could see – far away, much further off than she thought she could have run – were small yellowish lights, motionless in the distance, and the powerful white beam of a torch, probing the darkness continually, jerkily, enigmatically.

At dawn she realised, before she had even opened her eyes, that what had aroused her was not anxiety, nor the sharp pain in her calf, nor the still feeble brightness of the day but the feeling, from an imperceptible sensation of tingling on her skin, that someone was staring motionlessly at her. In order to give herself time to regain her composure she pretended to be still asleep, whilst remaining very much on the *qui-vive*.

She suddenly opened her eyes and sat up on the sand.

A few yards away a young man was kneeling. He did not lower his eyes when she looked at him. He just cocked his head slightly and held his hands up with their palms towards her to indicate that she had nothing to fear. She scrutinised him furtively and cautiously. Flitting mentally through the images of the previous evening with a speed and coherence she no longer thought herself capable of, she recognised one of the faces she had glimpsed, pale in the beam of the torch, just before climbing into the boat.

He seemed younger than her, about twenty perhaps. With a high, shrill voice, almost like a child's, he asked:

"You O.K.?"

"Yes, thanks, and you?"

"I'm O.K. My name's Lamine."

She hesitated a moment, then, not quite managing to avoid a proud, almost arrogant note creeping into her voice, she told him her name: "Khady Demba."

He got up and sat down beside her.

The deserted beach of greyish sand was covered in garbage (plastic bottles, rubbish bags split open, and the like), which Lamine eyed with cold detachment, looking to see if any of it could possibly still be of use, passing from one item to the next, promptly forgetting each one the moment he had ceased looking at it, consigning it to oblivion as though it had never existed.

His eyes fell on Khady's leg. His face was twisted in horror but he tried to hide it clumsily behind a hesitant smile.

"You're badly hurt, aren't you?"

A bit peeved, she looked down in her turn.

It was a gaping wound, encrusted with dried blood covered in sand.

The dull nagging pain seemed to get worse the more she looked at her leg. Khady let out a groan.

"I know where we can get some water," Lamine said.

He helped her to her feet.

She sensed, like a coiled spring, the nervous strength of his raw-boned, tight body, as if it were being kept firm – were being held taut and constantly on the alert – by the hardships he had endured and by the ability to efface them, in the same way as he seemed, through denial, to erase from his vision any object on the beach that was of no interest.

Khady knew she had a slim and robust body but not, like the boy's, tempered in the icy water of unavoidable deprivation, so that for the first time in her life she felt luckier than another human being.

She checked to make sure that the wad of banknotes was still there, held in the elastic of her knickers.

Then, refusing his offer of help, she walked beside Lamine towards the row of houses and shops with corrugated iron roofs which lined the beach above the high-water mark.

At every step, the pain intensified.

And because, on top of that, she was very hungry, she wished passionately to be able to acquire an insensible, mineral body, with no needs or desires, a body that would be a mere tool in the service of a plan of which she still knew nothing but which she understood she would be made to learn about.

Well, she did know one thing. She knew it, not as she usually knew things – that is without knowing that she knew – but in a clear and conscious way.

I can't go back to the family, she said to herself, not even wondering (because it was useless) whether that was a good thing or just a supplementary source of unhappiness. Thinking clearly and calmly, she was well aware that she had, in a way, made a choice.

And when Lamine had told of her of his own intentions, when – in a rather strident voice interrupted by little nervous giggles when he could not think of a word or seemed afraid of not being taken seriously – he had assured her that he would get to Europe one day or die in the attempt, that there was no other solution to his problems, it appeared to Khady that all he was doing was making her own plan explicit.

So, in deciding to join him, her conviction that she was now in control of the precarious, unstable equipage that was her existence had not been shaken in any way.

Quite the opposite.

He had led her to a pump in the centre of town so that she could wash off the sand sticking to her wound. Then he had explained to her that he had tried several times to leave, that he had always been prevented by major or minor unforeseen circumstances (last night it was the dilapidated condition of the boat) but that he now knew enough about things to hope to counter, dodge or fearlessly confront the difficulties of which there could not be that many and all of which, he considered, he had experienced and thoroughly grasped.

Khady simply recognised that he was *au fait* with things she could not even imagine, and that by staying with him she would benefit from and absorb his knowledge, instead of having to grope her own way laboriously towards it.

How remarkable she found it that she had not said to herself, "What else can I do, in any case, but follow this boy?" but had thought, rather, that she could take control of the situation and draw benefit from it.

Racked with pain, she washed her torn calf.

The two pieces of flesh were clearly separated.

She tore a strip off the batik that contained her belongings and wrapped it tightly round her calf so as to bind together the two flaps of the wound.

Throughout the heavy, still days that followed, the place remained greyish but the light was bright, as if the shimmering metallic surface of the sea was diffusing a leaden glare.

It seemed to Khady she had been granted a reprieve so that she could steep herself in information such as she had never acquired in twenty-five years; and discreetly too, without appearing to learn anything, an instinctive caution having stopped her revealing to Lamine how ignorant she was.

He had brought her back to the courtyard their group had departed from.

Many new people were gathered there, and the boy went round collecting orders for food and water which he then ran to get in town.

He never asked Khady to pay for what he would bring back for them to eat (omelette sandwiches, bananas, grilled fish), and Khady never offered because she had decided never to talk about anything that had not already been aired, confining herself to short replies to questions that were equally laconic, not mentioning money since Lamine did not, questioning him on the other hand with restrained eagerness about the journey he was planning and the means of achieving it. On that topic she tried to conceal her hunger for information behind an air of constrained, bored glumness; she felt a veil of morose impenetrability covering her face, just as it had done in her husband's family, where she had adopted it to hide her pallid, lukewarm thoughts behind it.

Oh, how fast her mind was working now! Sometimes it got in a muddle, as if intoxicated by its own abilities.

It was not too sure now whether the ardent young man standing before it was Khady's husband or a stranger called Lamine, or why exactly it had to remember everything that came out of that mouth with the hot, almost feverish breath, and it felt tempted – at rare, very brief moments – to flush itself clean and return to its previous state where nothing was demanded of it except not to get involved in anything to do with real life.

At nightfall, then, lying in the courtyard, Khady memorised

the new pieces of information, filing them in order of importance.

What had to be kept continually in mind was this: the journey could take months, even years, as it had for a neighbour of Lamine's who had only reached Europe (what "Europe" was exactly, where it was situated, she put off until later to find out) five whole years after leaving home.

This too: it was imperative to buy a passport. Lamine had reliable connections for getting one.

And then: the boy now refused to go by sea from this coast. The journey would be longer, much longer, but it would go through the desert and arrive at a certain place where you had to climb to get into Europe.

And then, and then: Lamine had said many times – his suddenly mulish, inscrutable, smooth face shining with sweat – that he did not mind dying if that was the price to be paid for pursuing his aim, but to go on living as he had done until now, that he refused to do.

Although Khady spontaneously blotted out everything to do with the boy's earlier life, although she tried not to listen to anything she thought inessential, anything likely to upset or embarrass her, even, inexplicably, to fill her with a dull sadness as if her oldest memories were being revived even more than his own, she could not help retaining the fact that a stepmother – his father's new wife after his mother's death – had for years beaten Lamine so hard he had almost gone mad.

He pulled up his tee-shirt to show her the pinkish, slightly puffy marks on his back.

He had gone to the *lycée* and failed the baccalaureate twice.

But he wanted badly to go on studying, he dreamt of becoming an engineer. (What did that mean? Khady wondered despite herself, trying hard not to get interested.)

When after a few days she tried to remove the cloth protecting her calf, it was stuck so hard to the wound that she had to wrench it off, causing such pain that she could not help crying out.

She wrapped a strip of clean cloth tightly around it.

She limped from one corner of the courtyard to another, trying to overcome the inconvenience of her slow pace and constant pain by getting habituated to it, so that this new situation became a part of herself which she could forget or ignore by relegating it to other circumstances which, like the painful stories from Lamine's past, served no useful purpose but merely risked deflecting and putting a brake on the still raw, uncertain development of her thinking by insinuating into it elements of turmoil and ungovernable suffering.

She similarly let her eyes flit across the faces of the people who arrived ever more numerous each day in the courtyard; and her look, she knew, was neutral, cold and a permanent discouragement to anyone attempting conversation, not because she was afraid of being asked something (she had no fear of that), but because her mind panicked at the mere possibility of hearing about painful, complicated lives and being told at great length about issues which were difficult for her to understand since she lacked the principles for interpreting things in life that others seemed to possess as a matter of course.

One day the boy took her through narrow, sandy streets to a barber shop where a woman in the back took photos of her.

A few days later he came back with a worn, creased, blue booklet which he gave Khady, telling her she was now called Bintou Thiam.

His eyes had a look of pride, triumph and self-assurance that put Khady slightly on her guard.

She felt fleetingly that she was becoming feeble again and subject to the decisions, knowledge and indiscernible intentions of others. Through sheer weariness she was briefly tempted to accept this subordination, to stop thinking about anything and to let her mind once again drift in the milky flow of its dreams.

Feeling a little disgusted, she pulled herself together.

She thanked the boy with a nod.

She felt terrible shooting pains in her calf which made it hard for her to think straight.

But though she was still determined not to discuss money before he did, she could not ignore the issue, nor the fact that Lamine had bought a passport for her and was behaving as if it was obvious that she had no money, or that one way or another she would pay later. That worried her to the point that she sometimes wished he would disappear and vanish from her life.

But she was becoming attached to his eager features, his adolescent voice.

She caught herself looking at him with pleasure, almost with tender amusement, when, hopping about the courtyard like the delicate birds with long spindly legs which she remembered seeing as a child on the beach (although she thought she could not now remember what they were called, she could understand that everything had a name even if she did not know it, and realised with embarrassment that she had once believed that only what she knew possessed a name) he moved from one group to another, busying himself with a spirited, childlike innocence that inspired confidence.

He was possessed of a particular intuition.

She was beginning to find time dragging (but never for a moment thought to complain about it), when he announced they would be leaving the next day. It was as if – she thought – he had guessed that without realising it she was starting to get bored, and had decided it was a bad thing: but why?

What could that matter to him?

Oh, she certainly felt affection for the boy.

That night, in the darkness of the courtyard where they were lying, she felt him moving close to her, hesitantly, as if unsure of her reaction.

She did not rebuff him, rather she encouraged him by turning towards him.

She pulled her batik up and, carefully rolling the banknotes in them, slipped her knickers off and laid her head on them.

It was years since she had made love: not once since her husband's death.

She carefully stroked the boy's heavily scarred back and was surprised at the same time by the extreme lightness of his body and by the almost excessive gentleness and delicacy (because she could barely feel he was there) with which he moved within her. Almost as a reflex, recalled by the sensation of a body on top of hers, even if this one was so different from her husband's compact, heavy frame, there came back to her the prayers to be got with child which she had never ceased murmuring at the time and which had prevented her having an orgasm by distracting her from the necessary concentration on her own pleasure.

She vehemently chased all such prayers away.

She was filled with a kind of well-being, a sort of physical comfort – nothing sharper than that, nothing at all like what her sisters-in-law giggled and sighed about between themselves – but it made Khady feel happy and grateful to the boy.

As he pulled away from her he inadvertently bumped against her calf.

An explosion of pain tore through Khady.

She was panting and almost fainted.

She could hear Lamine murmuring anxiously in her ear and – suffering so much that she felt surprised, almost detached, a stranger to a self that was in such violent pain – she said to herself, "Who ever cared about me the way he does, this boy, and so young too! I'm lucky, I'm really lucky . . ."

They clambered before dawn onto an open-backed lorry where so many people were already huddling that it seemed impossible for Khady to find any room for herself.

She perched on a pile of sacks at the back of the lorry, high up above the wheels.

Lamine advised her to grip the string on the packaging firmly so as not to fall off.

He was sitting astride a box right next to her and Khady could smell on their arms, pressed close together, the slightly sharp odour of his sweat mingling with hers.

"If you fall off, the driver won't stop and you'll die in the desert," Lamine whispered.

He had given her a leather bottle filled with tepid water.

Khady had seen him give the driver a wad of banknotes, explaining he was paying for her too, then he had helped her on to the lorry since her leg seemed to have become so heavy, she could not have managed it alone.

Lamine attempted to conceal his barely contained excitement by fussy, precise gestures (such as checking many times that the top of the water-bottle was screwed on fast) and by continual warnings, repeated in a soft, slow voice ("Hang on tight, if you fall off the driver won't stop and you'll die in the desert"), but she could sense it from the way his face twitched a little. She found herself infected by his slightly intoxicated eagerness, so that she felt neither afraid nor humiliated at being helped in the simplest ways by the boy, nor by the constant support he gave her, such as cupping his hands together and then lifting them up vigorously to hoist her onto the lorry. None of that called into question the idea she now had of her own independence, of being free from constraints imposed by the will of others. In much the same manner she endeavoured not to see, in the money which Lamine had given the driver on her behalf, anything that amounted to a personal commitment on her part.

For Khady Demba, none of that was of any consequence.

If it pleased Lamine to play a crucial role in her liberation, she was sincerely grateful to him for that – yes, she felt a great deal of affection for the boy, but it did not make her accountable in any way.

Her head was spinning a little.

There was no relief now from the intense pain in her leg. It mingled with a feeling of joy which appeared similarly to be urging her fiercely onwards.

As it moved off, the lorry juddered so violently she was nearly thrown from her perch.

Lamine grabbed her in the nick of time.

"Hold on tight, hold on tight!" he shouted in her ear, and close up in the rosy light of dawn she could see his thin, hollow cheeks and the pale chapped lips he moistened with many licks of the tongue, and his eyes: a bit wild, a bit frantic, she thought, like those, dark and terrified, of a large yellowish dog which had been cornered in the market by women armed with staves and was about to be made to pay for the theft of a chicken. Lamine's were just like the dog's eyes, filled with innocent terror, that had met hers in the market and pierced her numb, cold heart and had for a brief moment aroused in her strong feelings of sympathy and shame.

Was it for her that Lamine had been so afraid?

She was to recall, with dull sadness but without bitterness, how very attentive Lamine had been towards her.

She would remember all that, never thinking however that he had sought to deceive her. In thinking back to the concerns he had had for her, the distant sadness she would feel would be more about him than about her: it would be the boy's fate that would affect her so much as to make her shed a few cold tears, whereas she would judge her own destiny neutrally, almost with detachment, as if she, Khady Demba, who had never wagered on life the same sum of hope as Lamine did, had no reason to complain about losing everything.

She had not lost much, she would think – thinking too, with that imponderable pride, that discreet, unshakeable assurance, "I'm me, Khady Demba", when with sore thighs, swollen vulva and hot, inflamed vagina she would get up several times a day from the apology for a mattress, a piece of greyish, stinking foam, that throughout all those long months was to be her workplace.

She had not lost much, she thought.

Because never, however great her exhaustion or intense her affliction, would she regret that period of her life when her mind wandered in the confined, foggy, numbing, protective space of her static dreams, during the time she lived with her husband's family.

She would not miss either the years of her marriage when the longing to get pregnant occupied every thinking moment.

Truth to tell, she would regret nothing, plunged in the reality of an atrocious present which she could see clearly, to which she would apply thinking that was replete both with pragmatism and with pride (she would never have pointless feelings of shame, she would never forget the value of the human being she was: Khady

Demba, honest and true), a reality which above all she considered transitory; she was convinced that this period of suffering would have an end, and that she would certainly not be rewarded (she could not believe she was owed anything for having suffered) but would simply move on to something else. She did not yet know what that would be but she was curious to find out.

As for the chain of events which had brought them – her and Lamine – to this point, she had a precise picture of that and was trying, calmly and coldly, to understand it.

After a day and a night on the road, the lorry had stopped at a frontier.

All the passengers had got down, formed a queue, and shown their passports to soldiers who shouted a single word which Khady understood even though it was not her language.

Money.

Those who put their hands up to indicate they had none, or who offered too little, were then so badly beaten up that some fell to the ground, where they lay unconscious and were sometimes even thrashed further by a soldier whose hard work in hitting people, the trouble they made him go to, seemed to drive him mad with rage.

Khady began to tremble all over.

Lamine, next to her, had gripped her hand.

She could see his jaw quivering as if behind those tight-set lips his teeth were chattering.

He had held out his passport to the soldier and a roll of banknotes, pointing to Khady and then himself.

The man had taken the notes with the tips of his fingers, contemptuously, and thrown them on the ground.

He had given a soldier an order. The soldier hit Lamine in the stomach.

The boy was bent double and fell to his knees without a word, without a groan.

The soldier had taken out a knife, lifted one of Lamine's feet and slashed the sole of his shoe. He had felt the slit, then he had done the same with the other foot.

And when, his bony knees knocking, Lamine had straightaway staggered to his feet as if it was more dangerous to lie prostrate than face his enemy, Khady could see two thin lines of blood running into the dust from under his shoes.

The man in command had then turned to her. Khady had shown him the passport that Lamine had procured for her.

Clear-headedly, even though she could not stop shivering, she had slipped her hand under her batik and drawn out the thin wad of banknotes which, soaked in sweat from being held in the elastic of her knickers, looked like a piece of greenish rag. She had placed the money delicately and respectfully in the man's hands while clinging tight to Lamine to make it clear that they were together.

It was now several weeks – she was not sure how many – that they had been holed up in this desert town, not where the soldier had slashed the soles of Lamine's feet but in another town, further on from their original point of departure, where, once through that first checkpoint, they had been brought by the lorry.

Those travellers who still had money, either because they had managed cleverly to hide it or because for some obscure reason they had not been beaten or searched, had been able to pay the driver to take them on the next leg of their journey.

But Khady, Lamine and a few others had had to stop here, in this town invaded by sand, with low sand-coloured houses and with streets and gardens covered in sand.

Exhausted and famished, they had lain down to sleep in front of a sort of bus station where the lorry had dumped them.

Other lorries, laden with their human cargo, were waiting, ready to leave.

When Khady and Lamine had woken at dawn, numb with cold, they were covered in sand from head to foot. Khady's leg was hurting so much that it seemed to her, in flashes, that her suffering could not be real, either because she was struggling inside the cruellest nightmare of her entire life, or because she was already dead and was being made to understand that her death was just that: an unbearable – albeit durable – permanent physical pain.

The cloth she had used to bind her calf several days earlier was encrusted in the wound.

It was damp under the grains of sand, impregnated by the seepage of a foul, reddish liquid.

She had not the strength to take it off, even though she knew she ought to – all she managed to do was gently move her leg which was stiff and shot through with pins and needles. In the end she got up, shook the sand out of her hair and clothing.

She hopped around a bit.

On the ground sand-covered shapes were stirring.

She came back to Lamine who was now sitting up. He had taken his shoes off and was inspecting the soles of his feet, cut by the soldier's knife at the same time as the soles of his shoes.

A crust of dried blood made a dark line on the hard, broken skin.

She knew that the boy, though in pain, would not show it or ever speak about his wounds; she knew too that her questioning look would be met only by a deliberately gloomy expression masking his humiliation (oh, how humiliated he was, how sorry she was for him and how upset too at not being able to take on the humiliation in his stead, she who could bear it, who was so little affected by it), because what convincing explanation could he give, if not of their failure, at least of such a setback occurring so early in their journey, he who had assured her that he knew all about the obstacles and dangers likely to be met with on the road?

She was fully aware of it, she understood and accepted it: the mortification he was feeling which gave him that blank look and made him seem remote, so different from the intense, friendly lad he had been.

Understanding it, she did not hold it against him.

What she did not then know, what would only gradually become clear to her but what at the time she was not equipped to envisage, was that the boy was greatly, doubly humiliated, both by what had happened the day before and, as a direct consequence, by something that had not yet happened, something which Khady, who was not naïve but who was inexperienced, had not yet intuited but which he, Lamine, knew would happen. That was why – Khady was later to understand – he had felt ashamed in her presence, ashamed both at knowing what she did not know and ashamed at the thing itself: that was why, through fear and through not wishing to have anything to do with Khady's innocence, he was so withdrawn, why he had clammed up on her.

Had he, later on, said anything specific to her?

She was unable to remember exactly.

But it would seem to her that he had not.

They had simply wandered around, both limping in different ways (he trying to put only the outer edge of his feet on the ground, she, hopping irregularly along, trying not to put her weight on her lame leg) through streets heavy with dry, dusty heat under a yellowish, shimmering, sand-coloured sky.

Lamine's close-cropped hair, face and chapped lips were still covered with sand.

In a daze and desperate to find some shade, they had taken refuge in a cheap eating place with earthen walls and no windows where, in the semi-darkness, they had eaten hard, stringy pieces of grilled goat's meat and drunk coke, both knowing that they had no money left to pay even for this meagre fare. Lamine retreated into a bitter, heart-rending detachment behind which, he perhaps thought, he could take refuge alone with his indignity and prevent it contaminating Khady, he who knew what was going to happen while she – he perhaps believed – still did not. But she had had an inkling when, chewing the last piece of meat and washing it down with a last gulp of coke, her eyes had met the hostile, half-closed eyes of the woman who had served them and who, breathing noisily, slumped on a chair in the darkest corner, had been scrutinising the two of them, her and the boy. Khady had wondered then how they were now going to pay what they owed. In its own way the woman's unfriendly, judgemental, inquisitorial gaze had given her the answer.

Throughout this period she would cling ferociously to the conviction that only the reality of physical pain had to be taken into account.

Because her body was in a permanent state of suffering.

The woman made her work in a tiny room that gave on to a courtyard at the back of the chop-house.

There was a foam mattress on the hard floor.

Khady spent most of her time lying on it, dressed in a beige slip. The woman would bring a customer in, usually a wretched-looking young man who, like Khady and Lamine, had fetched up in this town where he scraped a living as a houseboy, and who often on entering the hot stuffy room would cast frightened looks around him as if caught in a trap of what was hardly – Khady thought – his own desires but the machinations of the woman who tried to inveigle every diner into visiting the room at the back.

The woman would then lock the door and go away.

The man would then lower his trousers with almost anxious haste, as if it were a matter of getting a tiresome and vaguely threatening obligation over with as quickly as possible. He would lie down on Khady, who – to avoid jolting it as far as possible – would move aside the injured leg on which the woman put a fresh bandage each day. He would then enter her, often groaning in surprise, because a recent attack of pruritus which made Khady's vagina dry and inflamed also caused his penis some discomfort. She summoned all her mental strength to counter the multiple shooting pains in her back, her lower abdomen and her calf, thinking "There's a time when it stops," feeling on her chest half-hidden by the lace edging of her slip and on her neck the man's copious sweat mingling with hers, thinking again "There's a time when it stops," until the man finished laboriously and, in a murmur of pain and disappointment, had withdrawn promptly.

He would then bang on the door and they both heard the slow, heavy tread of the woman coming to open the door.

Some customers would complain, saying that it had hurt, that the girl was infected.

And Khady thought with surprise, "Ah, 'the girl', that's me," almost amused – she, Khady Demba in all her singularity – to be called that.

She would remain lying there a while after the other two had gone.

Breathing slowly, with her eyes wide open, she would calmly inspect the cracks in the pinkish walls, the corrugated-iron ceiling and the white plastic chair under which she had put her bundle.

Lying perfectly still, she could hear the blood throbbing calmly, softly, in her ears, and if she moved slightly, the sucking sound of her wet back on the mattress – which was also soaked in sweat – and the tiny lapping noise made by her burning vulva, and then, feeling the pain oozing gently away, conquered by the youthful, impetuous strength of her solid, determined constitution, she would think, calmly, almost serenely, "There's a time when it stops," so calmly, so serenely, that when the woman came back not alone, as she usually did, to wash her, nurse her and give her something to drink, but in the company of another customer whom – with a vague gesture of regret or excuse in Khady's direction – she would bring in: even then Khady would experience only a brief moment of dejection, weakness and disorientation, before once more thinking calmly, "There's a time when it stops."

After imposing one customer after another upon her, the woman would take care of Khady with motherly solicitude.

She would bring a towel and a bucket filled with cool water and gently wash Khady's nether regions.

In the evening they would sit down together in the courtyard and Khady would eat a solid meal of goat's meat and boiled maize washed down with coca-cola, keeping back a portion for Lamine.

The woman would take off Khady's bandage, smear fat on the wound which was swollen and foul-smelling, and bind it up again with a clean piece of cloth.

And as they sat there, full up, enjoying the quiet of the cool evening, Khady would turn to look at the woman. In the dusk she could see only the outline of a round, kindly face, and it sometimes seemed to her that she had gone back to the time of her childhood which, although harsh, muddled and often grim, had had its happier moments, such as when Khady sat in front of the house at her grandmother's feet to have her hair done.

Just before nightfall, Lamine would arrive.

He slipped into the courtyard – Khady thought with a touch of pity and disgust – like a dog afraid of getting a hiding, but even more of finding his bowl empty. Lamine was at once quick and stooping, keen and furtive. Khady and the woman pretended not to notice, Khady out of delicacy and the woman out of scorn, and Lamine would pick up the full plate and carry it to Khady's room, where the woman allowed him – or at least did not forbid him – to spend the night, on the unspoken proviso that he would be gone by dawn.

Before going to bed, the woman would give Khady a small part of the money she had earned.

Khady would also turn in, going back to the pinkish room lit by a grimy bulb hanging from the tin roof.

Seeing Lamine, once so energetic, crouched in a corner scraping his plate with his spoon, made Khady feel her aches and pains all come flooding back.

Because what – beyond the faintly tired evidence of her own honour now for ever secured, and the rather weary awareness of her irrevocable dignity – could she set against the incurable shame the boy felt?

Perhaps he would have preferred to see her humiliated and in despair.

But he carried the whole burden of humiliation and despair. Khady felt that, without realising it, he held it against her. That was why she would have preferred him not to be there in the evening, filling up the cramped space with his bitterness and his silent, obscure, unjust reproaches.

She also knew that he bore a grudge over her refusal to let him now make love to her.

Her reason – the one she gave herself and the one she told him – was that her swollen, ulcerated vagina needed a rest.

But this she guessed too: Lamine was ashamed of her, and for her, as much as he was ashamed of himself.

That annoyed her.

What right had he to include her in his feelings of abjection just because he lacked her strength of spirit?

She did not see why she should put up with pain in her genitalia just to satisfy his needs.

Silently, wearily, she would slide down onto the mattress.

What he did all day long in the dry, suffocating heat of the town, she did not care to be told.

She would feel a sullen pout beginning to play on her lips, aimed at discouraging any timid wish he might have for a chat.

Meanwhile her fingers would start moving mechanically towards the wall to stroke its nooks and crannies and, just before she fell asleep, a wild surge of joy would make her exhausted body quiver all over as she recalled suddenly, pretending to have forgotten, that she was Khady Demba: Khady Demba.

She awoke one morning to find Lamine gone.

Curiously, she understood what had happened before noticing his absence; she understood as soon as she woke up and leapt towards her bundle, which was wide open. She had left it, tightly knotted, under the chair. She pulled out its meagre contents – two T-shirts, a batik, a clean empty beer bottle – and groaned as she took in what she had guessed before remarking anything else: that all her money had gone.

It was only at that instant she realised she was alone in the room.

In her distress she started making little whimpering sounds.

She opened her mouth wide. She felt she was suffocating.

Having awoken in the certainty that something bad had been

done to her, had she, during the night, heard something, or had she had one of those dreams that foretell in precise detail what is about to happen?

She rushed out, limping so badly that she nearly fell over at every step, crossed the courtyard and went into the chop-house where the woman was drinking her first coffee of the day.

"He's gone! He's stolen everything from me!" she said.

She slumped down onto a chair.

With rather distant pity, the woman eyed her coldly and knowingly.

She finished her coffee, slightly spoilt by Khady's entry, and clicked her tongue. Then she got up heavily and, taking the girl in her arms and cradling her gauchely, promised she would never throw her out.

"No risk of that," Khady said, "with what I bring you."

In utter dejection she thought that she would have to start all over again, that everything had to be endured once more, and even worse, because her body was so horribly bruised, whereas the night before she had worked out that a further two or three months' work would suffice to enable her and Lamine to continue their journey.

As for the boy, well, she had already forgotten him.

It would not be long before all recollection of his name and what he looked like would fade from her mind. In retrospect she would see his betrayal as just another of fate's cruel blows.

Whenever she looked back to that period, she would round down to about a year the time she had spent at the chop-house and in the pinkish room, but she knew that it had probably lasted a great deal longer and that she, too, had got bogged down in the sand of the desert town like most of the men who visited her, who had come from several different countries and who had been wandering around the place for years, their eyes flitting apathetically over everything but seeming to take nothing in. They had lost count of how long they had been there, and people back home must have thought them dead because, feeling ashamed of their situation, they had failed to keep in touch with their families.

Inert and impenetrable in manner, they would often linger by Khady's side, having seemingly forgotten what they had come for or thought it so exhausting and pointless that in the end they preferred just lying there, neither asleep nor really alive.

Month after month Khady got thinner and thinner.

She had fewer and fewer customers and spent a good part of her day in the semi-darkness of the chop-house.

Still, her mind was clear and alert, and she was sometimes overwhelmed with joy when, alone at night, she murmured her own name and once again savoured its perfect affinity with herself.

But she was losing weight and getting weaker all the time, and the wound in her leg was slow to heal.

One day, though, she reckoned she had saved up enough to be able to try and leave.

For the first time in months she went out into the street, and limping in the scorching heat, she made her way to the parking-lot where the lorries left from.

She came back stubbornly each day, trying to work out which of the numerous men hanging about place she should link up with so as to be able to get onto one of the lorries.

And she was no longer surprised by the harsh, combative tone in her own hard, sexless voice as she asked questions in the few words of English she had picked up at the chop-house, any more than she was surprised by the reflection, in a lorry's rear-view mirror, of a gaunt, grey face with matted, reddish hair, a face with pinched lips and dry skin which happened, now, to be her own and which, she thought, one could not be sure was a woman's face, any more than it could be said that her skeletal body was a woman's, and yet she was still Khady Demba, unique and indispensable to the orderly functioning of the things of this world, even though she now looked more and more like the lost, sluggish, scrawny creatures roaming the town, in fact so much like them that she thought, "Between them and me, what difference, basically?" after which she laughed inwardly, delighted to have told herself a good joke, saying, "That's because I'm me, Khady Demba!"

No, nothing surprised her any more; nothing, any longer, made her afraid, not even the great weariness she felt all day long that caused her thin limbs suddenly to feel so heavy that she laboured to lift her spoon to her mouth and to put one foot in front of the other.

To all that, too, she had grown accustomed.

Now she looked upon exhaustion as the natural condition of her organism.

Weeks later, in a forest the name of which she had forgotten, among trees that were unfamiliar to her, her state of great weakness would prevent her leaving the makeshift tent of plastic and foliage in which she was lying.

She had no idea how long she had been there, nor how it was possible for the sunlight filtering through the blue plastic to reveal her arms, legs and feet that were so thin and so far off. She felt herself weighing so heavily on the earth that gravity seemed to cause her to sink into it as soon as she closed her eyes.

And she, Khady Demba, who was ashamed of nothing, was

dying of shame at seeing herself like that: huge, unwieldy and immovable.

A damp, strong-smelling hand was lifting her head, trying to put something into her mouth.

She tried to prevent it, because the smell of that something and of the hand holding it sickened her, but she had so little strength left that her lips parted in spite of herself and she let a sort of insipid, sticky paste slide down her gullet.

She felt cold all the time. The cold was so deep and awful that it could not be assuaged either by the blanket covering her or the warm hands which occasionally massaged her.

And whilst she hoped to find in the earth, hollowed out under the weight of her enormous body, the heat which she thought would put her back on her feet, as soon as she closed her eyes she encountered an even greater cold which the bluish sun filtering through the plastic could not cope with, any more than could the humid, stuffy and (since she was sweating profusely) probably warm air in the tent under the trees.

Oh, she was certainly cold and every inch of her body was hurting, but she reflected with such intensity on how she could forget the cold and the pain that when she saw again in her mind's eye the faces of her grandmother and of her husband – the two people who been good to her and had reinforced her in the view that her life, her person, had no less meaning and value than theirs – and when she wondered if the child she had so longed to bear could have prevented her falling into such a wretched situation, she realised that these were only thoughts and not regrets, because she did not lament her present state, did not want to change it, and even found herself in a way delighted, not at her suffering but simply at her condition as a human being confronting all sorts of perils as bravely as possible.

She got better.

She could sit up and eat and drink normally.

A man and a woman who appeared to be living together in the tent gave her a little bread and some boiled wheat which they prepared outside on a log fire in an old saucepan without a handle.

Khady remembered she had travelled in the lorry with them.

They were both taciturn, and Khady and they had no language in common except a few words of English; still, she grasped eventually that they had been trying for years to get to Europe and that the man had managed to live there for a while before being expelled.

They both had children somewhere whom they had not seen for a long time.

The tent was part of a vast encampment of shacks or tarpaulins on poles, and men in rags were moving between the trees, carrying branches or tins.

Khady had noticed she had nothing any more: no bundle, passport or money.

Both the man and woman spent their days making ladders. After watching for a while how they did it, Khady went in search of branches and worked in her turn at building a ladder, dredging up from memory a story she had been told (by the nameless faceless boy of her *ascension manquée*) about a wire fence separating Africa from Europe, and questioning in her new hoarse, rough voice the man and the woman, who replied with a few words which she did not always know but which, linked to others she had learnt, or translated summarily by a sketch drawn on the ground, ended up representing fairly closely what she had gathered from the boy. The couple tossed in her direction bits of string which they used to tie each rung of the ladder to the uprights. They did so reluctantly and with some annoyance, as if, Khady thought calmly, having robbed her of all she possessed, as she assumed they had, they could hardly refuse to help her, however little they liked it.

She left the forest with the woman, and they followed a tarmac road to the gates of a town.

She was limping badly and her damaged calf could be seen below the edge of her old batik.

They begged in the streets.

Khady held her hand out as the woman did.

In an incomprehensible language people hurled what must have been insults at them. Some spat at their feet. Others gave them bread.

Khady was so hungry she bit violently into the bread.

Her hands trembled.

Her gums were bleeding. They left traces of blood on the bread.

But her heart was beating gently, calmly, and she felt the same: gentle and calm, beyond reach, shielded by her unshakeable humanity.

A short time later barking, shouting and the sound of people running echoed through the camp.

Soldiers were pulling down the shacks, tearing off tarpaulin covers and scattering the stones where cooking fires had been lit.

One of them grabbed Khady and ripped her batik off.

She saw him hesitate and realised he was repelled by her thin body and the blackish marks on her skin.

He punched her in the face and threw her on the ground, his mouth twisted in anger and disgust.

*

Later, much later, weeks and months later perhaps, with every night in the forest feeling colder than the last and the sun seeming every day to look paler and hang lower in the sky, the men who had been elected – or who had appointed themselves – as leaders of the camp announced that the attack on the fence would take place the day after next.

They set off at night, dozens and dozens of men and women amongst whom Khady felt particularly diaphanous, almost impalpable, a mere puff of wind.

Like the others she was carrying a ladder which, though light, seemed to weigh more heavily than she did, just as things sometimes – absurdly – do in dreams, and yet, her enormous heart beating within the little bony cage of her fragile, burning chest, she was limping along at no slower a pace than her companions.

They walked for a long while in silence through the forest, then over stony fields where Khady stumbled and fell several times, but she picked herself up and returned to her place in the group, feeling herself but an infinitesimal displacement of air, a glacial subtlety of the atmosphere, she was so cold, she was cold through and through.

They arrived at last in a deserted area bathed in a white light that resembled the brightness of the moon made incandescent, and Khady saw the fence they had all been talking about.

As they moved forward dogs began barking and shots rang out. Khady heard a voice made strident and uneven by anxiety announcing "They're firing in the air", then the same person, perhaps, shouted an agreed signal, a single word, and everyone began running towards the fence.

She ran too. Her mouth was wide open but she could not breathe. Her eyes were staring and her throat was blocked. Already the fence was there and she leant her ladder against it. Then, rung by rung, she climbed up until she reached the top and gripped the fence. She could hear all about her shots being fired and cries of fear and pain. She could not tell if she was shouting too, or if it was the sound of her blood throbbing in her skull that was wrapping her around in an unending threnody. She tried to go higher and remembered that a boy had told her that you must never, never stop climbing until you have reached the top, but the barbed wire was tearing the skin off her hands and feet and she could now hear herself screaming and could feel blood running along her shoulders and down her arms. She kept telling herself never to stop climbing, never, repeating the same words over and over again without any longer understanding them, then giving up, letting go, falling slowly backwards, and thinking then that the essence of Khady Demba – less than a breath, scarcely a puff of air – would surely never touch the ground, would float eternal, inestimable, too evanescent ever to be made to crash in the cold, blinding glare of the floodlights.

She was still thinking "It's me, Khady Demba" the moment her skull hit the ground. With staring eyes she saw a bird with long grey wings hovering above the fence. "It's me, Khady Demba," she thought, dazed by the revelation, knowing that she was the bird, and that the bird knew it too.

COUNTERPOINT

Every time Lamine was given money for his work, in the kitchen at the back of the restaurant *Au Bec Fin* where he did the washing-up in the evening, at the warehouse where he unpacked goods for supermarkets, on a construction site or in the *métro*, wherever he went to sell his labour, every time euros passed from a foreigner's hand to his own, he thought of the girl. He silently begged her to forgive him and not to pursue him with curses and poisoned dreams. In the room he shared with others he slept with his money under the pillow and dreamt of the girl. She was either protecting him or – on the contrary – wishing he was in the pit of hell. And when, on bright days, he raised his eyes and let the sun warm his face, it was not unusual for the sky to cloud over suddenly for no obvious reason, and then he would talk to the girl and tell her softly what had become of him. He would then give thanks to her. A bird flew away: far, far away.

MACLEHOSE PRESS

~ Read the World ~

www.maclehosepress.com

VISIT OUR WEBSITE
OR JOIN US ON TWITTER AND
FACEBOOK FOR:

• Exclusive interviews and films
from MacLehose Press authors

• Exclusive extra material

•Pre-publication sneak previews

• Free chapter samplers and
reading group material

• Competitions and giveaways

And to subscribe to our quarterly newsletter

www.maclehosepress.com
twitter.com/maclehosepress
facebook.com/maclehosepress